The road surface was hard and the echo of her footfalls were as the sound of an army following, halting, stumbling but always close behind.

She knew she would never again feel quite the same crushing loneliness. There went with her all those others who have been turned back from the gates of paradise on earth because their passports are made out in a strange, unknown language. The inventor who has brought forth a brain child that the world calls a monstrosity . . . who prefers those plans to any human infant. The explorer, who scorns ease, beauty, life itself, to scale a peak that is unclimbable. All the dreamers who prize their dream above reality . . . And the rebels who would rather go on kicking against the pricks to the bitter end, than settle down to the yoke.

All these . . . went the same way as the girl who refused to marry because her deepest love had been given to another girl.

# SURPLUS

a novel

# SURPLUS

a novel

by

## Sylvia Stevenson

the NAIAD PRESS inc.

1986

Surplus was first published in 1924.

Cover by Tee A. Corinne

ISBN 0-930044-78-9

TO THE
"SURPLUS" WOMAN
*"I have spread my dreams under your feet;
Tread softly, because you tread on my dreams."*
W. B. YEATS.

# SURPLUS

a novel

# SURPLUS

## CHAPTER I

OFTEN the road to heaven on earth—which
some call happiness, and some mirage—is a
tangled pathway, broadening slowly as it
winds along, till at last the haven is in sight. But now
and again, there is no road at all. One step out of the
thicket, and there are the white walls and golden turrets, so near that they dazzle you.

So it was for Sally Wraith. She came out that
June morning on to the Salter's Ridge golf-course,
expecting simply to give a message to a friend of
Miss Landison's. And that morning she first met
Averil.

The girl was sitting cross-legged on the turf with
her back to a late flowering gorse bush, looking out
over the green and gold ravine scored slopes of the
most beautiful course in England. Approaching her
from the side, Sally noticed how still she sat, the still-
ness of strength in repose, not of lassitude. Her head
was tilted slightly backwards to meet the wind, so that
a pennant of thick, dark bobbed hair swung out from
it. Then she turned, and her eyes were green and gray
and violet, like patches of deep, cloud mirroring sea,
with a litttle light shining from far down.

"Remarkable eyes," Miss Landison had said,
describing her. To Sally the most remarkable thing

about them was that you saw at once they would never flinch, never betray you, even if you betrayed them.

The owner of the eyes acknowledged that she was Miss Kennion, with a smile so swift that it was gone before you could see whether they danced with it or not. Her square-tipped, deeply browned fingers had a grip that was startling in its strength.

"I'm to tell you, from Miss Landison, that she's expecting you and your uncle to lunch any time," said Sally. "He's not to hurry through his round."

"Right," said the girl. She had a soft, low-pitched Irish voice like the ringing of a muffled bell, but did not seem anxious to use it. She just stood there, looking up at Sally, while a bumble-bee explored the gorse behind her, and a gate clanged from the club-house down below.

"As you're not playing yourself, d'you mind if I wait with you? It seems a shame to go back indoors, on a day like this."

It was the best excuse that Sally could think of, and it drew another fleeting smile from Miss Kennion.

"I do play," she volunteered, "whenever I can get over. But uncle's got a match on this morning."

She was obviously as happy sitting there alone, listening to a bumble-bee, as she would have been playing golf, or nursing a sick child, or leading a forlorn hope on the field of battle. And in all those things she would find an interest, a fascination, that nobody else could find.

"You live out at Hinstead, don't you? It must be pretty dull out there."

The conversation might as well have been about

2

the weather and the crops, thought Sally. But it was impossible to say to a perfect stranger, without any notice, "I believe you're the person I've been looking for all these long, dreary years, till I'd given up hope—only I find you're a girl, instead of a man."

The girl was saying:

"It's not at all bad. I'm only just beginning to get used to it, though, after the war."

"Miss Landison told me you were an M.T. driver, that's why she thought we'd like to meet each other. I was one, too," said Sally.

"Were you? How splendid! What were you—cyclist or cars? Oh, both, so was I. It's ages since I met one of the old crowd."

The brown face, with its slightly broad cheek bones and brows that very nearly met, was alight with interest now.

"Where were you stationed—Longthorpe? I was at the Central Flying School. No wonder we never came across each other. Those days seem a long time ago, don't they?"

"I wish—just from my own particular point of view, I wish they were back again."

Having said it, Sally held her breath. Would this dream girl protest, like everybody else. "How *can* you! Abominably selfish—think of the suffering——"

But she only nodded.

"One had one's definite job to do then, and one went ahead and did it. Now—it's not so easy to break free again."

"Break free"—it was the cry of Sally's heart. And on that June morning, at the disgraceful age of twenty-six and a bit, her career was still a thing of the future.

There was very little excuse. Her education had been well started—that was before her mother, so indifferent about most things but so determined on this one point, had decided that the battle of life was not worth fighting any longer, and surrendered to an ordinary chill. It had been finished at Sally's own discretion, and that was just too early.

Those had been the days when teaching and clerking had been still the only professions, barring domestic ones, that suggested themselves for women. And Sally did not want to teach. She saw that teachers were what she called narrow—they played about in a little world of their own, with its small triumphs, excitements, jealousies, while Sally wanted nothing less than the whole big world to play about in. She was quite ready to admit that they were doing a great work for the coming generations, but unfortunately she could not summon up much interest in coming generations. She was perfectly ready to oblige them by discovering a new continent or a star, painting a masterpiece, occupying the throne of a savage kingdom—anything spectacular, and preferably out of doors. But when it came to sitting cramped over a desk, day in and day out, delving a living out of little musty manuals or ledgers, the prospect was too much for Sally.

Her father, wrapped up in the school progress of her only brother Ronald, and in the lowering of his own handicap at golf, had been content to leave it at that.

"She'll always be able to make a living somehow, if she doesn't marry," he argued. "She's got more

4

sense than one would think under that dreamy manner of hers. Bit queer tempered, like her poor mother, of course. The only thing to do with women like that is to leave 'em alone."

This course, therefore, he pursued. And Sally left school, just before taking her degree—because it seemed to lead nowhere, except to teaching—and tried Society, of which there was a good deal in Leamingham, of the anxiously non-surburban, Anglo-Indian type. And here, also, she just missed being a success.

Women mostly liked her, because she listened with an obviously genuine interest to their love affairs and sentimental adventures. They would have been surprised to learn that her interest sprang chiefly from a desire to find out why it was that the men they thrilled over seemed to her so extraordinarily commonplace, so unworthy of the girls. Then, when she knew the girls a little better—this was after she had been chief confidante of several in succession—she marvelled that there could be a thrill on either side. Sally acquired a reputation for fickleness, about that period, which did nothing to enhance her popularity.

Sally could not help seeing the flaws in other people of both sexes, and her manner. despite her best endeavours, showed plainly that she saw them. She might try to cover her real opinions with a smiling mask, but the scorn would still be there in the curl of her lips, or the hurt and disappointment in the droop of them—the anger in her hard, unsmiling eyes would still look out from the holes in the mask. She had, as a photographer once told her, a "terribly changeable face." He might have added that it was a dastardly betrayer.

5

# SURPLUS

It followed that her experiences with young men were equally unsatisfactory. They were scarce and precious articles in pre-war Leamingham, and she realised at once that success at any social function depended on the acquisition of a faithful escort—exchangeable, of course, but not too frequently—with whom to pair off. Sally therefore did her best to attract one to herself, selecting the best dancer or the best tennis player or the owner of the fastest car she could find, who seemed at the moment to be unappropriated. To this end she endeavoured to suit her step to theirs, to improve her tennis up to their standard, and generally to show how much she appreciated their action whenever they asked her for a dance or a game.

And the males reacted to this expression of her preference, each according to his nature, but not one of them suspected that it might be simply what it seemed—a desire to dance, and to be seen dancing, with the best dancer in the room. Instead the ones who admired her style—the slim figure, and the wistful appeal in the eyes—went straight ahead with the affair according to custom. And these, finding she had a perverse and ridiculous objection to being kissed, insisted on talking "shop" instead of sweetnesses, and—worst sin of all—gave them whichever dance they asked for, instead of searching through an overcrowded programme to see if she could manage to spare one, soon deserted her for more elusive and provocative partners. While the cautious ones, who took themselves seriously, believed she was out to chase them into the matrimonial corral, and withdrew with all speed from the neighbourhood of danger.

To the latter class there were a few exceptions.

6

# SURPLUS

Two of them, both ineligible at the time, but with the hope of having only a year or two to wait, to offer her—actually got so far as to propose to her. This was after she had found out that it was essential to allow one's partner-in-chief other liberties, besides the privilege of one's society, if one wanted to keep him long enough to be any good. Had discovered, on trying it, that a kiss or two was a mighty pleasant adjunct to an evening's entertainment and had omitted to pretend otherwise. Which development merely resulted in a fresh access of panic, among the frivolously inclined and the serious minded alike. She was the sort of girl, one of them remarked, that you couldn't play about with—if you didn't want to get engaged to her, you'd do better to leave her alone. (Poor Sally—who, even when she wanted to be a flirt, was not allowed to be!)

And the two who really wanted to marry her were saddened and annoyed beyond measure, when she explained that she had never had the least intention of going beyond the kissing stage. It may be gathered that Sally's methods of refusing an offer were only moderately successful, like the rest of her Society campaign.

As a matter of fact, marriage was not outside her scheme of desirable possibilities at that period, but it depended on the apparition in the flesh of a vague being at the back of her mind, a kind of story-tale fairy prince, not in the least like any of the men she knew.

The war came just as she had discovered that life at home, waiting for this mythical gentleman to materialise, was the littlest and dullest thing imaginable. The war—was not that hydra-headed monster

7

kind to the women whose hearts it did not devour, a foster-mother to ambitions, a nurse of dreams?

Sally turned straight to the open air, and became an M.T. driver. Life became full of swift motion, discomfort and glory—she was wanted, then, by everybody. The very shop assistants served her first, at sight of her uniform. That is, until they got used to it.

There was no going alone among strangers, either, because another Leamingham girl went through it all with her. Not a great friend—Sally had none—but someone to pair off with, as the others did. Because this Cecily Winter did not want to go out to France, Sally did not apply to be sent there. There were times when she regretted it—it was the top, the apotheosis of service—but she preferred to stay among the rank and file in England, if by so doing she could be certain of always finding a familiar face in the drivers' quarters.

When peace came Cecily, wise in her generation, married a youth she would have scorned in the old society days, a temporary captain. Sally, then twenty-five, had decided—with a loophole, still, for miracles—that she was not a marrying woman. Apparently affection of any sort was to be rather a minus quantity in her life, for she had given up pretending that there was, or ever could be, anything but a state of irritated tolerance between her family and herself. Which state of affairs left an aching void that could only be filled by work and independence.

But she quickly discovered that it was one thing to spell these desirable conditions with a capital letter, and another thing to attain them. For the world oyster had closed itself again to such as her. No-

SURPLUS

body wanted the girl of all round intelligence, unless
she was specially trained—preferably as teacher or
domestic worker. It seemed the posts open to women
were the same, after all, as when she had left school,
except that the applicants had to have all sorts of
degrees and qualifications. Those who escaped from
the rut were the shining exceptions. Indeed the old
order had merely turned over in its sleep and was the
same fat beast seen from another angle.

So Sally tried in vain to get employment as a
chauffeuse—she might as well have tried to gain the
throne of a cannibal island. And her father, taking
fright at a greatly diminished income, with a son who
was still an expensive item, bethought himself that
she had all the qualifications for a lady's companion.
He even found a suitable elderly dame who would take
her.

And Sally refused, saying that he had forgotten one
qualification, essential for companioning, that she did
not possess—a cheerful, even temper. The while she
inwardly cursed herself for a good-for-nothing failure.
Had she not already failed, by a neck, to put the crown
of a degree on her scholastic achievements, failed to find
a husband, failed to do anything special in the Great
War? And now she was failing to find work, and no
excuses could take away the bitterness from that.

Not being a thought reader, Colonel Wraith complained that his daughter's education had been wasted,
that she was a fraud, refusing posts for inadequate
reasons, because she did not really want one at all.
And the more hotly Sally repudiated that suggestion,
the more she suspected that there was an uncomfortable
amount of truth in it. Each advertisement answered
in vain gave her a guilty moment of relief.

9

SURPLUS

She was mentally alone in her father's house, but at least he was used to her. Strangers, especially strange employers, had to be placated, superficially deferred to, while one's real self hid behind an indifferent, defensive mask. And that Sally had never yet been able to achieve. It may have been a contradiction in terms, but it was a fact that she wanted desperately to be independent, yet feared to do it alone.

Matters were thus when the invitation had arrived from Miss Landison, who had been a girlhood friend of Sally's mother.

"Years ago your mother wanted me to ask you, but I've waited, knowing how boring an invalid is for the very young. I warn you I don't go out at all, and know no one. But the house is full of books; if you're like her at all, that will encourage you."

So Sally had arrived at the round "Turret House," clinging to the edge of the forest behind a flaky, grey stone wall. And here, on the very first day, was this Averil, who knew how hard it was to break away. But did she also know what it was to be afraid of doing it alone?

"Are you trying for a job, too?" Sally asked her.

"I've got one. At least, I'm a miniature painter of sorts, and I've started a correspondence course in poster designing. But it's difficult to work properly at home. Mother can't help interrupting, and if there's a tea fight within ten miles, she drags me to it."

Averil said it with a smile, but Sally cried.

"So you hate that sort of thing, too!" And she went on, before she could stop herself, "You'll think I'm mad, seeing we've only just met, but is there any chance you'd come away with me, if I can get any kind of work, and let's share rooms?"

SURPLUS

Then she remembered, and apologised for forgetting, that this girl must have any amount of friends
with whom she could have gone off long ago, if she
wanted to. But fate was kind, and the dream girl
shook her head. All her old friends were married or
abroad, she said. But—her mother didn't like being
left, with her father out in Siam, where she wouldn't
join him because she hated the climate.

"But you must be about as old as I am—it isn't
fair! Can't you just insist, run away?"

"I'm afraid not," she said. "But I could think it
over."

Sally could see it was no use pressing her further
just then, but there was hope enough to set her heart
singing. It *was* some good having impossible ideals,
then, waiting for dreams to come true and refusing
substitutes!

## CHAPTER II

SIX weeks later, they were settled in two rooms in Farthing Lane, which maintained an attitude of aloofness (being a no-thoroughfare) in the blustering region between Euston and St. Pancras. And this result was owing almost entirely to the efforts of Miss Landison.

A singular woman, this Miss Landison. Sally could not quite decide whether she liked her or not, and had no time to give the question the consideration it seemed to need. Her age might have been anything from forty to fifty-five, but was probably somewhere near the latter figure. Her hair looked as if the dark grey streaks had always been there. She did it in a plain knot, which accentuated the classical lines of her nose and her high cheek-bones. Not an ascetic's face, though—rather the face of a child of the soil, with wind roughened complexion, a little sallow now from enforced indoor life. Her eyes were her most striking and incongruous feature, and they were brilliantly dark, far seeing, untroubled eyes—those of a Sybil, who has no part or lot in the lives of common mortals, yet can be sorry for them, and laugh at them, and love them a little.

Apparently she had been an invalid ever since her coming, ten years ago, to Salter's Ridge.

It was no more than the truth that she had few acquaintances in the place. Originally, she had brought no introductions, and it was hardly to be ex-

12

pected that the residents should be in a hurry to call upon her. Moreover, she could not for obvious reasons play golf or hunt, and she did not play bridge— which was sheer obstinacy on her part, as the few whose kind hearts and curiosity had led them to her door agreed. She refused, also, to talk about her symptoms. Said she had come to Salter's Ridge "for the air"—no word as to why she had come alone, mark you!—and appeared quite satisfied with an existence that was bounded by books and a couple of Airedales.

The Salter's Ridge ladies had every sympathy for her canine tastes, but none for her literary ones. As one cannot sustain intercourse upon the vagaries of dogs and the weather alone, and as none of the callers were pressed to call again, the mistress of "Turrets" was soon left entirely to her own devices.

These included the holding of weekly "book teas" for the people who merely lived in Salter's Ridge, and were not numbered among the residents. The girls from the little shops in the High Street, the butcher's boy and the carpenter's young man—these, with the servants from the big houses, were welcomed every Saturday afternoon at the "Turrets." Miss Landison let them choose their own books from her collection, and each person present had to take his turn in reading aloud. She gave them a plain tea, but her advice, which was given only to those who sought it, was found to be worth more than many sugared cakes.

Later, when war had brought the inevitable shifting of population, she became more of a recluse than ever. The post-war residents had become birds of passage; in the summers they let their houses to wealthy business folk who could afford to pay for their entry into such an exclusive little sporting fraternity as Salter's

13

# SURPLUS

Ridge. Meanwhile, the members of this fraternity had themselves migrated to inexpensive rooms in Eastbourne or a pension in Dieppe, leaving the golf club to the visitors. A state of affairs which was responsible for not a few heart burnings, in spite of the fact that the prize list for the monthly competitions now included diamond necklaces, where formerly it had not risen above a paltry silver spoon or two.

At the time of Sally's visit, Miss Landison spent most of the long days in her garden, with its high grey wall on the road side, and on the other a sloping lawn, merging by imperceptible degrees into the forest. Once there had been a hedge to mark the boundary, but she had pulled it down. She said she did not mind the forest coming into her garden, and she supposed that its absentee owner would not object to her garden encroaching on the forest in return. So a few bold daffodils had pushed over the line, and the forest had sent an advance guard of larch saplings. There was a carpet of pine needles all across the lower half of the lawn, that summer, sending up a wave of bitter sweetness into the still, dry air.

Here, on the evening after the Kennions' departure, Sally sat by the invalid's couch and talked about Averil. And Miss Landison listened, her eyes searching the other's eager face. Then she said, "An attractive girl, very. Her uncle mentioned to-day that she used to be a regular breaker of hearts, before they moved to Hinstead. He said he couldn't think why she hadn't married yet."

"Oh, men——" repeated Sally slowly.

Somehow, she had not once thought of "that sort of thing" in connection with the dream girl. Remembering those steadfast eyes, the wiry brown hands, the

14

SURPLUS

diffident brevity of her speech, it was impossible to
picture her a deliberate scalp hunter, luring men on,
playing hot and cold, all the bag of super-feminine
tricks.  As impossible as it was to imagine her being
catty to another woman.  One saw that she had other
and more important aims than the subjugation of the
male.

"I don't think there's any sentimental stuff about
her," declared Sally.  "It's her career she's keen
on."

Miss Landison did not say, "You seem to know a
lot about her, considering you've only seen her once,"
which was the kind of fatuity any ordinary person
would have achieved.  Instead, "You may be right.
I'll do anything I can to help you both.  It is the kind
of thing I should have liked to do myself, if I'd been
fit."

Sally would have liked to ask how it came about
that Miss Landison was not fit—nobody had told her
—and to say how sorry she was.  But the invalid's
expression did not invite sympathy; she seemed to
want nothing from other people.  All one could do
was to take gratefully what she gave, as Sally now
took her playing of the part of audience.

It proved impossible to hurry Averil, though the
sole obstacle to her immediate departure from home
appeared to be her mother.  Though the elder woman
apparently did her best, by adopting a helpless pose,
to thwart and hamper her daughter's career, there was
between them the tie of a strong family affection that
was incomprehensible, as such, to Sally.  She could
understand loving a mother because she was a lovable
human being—because she was herself.  But when it
came to loving her simply because she was your

15

mother—really caring, not only in public—the thing was a mystery to Sally.

"She'll feel it much more now," said Averil, "than she would have directly after the war, when she's got used to my being away. It's the idea of my going that she hates."

There was, it appeared, an aunt who would gladly live with her if it were simply a question of loneliness. But the aunt insisted on late dinners, and Mrs. Kennion liked them in the middle of the day.

"Absurd!" thought Sally.

But she exulted that Averil had a tender heart under that cold manner of hers; though outsiders wouldn't know it, which made the discovery correspondingly valuable. Also that Averil, as she had already found out, could beat her at every kind of game and was a perfect motor driver. Surely it could not be possible that such a wonder would ever throw in her lot with a semi-failure? Yet all the time she felt that it was pre-ordained.

"You must come," she said. "We haven't met like this, by accident, for nothing. We want exactly the same kind of life—success, and a home of our own. I've got fifty pounds that mother left me, we can live on that till I find work."

"I've a small allowance from father, as far as that goes," said Averil. "But—there's mother to be thought of."

But Miss Landison had said she would help, and one scorching July day a letter came from London. The writer, to whom she had appealed, breaking the silence of years, knew of a small motor firm not long started, where a salesman-demonstrator was wanted. He had persuaded the proprietor to give Miss Wraith a trial, if she were willing to accept a small salary, and a microscopic commission on sales.

"Exactly what I wanted!" cried Sally, who had never thought of such a thing before. "Now, if only Averil will make up her mind——"

That day, Averil said she would go.

Back in Leamingham, the family took it just as Sally had expected. Colonel Wraith said:

"Good idea, so long as you take care of yourself," which was his formula for all occasions of departure.

Ronald, on vacation, remarked:

"Catch you sticking to this job, Sara! You'll never be on the spot in time—or else you'll crash their best Rolls. And anyway you'll fight with this Miss Kennion, girls always do."

But nothing marred the perfection of the first day in town together. Hot grey streets took on another colour and scent when Averil was in them. London, instead of an inferno full of hurrying strangers with indifferent or hostile faces, became thronged with tube conductors who were only anxious to be helpful, with police who thought nothing of going a block out of their way to direct, with men and women whose eyes met hers from the tops of 'buses, from pavements, from the reflections in shop windows—all with a friendly look in them, that said, "You're happy about something. We're glad you're happy!"

In the matter of lodgings, Sally insisted obstinately on quiet situation and comfortable beds; she was a pernickity sleeper. It amazed, and then delighted her to find that these details were a matter of perfect indifference to Averil.

"As long as I can get a good light to paint in—" said Averil.

17

And Sally thought, remembering Miss Landison's remarks, "That shows how fearfully keen she is. Marriage, indeed!"

When finally they came to No. 17, Farthing Lane, there were only two available rooms, clean, but with windows looking over the street.

"Look here, Sally, I'm tired of wandering about," said Averil. "You take the top room—that'll be quiet —and I'll have a camp bed in the studio. I can sleep through any noise."

Mrs. Dunn, the landlady, began to talk, throwing out her sentences in great jets, like the tap from a full charged main. She explained that there never was no noise in that street, only milk carts in the mornings, and the Tube underneath that you got so used to you missed it on Sundays, and sometimes the shunting over to St. Pancras—she had a cousin George who owned his own fish shop near St. Pancras, and you wouldn't believe what a bad summer he'd had, he thought it was on account of ice being the price it was—

But Sally was thinking that Averil was unselfish, as well. Slowly, bit by bit, she was revealing herself, and so far she was up to the standard of the fairy prince in every way. If she had not looked so much alive, one would have expected her to vanish suddenly.

That evening Sally told a little of the truth, with Averil sitting cross-legged on the floor beside her, as if she belonged there and had never sat anywhere else. She could see the line where the cropped hair curled inwards on the nape of the brown neck.

"I don't know what would have happened to me, if I hadn't met you. Father and I had given up speaking to each other."

18

"Why didn't you go off on your own, and hunt for something?"

"I—hadn't the courage, alone. I just stayed there, sunk in heaps."

"You strange girl, don't you like being alone? Why, I should have had a studio of my own long ago, if it hadn't been for mother."

There was a short silence. Then Sally said:

"Did she take—this—very badly? You never told me."

"Oh, she made a fuss when I told her it was settled. Now I must get on as fast as I can with my work, and show her I was right."

"You aren't sorry you came?"

"Goodness, no!" said Averil, and laughed. "Not now it's done. I don't say I feel proud of myself, though."

(Sally thought, "She needn't worry. Mrs. Kennion has had her all these years. And she's got a husband, anyway.")

Aloud she said, "I've got you now, anyway, Averil the Silent. And I feel like celebrating for the rest of my life."

"Silly!" said Averil.

But she caught Sally's hand in a lightning grip, and that was good enough, from Averil. Sally should have known it, even though she flung the hand quickly from her with "Nasty thin claw you've got!"

But Sally was hurt, and looked it.

"You think so, do you?"

Averil turned to stare at her.

"You didn't take that seriously? Haven't you ever been ragged?"

# SURPLUS

"Yes, of course," Sally hastened to affirm. "But —you sounded as if you meant it."

"It *is* a claw. Did you want me to call it 'lily white fingers'?" smiled Averil. "You must have known I didn't mean to be nasty."

It had been hard to be laughed at by the dream girl, even in a friendly spirit. Sally swore to herself she would henceforth remember that it was a proof of affection, to be teased. She forgot that a naturally suspicious nature finds it impossible to become trustful to order, all in a moment—forgot, in fact, that the porcupine cannot at will discard his prickles.

# CHAPTER III

MR. SAMPSON, of the Euston Road Motor Agency, proved to be a pale person with an underslung, rabbity jaw, who inhabited a hutch, six foot by three, designated in large white letters "The Office." As soon as Sally arrived, he informed her that as there was not much actual demonstrating to be done at present, he could find her plenty of employment looking after his correspondence. He had been doing without a clerk since the firm started.

"You know, Miss Wraith"—he drew back his lips in what was evidently meant to be a smile—"you are the first lady we have employed. But I feel sure the innovation will be a success."

It was a dreary morning, and the afternoon was not much better. Only one promising looking customer came into the shop, a tall man with a long, easy stride, who picked his way among the cars on exhibit like a mastiff in a drawing room. Sally noticed him from the peephole window in the hutch, and took advantage of Mr. Sampson's temporary absence to make a move towards him. Only to be forestalled by Jelks, the foreman, with his "Yes, sir, what can we do for you?"

Eventually the customer did not decide on anything. Sally, from her lair, could hear him promising to call again, at which well-worn formula Jelks shrugged his shoulders as soon as he had gone.

Already she saw that it would need great finesse on

her part, if her title of salesman-demonstrator were ever to be anything but a polite fiction. She would have to outwit the more skilled manœuvres of both Jelks and Sampson himself, with the added handicap of her imprisonment in the "office." And she had been rash enough to expect fair play!

"If only I'd never admitted I could use a typewriter a little," she thought. "I'd love to tackle Sampson about it at once. But—no, I don't think I'd better."

She must keep this post, whatever happened, because if she lost it, and could not get another, Averil and she would have to part. It did not strike her that she was a victim of a state of affairs that has been the despair of strike leaders since time began.

Averil had tea laid when she got back to Farthing Lane. It took Averil to look charming in a four square, paint smeared overall that rivalled Joseph's coat.

"You shouldn't have waited for me!" said Sally, glorying in the fact.

She could not remember that anyone had ever waited tea for her at the house in Leamingham which had hitherto masqueraded as her home.

When she bent to kiss the top of the bent dark head, it moved slightly under the caress. She was becoming daily more demonstrative in her affection, and the obvious fact that Averil was not accustomed to it, and did not particularly like it, was powerless to check her. She, who had given so few kisses in her life, and wanted to give still fewer, now felt the urgent need to express love in all its outward symbols.

"I'm too disgusted to want any tea myself," she added. "Oh, it's a hopeless business!"

"What's happened?" asked Averil quickly. "Hasn't it been a good day?"

Sally explained, and she laughed soft encouragement.

"How do you know you won't get all the customers to-morrow?"

"I can't believe it, somehow. I've never yet made a success of anything I've tried. That's why I don't expect to now, I suppose."

"Silly," said Averil. "Of course you will! You have the knowledge, it's only a question of holding the job down."

But Sally would not let this pass; that was by no means all, she said. How could one save, how could one feel any sort of security as to the future, unless one got on, nearer the top? There were too many women already in every trade who were content to remain underlings from beginning to end, or rather, who had to be content.

"Not you," said Averil. "You won't end like that."

She had always found that the best way to surmount difficulties was to ignore them, and the thing had become a habit, as natural to her as was the opposite course to Sally. But Sally took this belief in her ultimate success as a personal tribute to her capacity, and for the moment she too almost believed.

"Think how splendid it will be, when you're a famous artist and I'm the head of a motor firm! We'll have all the interesting people of both worlds dropping in in the evenings."

"Can't see as far as that yet," said Averil. "I've got to get some commissions, first."

Averil had fixed up a makeshift studio in one corner, where a sugar box stood against the wall, draped with a man's size silk handkerchief. On this stood a miniature, the daintiest ivory thing of misty blues and greys, in striking contrast to the vivid posters pinned to the wall. It seemed to Sally that two different personalities wielded Averil's brush, one bold and masterly, the other tender, almost childlike.

The latest poster represented the figure of a girl, decked in the battle array of a Gilbert and Sullivan, Princess Ida, her short tunic and gleaming shield standing out against a background of bright green hills and purple trees.

"It's for 'Regina Soap,' " explained Averil. " 'The Armour of the Modern Woman.' She's got wings on her heels, you see, and a spear in one hand. I'll have to put a cake of soap in the other, I suppose."

But Sally was not listening.

"Wings for progress, and a spear for the destruction of the old ideals," she said. "Who was it said the other day they had no imagination?"

But Averil declared she had never thought of that inner meaning, though she saw now that it applied.

"The trouble is, I haven't got the face right," she said. "My drawing's very weak, really—that's because I've never been properly trained. I ought to have a model." She turned from the poster to Sally. "Now I come to think of it, I'm not sure you wouldn't do. Would you mind awfully?"

"I can't sit still. But, of course, if you really want me to—— You'll get a bad specimen as far as looks go, though."

"Don't want prettiness, I want good bones. You've got them," said Averil briefly.

24

# SURPLUS

And, so her face was the kind that Averil wanted, Sally was content. She had regretted, in the old Society days, that it was not a pink and white talisman to male admiration. Now she was only grateful to have it thin and brown and bony.

Days later it occurred to her that it must be rather dull for Averil, during the hours from nine to five when she was away. Averil had admitted, once, that she had been one of a "big crowd" of cousins and friends in Marchester, before the war. Even at Hinstead she must have had many more outside interests than now fell to her lot, considering that now she had nothing to do but work all day, no one to talk to except Sally in the evenings. Could one be certain that she was not missing that life, comparing it unfavourably with this?

"I wish we knew someone who would come in and have lunch with you. It must be pretty lonely."

"I don't want anyone, thanks! I'd rather bolt it, and get back to work."

(So she needed looking after about her meals—there was just that little touch of weakness in her strength!)

"You needn't worry, I'm just as used to being alone. It's whichever comes along. I made a friend over the way, to-day, too."

"Who on earth——?"

"A baby. The pram was standing outside by itself. The mother's quite young—an untidy sort of creature. But the kid wasn't too dirty."

The dark girl lay back in her chair blowing smoke rings one through the other, watching their little parachutes as they drifted ceilingwards.

"I'm afraid it would have been wasted on me,"

25

laughed Sally. "I'm not a baby maniac. I don't feel I want to slobber over every pram I meet, like the womanly woman's supposed to do."

"Not every one, of course. But this really was rather a fine chap. Just five months."

"Five months—that settles it! Why, they can't even coo intelligently at that age."

Sally ran her fingers through the soft brown hair that clung to her forehead; the "office" had been like an oven. In her corner of the dingy room, Averil looked infinitely cool and still. She had taken up a silken garment she was embroidering—doing all the seams by hand, too. Sally would have bought a strip of ready-made embroidery and put it together with a machine. It was Sally's turn to clear the table that night, therefore it had not yet been cleared. A single shaft from the sunset, creeping between the houses over the street, touched first the rubber-spouted tea-pot, then a cracked, blue-rimmed plate, then the cloth itself with ruddy gold.

"You surprise me—you and your baby."

"Mine, indeed, and it not even clean!" protested Averil.

"Would you like one of your own?"

"I suppose so—if it came along."

Averil had withdrawn into her shell, like a snail that has been touched on the horns. But Sally was learning the way to bring her out again.

"Well, I shouldn't," she pronounced. "It's not so much the bother of having one—though I should hate that quite enough—but I'd hate to put anybody like me in the world. One of us is enough and to spare. The race won't lose anything particular when the mould's broken."

"It would be like somebody else, as well," suggested Averil.

"Like its father? That might improve matters, if he was a very splendid person—the kind that doesn't exist. But even then it would be half me, if not more. No, it's too much responsibility. And, anyway, I can't see the attraction."

"Not to have something of your very own?"

Sally stared at her blankly.

"My dear old thing, you're talking like a novelette! A lot of cuddling any kid of yours would get. More likely a smack on the head."

"Oh, it would be smacked, too, of course," laughed Averil. "Quite often, I expect. It does 'em good. I had a lot of it myself."

"This saying beforehand that a baby is 'something of one's own to love,'" pursued Sally. "It makes me furious. That's the way every woman worth the name is supposed to feel—as if that was the only sort of love in the world!"

"It must be different, anyhow. Stronger, I suppose," ventured Averil.

"Whiskey's different to water—and stronger. Some people prefer water, though."

"You perfect idiot, Sally! Suppose you think you're being funny."

Averil was only too glad to find that the conversation had got back to the ragging plane again. But Sally had not yet finished her say.

"I think this idea that a woman's wasted her life unless she's a mother is the most pernicious bilge that was ever invented by Adam—or the serpent, more likely. Are we wasting our lives? When you're a famous artist and I own a motor business, and we're

27

getting on in years, will you weep buckets every night because you haven't got a che-ild?"

"Rather not!" said Averil, with intense conviction. "I don't go in for regretting things. It's waste of time."

## CHAPTER IV

LIFE in the little house down Farthing Lane soon acquired a routine of its own. Averil had the gift for settling down at once in whatever spot she might chance to find herself, and the sitting-room now looked as homelike and attractive as she could make it. She had hung plain blue cretonne curtains at the windows in place of the old flowery abominations, and a couple of her own water-colours—arresting little pieces of colour, with sharp, clear outlines—instead of "The Soul's Awakening." She had hidden away the hideous china ornaments, and replaced them with a silver cigarette box bearing a military crest, and a few small pieces of brass work. The cushions she had covered with deep crimson silk.

"What's the good of wasting time making this place look decent?" Sally had objected. "Let's hope we're not going to stay here long. The minute I can hear of a better job, we're off."

It's a fatal thing to keep on changing jobs," said Averil. "We might as well make ourselves comfortable now, anyway. There's no sense in looking so far ahead."

And Sally saw that the dream girl was right, as usual. But she went on seeing in her mind's eye the kind of house that would fit their life togther—the ideal house, without a single flaw.

Averil's scheme of decoration was completed by a selection of artistic photographs, mostly of men. The first time they appeared, Sally had made full enquiries about the originals, and by now she felt, not that they were friends, but that she knew them well.

They were the "old crowd" of Marchester days, who had lived in each other's houses, and Sally tried hard not to be jealous of them. But she resented desperately the fact that Averil had had a life of her own before she met her; she would have liked to wipe it all out, so that they two might start together from the beginning.

Averil's monosyllabic descriptions of them, and of their relations with her had to be pieced together at different times. But it was obvious without telling that they had one and all been her ardent admirers. They were cousins Bobby and Jake Hepworth, strapping, athletic looking youths, so alike that Sally could only tell them apart by the "Thine, Bobby" and "Thine, Jake" scrawled across their respective legs. They lived on the mantelpiece, in large silver frames.

Dina, their sister, had no frame, but she was pinned to the wall over Averil's bed. The photograph showed a tall, serious-looking girl, evidently a good deal older than Averil, holding a single rose in what Sally privately characterised as a silly, self-conscious attitude. The face was in profile, and nose and cheek-bones stood out with an almost Jewish effect—or no, perhaps it was more Greek, Sally admitted, trying to be fair. A strong face, certainly, but not beautiful. Yet Averil, whenever she mentioned Dina, implied that she was always besieged by a horde of suitors. Dina, apparently, had succeeded in the Society game without the kind of charm and prettiness that Sally also lacked.

"Didn't you say she's out in India somewhere?"

(It was easier to be a success in India.)

30

"Yes, keeping house for Uncle. She's been out ever since the war; we were together all through as drivers, you know. She's always wanting me to go out there."

"Didn't you miss her when she went?" asked Sally, with elaborate carelessness. "After driving together, and all——"

"Rather. But she writes fairly often, though I've not heard for months now, as it happens."

"Letters—that's not the same as having a person with you," objected Sally.

"As long as you're friends, you can go on being just as good friends apart, surely?"

Sally emphatically disagreed with this point of view, but policy demanded that she should not say so. If Averil felt like that about this Dina, why attempt to object? It seemed sufficiently obvious that the Sally-Averil partnership was in a different category.

Then there was the head of one Will Dowson, a poet of sorts who hadn't a penny, and of Eustace Sandiman, commonly known as "Bye-byes," who was making lots out in Australia. Both very good sorts, and both—as she admitted, when closely pressed—having proposed to her more than once. To the latter she had been secretly engaged, for a period of two weeks and a half, because she was so sorry for him.

"But then I saw it would mean chucking my painting, practically, if I went out there. And I'd only just taken it up seriously, then."

"You found you didn't care enough," asserted Sally, from her own experience, and Averil nodded. Adding that he was married now, and she still heard from him every now and again.

There was another, a much older man in uniform,

31

with a round, jolly face and little twinkling eyes to match.

"Major Barrington Hope, my old M.O.," Averil explained. "You'd like him, Sally. Awfully clever, and a good sport. We were just pals; he hasn't written for ages now, but last time I heard he was starting to take up psycho-analysis and that sort of thing."

"He doesn't look like it," pronounced Sally.

She was not surprised, and, after a while, not altogether sorry, that so many men had loved Averil. It showed that she was not alone in placing this girl in a class by herself. She felt a kinship with them, she was sorry for them, she almost loved them—as long as Averil did not love them.

As to that, there seemed no reason for alarm. They all belonged to the days of Averil's green youth, before she had started her career in earnest, and they had served to while away free hours. When it came to the point, she had not wanted one of them enough to marry him, any more than Sally herself had done. They were just good pals, who had been turned down so gently that they still merited that description. They wrote to her quite often, some of them—enlarged on their wives and children, looked her up whenever they got a chance. But Averil was satisfied with their letters only.

Most times, though, they talked of other things in Farthing Lane. Those evenings were so eminently worth the rest of the day! There was the excitement, for Sally, of finding one taste after another that they shared. It was the aftermath of love at first sight, being able to say to oneself, "I was right, of course! I knew nothing about her, and yet I knew that all my thoughts of her were true."

# SURPLUS

Averil had read very little, her life so far having been spent in learning to do a number of things superlatively well. It was pure joy, being able to introduce one's favourites among the younger school to her, and finding they became hers also. And the plays Sally most wanted to see proved to be the very ones Averil had a hankering for. And they laughed, from the pit, at the same point in the subtlest jokes, though the rest of the audience might keep straight faces.

In Mr. Sampson's establishment, matters showed little sign of improvement. Sally found that he was never happy unless she was safely boxed up in the hutch with his correspondence and accounts, so she seized the moments when his back was turned to slip through into the repair shop behind. Here at least was one part of the business she had to learn thoroughly, before aspiring to be a manager herself.

Martin, the elderly and dour head mechanic, tolerated her presence once she had shown herself capable of picking the tool he wanted from a tangled heap without being asked. And he told her she was not likely to do any actual demonstrating if she stayed ten years.

"You're cheering, I must say!" laughed Sally. "Why not?"

"*Be*cause it 'aint no job for a woman," declared Martin. "I don't deny as you seem to know a bit about engines, but what do you know about selling a car? Tell me that."

"Can't I learn?"

"And lose the boss all 'is customers, while you're learning?"

"Well, everybody's got to start some time," protested Sally.

"There's 'undreds of boys what have learnt the trade right from the bottom, in little one-'orse shops this one's a palace to. The boss could get one of them this minute, if 'e stretched 'is finger. No, 'taint education you want—'tis practice."

It seemed a vicious circle from which there was no escape. How could one get practice without starting somewhere?"

"*Be*sides which," pursued Martin, who, having once started talking, seemed in the mood to go on. "*Be*sides which, women ain't wanted in this trade, except in the office. They're well enough off there. Why can't they stay there?"

"But supposing they happen to hate offices, and love motors, and supposing they want to make money and have a business of their own some day?"

" 'Tain't a job for females," Martin repeated, ignoring this outburst. "Why, if I had a daughter——"

Here the figure of Mr. Sampson appeared in the doorway, wearing white spats and stepping delicately over pools of oil.

"Have you got off that letter to Bollard and Sons, Miss Wraith?" he called. "And I expect you're worrying Martin, if you'll excuse my saying so."

Martin looked up at his employer. He thought Sampson a "mean little skunk, what would boil down 'is own mother and sell the fat." Sampson thought him a burly brute, but knew that his value as a mechanic was too great to risk telling him so.

"She don't worry me, not as I've noticed," said Martin deliberately. The accent on the pronoun was unmistakable.

And that was the first bit of encouragement Sally had had.

# SURPLUS

She recounted this incident to Averil in the evening
—Averil in a straight, short dress of vivid green crepe
that clung about her knees, making her figure look
shorter and more thick set, but emphasising the grace
of her brown throat.

"I tell you, it's the thin edge of the wedge! Once I
get into the back shop, Sampson won't be able to keep
me out of the front. Why, I caught one customer to-
day. He only wanted a repair outfit, but still, it's a
beginning."

"Of course. It's splendid!"

The light in Averil's eyes was dancing. Nobody
else, thought Sally, would have shared her excitement
over such a trifle as the sale of a repair outfit. Because nobody else would have taken the trouble to realise how much it meant, making a start.

It was later, when the gas saving pair of them sat
in the misty September dusk, that she remembered
to ask after Averil's work. How was it that seemed
to hide itself in the background, behind one's own?
Now she learnt that a little art shop had been persuaded to show a specimen miniature in its window.

"Oh, and who *do* you think I met in Piccadilly?"
added Averil. "I nearly forgot to tell you."

"No idea," murmured Sally.

"Why, old Midge—Hilliard Earnshaw, one of the
old Marchester crowd. I haven't a photo, but I know
I told you about him. He's just come back from
India, been transferred to the head office of his firm.
He was so surprised to see me! I brought him home
to lunch."

It was such an unusually long sentence, for Averil,
that she wondered why Sally had not yet interrupted.
But Sally was gazing across the street at the lighted

35

windows of the wine merchant opposite, and seeing
through them into darkness.

"When's he coming again?" she asked—and then,
excitedly, "How nice for you, old thing!"

But Averil was not so easily deceived.

"You're not really pleased, Sally. Why? Don't
you think it'll be nice, having someone to take us
about a bit?"

"If—it doesn't mean you're tired of being alone
with me, already."

(Why will one's lips persist in saying the things
one's will has firmly decided not to say?)

"Of course, it means I'm sick of the sight of you!"
laughed Averil. "You creature! Come on, now, and
look at the poster I've begun to-day. It's going to be
the best I've done yet, I believe. Midge says he knows
someone who might buy it."

She turned towards the studio corner, and Sally followed, wrestling with her tell-tale face.

"I'm not going to be a fool," she was thinking. "I
know Averil doesn't want men around—not in that
way, anyhow. It's only because he's an old friend.
One of those jolly, rag-loving old friends of hers—
loathsome word, jolly—just the opposite to me, of
course."

But when you came to consider it calmly, you knew
with certainty that Averil would stick to her career,
and to the partnership. Otherwise—if she wanted to
marry—why had she not married one of those old
friends long ago? It all came back to that.

"It'll be interesting to see what he's like," she said
aloud. "I haven't met any of your friends of the
old days. Do hope he'll come soon."

She pictured, from what she could remember of

# SURPLUS

Averil's vague descriptions, a man of the world—the heroic, scandalous Anglo-Indian world of books—rather silent, perhaps, but keeping a fund of funny stories up his sleeve wherewith to amuse Averil. With an acceptance, grown matter of fact by now, that she would never be anything but a good pal to him.

Of course, he must have lots of other qualities besides his jolliness, or Averil could not count him as a real friend. Jolliness is a surface ebullition which almost always marks the presence of inexhaustible waters of honest-to-God dependability underneath. So Sally told herself, being careful not to attempt the proof of this axiom by recalling examples from her own experience.

In fact, Sally made up her mind that she was going to approve of Midge.

# CHAPTER V

WHEREFORE, Midge Earnshaw was a great surprise to Sally.

He proved to be a lanky youth, looking about nineteen (he was actually twenty-seven) with an accent that might have been attenuated Cockney, a preference for rather exotic tweeds, and an unbroken conviction that Averil was the only girl in the world.

He took to "dropping in" in the evenings, bringing bulky parcels from Lyons' for supper, containing dainties for which Averil might have once casually expressed a fancy. Averil would insist on leaving the honours of the establishment to Sally, herself taking a place in the background, whence she smiled on her partner's efforts to entertain her guest. So Sally, feeling like a performing dog, talked to him of everything she considered might be suitable for his mental equipment, which in her opinion was mediocre in the extreme. And he answered her in polite monosyllables, and at the first opportunity brought Averil willy-nilly into the conversation with a "do you remember——?"

It was quite painful to watch him following her about the room with gloomy eyes, asking her if she wasn't over-working (Averil, who never lost her fine bronze, even in London!), picking up her miniatures and putting them down again, as if his gross touch might defile their fairy lightness. While all the time Averil, who saw nothing painful about it, was teasing him with the solemn statement that she knew his favourite form of art was a "Pears' Annual" supplement.

Sally knew that it was because he did not understand Averil's work that he loved it so. It put her on a pedestal, crowned with the flame of genius—and Midge was a born hero worshipper. But it was only because Sally was one too that she saw so far into his heart, and was sorry for him, for he would not have recognised her as a separate entity if Averil had not insisted on it.

Sometimes, when he had arrived before Sally could get back from work in spite of her hurrying, she was informed that he wanted to take them both to the theatre that evening. Unless Sally was too tired, in which case Averil would not go. Meanwhile, Midge's glowering silence gave the lie to the fiction that he had wanted any such thing; but when Sally commented on his attitude, Averil laughed at the idea.

"Of course he wants us both—the more the merrier! You don't know Midge, Sally. He's like me, it takes him a long time to get used to a new friend, that's all. You must get out of that habit of thinking other people don't want you, it *is* so silly!"

It was later that Midge began to try keeping Sally occupied with a partner of her own. He provided her with a succession of several fellow bank clerks, who were each and all perfectly civil to Sally, which was more than she was to them. She might have tolerated them if she had picked them up herself, but when they were thrust on her she simply hated them.

The climax came when she discovered that Midge paid the whole bill for the little suppers and other foursome festivities. It was then she definitely stopped being sorry for him; it was detestable to feel

39

that he had to pay his friends to take her off his hands. But, of course, as Averil declared when Sally taxed her with it, it was no fault of hers.

She might easily have gone off with him alone, if she had liked. It was obviously true that she, at least, preferred having Sally.

Things were not progressing up to expectations in the Euston Road. Martin, once tamed, was always fairly accessible, and willing for Sally to help him with any job that came along, while seeing to it that she did only the unimportant parts. But he still held to it that the motor business was not the sphere for women.

" 'Tain't natural for them, and never will be," he said once.

"Well, is it natural for men to fiddle about with silks and satins and pins and bows? Yet all the biggest dressmakers are men. And all the best cooks, too—at least, the ones who get the biggest salaries. How do you make that out, Martin?"

This argument had not been presented to Martin before, in spite of its age. He thought it over for a moment, then dismissed it with a grunt as having a catch in it somewhere, that he had no time to waste in exposing.

Sampson and the foreman still attended to every likely customer, and things were so arranged that they were never both out of the shop together. One day, however, a miracle occurred, and Sampson called her out of the hutch.

"This gentleman wants you to take him out on one of the 'Fairy' light cars," he said. "He's thinking of buying one for his sister and wants to see if it suits a lady. You can manage it, I suppose?"

SURPLUS

The impudence of the question, in front of a
stranger, too!.

Sally turned to see what the customer thought of
it, and encountered a pair of blue eyes, too anxious to
be amused. Then she realised that it was the same
man who had promised to "call again," on her first
day at Sampson's. It was his bigness that she remembered. He was not really very tall, but one had
the feeling that he would knock his head against the
ceiling, or crush one of the clutter of little cars under
foot, if he moved suddenly.

He seemed to feel that way himself. He had a
habit, shared by certain large dogs, of treading delicately indoors, as though they have been often re-
proved for doing clumsy damage to the furniture.

"Will you, Miss Wraith?" he said, as one who asks
a favour.

He sat beside her in silence while she put the little
car through its paces, nodding once or twice as she
explained details. Sally thought he was noticing that
she was not too sure of herself—it was years since she
had driven in London—and was afraid of distracting
her attention if he opened his mouth. A piece of of-
ficiousness on his part.

As they turned in at the park gates she said, in a
tone that struggled between this reflection and the
fact that he represented her first chance of a commission:

"Do you think this car will suit your sister?"

She did not turn her head, but she could feel that
he was looking at her intently.

"I've got a confession to make. It's an oversight
on my part, but I haven't got a sister."

"Then what——" Sally slowed down, preparing

41

to turn the car. "Then you've brought me out on false pretences?"

"Not at all," said the man, quietly. "I'll explain. But couldn't we talk better if you stop?"

Sally weighed the matter in her mind. He was probably going to be facetiously apologetic, to gentle her as a rider soothes the horse he has forced over a leap—the sort of transparent manœuvre that a man always fancied one could not see through. But what did it matter how much he talked, as long as he bought a car in the end? So she drew up under a beech tree, from which a few late leaves were still fluttering like little flags of surrender on the frosty air. A boy ran past them, shouting after his hoop, but there was no one else in sight.

"I really do want to buy a car," he said. "I—my name's Carnier, by the way—I'm over in England for the first time in ten years, buying stock for my partner back in British East. I want to take it back there with me."

"But why did you want me to demonstrate it?" enquired Sally. Seen from close to, she noticed that his face was as brown as Averil's, but without the red glow under the skin. His eyes, also, were a different shade of blue, clear, and rather pale, uninteresting after hers, as any other eyes would have been. His tie had been clumsily tied, and one end hung down below the others. He sat there calmly, hands clasped over his knee, speaking slowly, with a pause between each sentence. The effect was somehow hypnotic, so that one could not interrupt, however much one wanted to.

"I saw you looked disappointed, that first day, when you were coming to serve me and got turned back. I made up my mind to come back again, with a good excuse for getting you. I would have come before, but I've been away on a trip."

"Very good of you," snapped Sally. "I was only disappointed because I wanted to get the commission" (why had she said that, that unnecessary, obvious kind of thing? Something in his tone must have suggested it). She mentally shrugged her shoulders, and went on: "The manager never gives me a chance at a customer. But I still don't see——"

"Well, you looked sort of honest, like a bit of open country, in the middle of—all this. I never did care for London, even in the old days when I knew people, but now I hate it more than you can think."

"Oh, so do I!" breathed Sally, surprised into the admission.

"Can't you get away from it?"

His tone was so impersonal that she answered with the truth.

"Not yet. I'm lucky to have a job at all. But when I've made enough money and had enough experience, I mean to set up on my own somewhere. Then we'll have a cottage in the country."

"I see. Then you're living at home?"

"No. With another girl. She's an artist."

Suddenly Sally realised that she was discussing her private affairs with a total stranger.

"If you've decided on this car, we'd better go back," she said.

As they drove in silence again, she did not wonder where Carnier's thoughts were leading him. What, to her, were the mental processes of a customer who told lies about his sister for the sole purpose of securing a woman demonstrator? Coming from the back-

43

woods as he did, such a branch of feminine activity was probably new to him, that was all. Two per cent. commission on three hundred and fifty—would they make it round figures, by any chance?

"I wonder," he said suddenly, as if a bright idea had struck him with such force that it pushed him through a whole sentence without a pause, "whether your firm would do another bit of business, now we've finished with this bit? Would you—would they undertake to sell an old motor cycle of mine for me? I've had it stored at a place in Portan Street since nineteen-eleven." He forestalled questions by adding, "You see, I must have a car out there—my partner insists."

"I don't think Mr. Sampson undertakes second hand——" Sally began.

Then an idea of equal brightness occurred to her.

"If you didn't want much for it—I suppose you must meet all sorts of people on your trips when you're buying cattle, owners of big estates, that kind of thing?"

"A certain number," he answered gravely. "Why?"

"Well, if I buy it myself—I've always wanted one to tinker about with—will you do something for me in return?"

"That sounds like bribery and corruption."

"Nothing of the kind. It's a business deal. If I find your machine suits me, and buy it, will you undertake to get customers for my friend's work, whenever you see a chance? She does lovely miniatures, but it's so hard to get together a connection just now. If you *could* take a specimen about with you, and show it to people, just casually—and, of course, it would be better if you had one done of yourself; she'd be only too glad to do it free, as an advertisement——"

If Sally had not been too excited, even she would have noticed the frown on his face.

"I'd do that much for your friend without your needing to buy my machine as a reward," he said.

But Sally shook her head.

"Shouldn't think of letting you. 'Nothing for nothing' is the only motto in business. Will you take it on? But you must see her work first."

"I'll come round and see it, if I may," he agreed at once. "But I've got to go off again to-morrow— to Scotland this time, to choose some Highland cattle —a longish trip, I'm afraid. Shall I come directly I'm back?"

"Splendid!" cried Sally. "And when can I inspect your machine?"

"I'll bring it round myself, this afternoon," he said. "You can have it on approval, if you like, while I'm away."

Sally was too busy with her own thoughts to answer. She had so longed for the chance of doing something for Averil, who, by her mere existence, had done so much for her. This chance seemed Heaven sent! She had fifty pounds in the bank, useless for financing her own career, but enough to give a helping hand to Averil's. If she bought this man's machine with it, and if he in return would find customers for Averil—for she meant to keep him up to the mark— his efforts might be the means of giving Averil a real start. And she would owe that start to Sally.

Incidentally, Sally herself would become the owner of a thing she had always coveted, but had hitherto found no excuse for buying. But Sally took this leap in her stride, and managed, in the hurry of it, to forget that her motives were mixed, if ever so slightly.

. . . . . . . .

That afternoon she burst in with—
"Averil, my dear, you're a made woman! I've found a man who's going to send you so many customers the studio will be crammed with them!"
Midge Earnshaw, draped over the window sill, stared at her as at an unwelcome intruder. But Averil played up, and put her two hands on Sally's shoulders.
"Is it really true? How ever did you manage it?"
Sally took a deep breath and told her.
"But that's impossible," broke in Averil. "You don't really want a motor cycle, and I know you can't afford it. Do you think I could let you spend all that money for me?"
"You've got to! I fixed it all up quickly, so you couldn't object." (Why can't I tell her it wasn't so much of a sacrifice?) "It really was a bargain, Averil," she added. "And I expect I can sell it again if I want to."
She was too triumphant to notice the other girl's slight hesitation before the eagerly expected gratitude came.
"I'll never be able to thank you properly! Even if it doesn't lead to anything—though I expect it will," she amended hastily. "But you shouldn't have done it, old thing—it was too much."
Averil was wondering whether she had done the right thing in making no further protest. On the other hand, had she thanked enough? By imperceptible degrees, she had begun to weigh her words, when dealing with Sally, even more carefully than she did

46

with other people. It was so easy to hurt Sally—
"Who is this chap, anyway?" asked Midge, from
the window.

"Oh, I don't know—a stock farmer of sorts, from
British East, he said. He seemed a trustful sort of
beggar, he took my cheque."

(She had told him so, and he had said, smiling,
"You're risking that I shan't turn up again to keep
my word." And she had agreed that they would have
to trust each other, that far.)

Midge insisted on celebrating at the Royalty, and
Sally walked home that night between the other two,
feeling that life was really beginning to come her way
at last. Under the stimulus of her own successful
seizure of a lucky chance, she even found her pitying
tolerance for Midge reviving. When they were still a
little way from No. 17, she said she would run on and
make some coffee for him.

They were rather a long time following, and she
went to the window and leant out to look for them.

They stood in the shadow of the half-open door.
His arms were round her, his head bent over hers.

Sally was staring into the fire, chin in hands, when
Averil came upstairs. She ignored a request to pass
the cigarettes.

"Got a headache?" asked Averil.

"No," said Sally. Then, unable to stop herself she
went on, "I saw you two, just now. Is that what
you've been doing all the time, while I've been away
at work? You don't—you can't—*care* for that
boy?"

Averil's brown glow deepened, but she laughed.

"There's nothing to get so tragic about! Midge is
one of my oldest friends—you're forgetting that.

47

Why shouldn't I say good-night to him, if I want to?"

"D'you say good-night to all your old friends like that—all the men you've got up there?"

Sally pointed a finger of denunciation at the photographs.

"Some of them. It pleases them, and it doesn't hurt me. Why, haven't you done the same yourself, Sally?"

Sally remembered the occasions during the Society period when she had not only been kissed, but had quite enjoyed it—until the kissers mistook her pleasure for the evidence of a more serious emotion, and betook themselves elsewhere with all haste. But that had been before Averil came—just the passing distractions of lonely youth, seeking a new sensation. Surely Averil, with her wide experience, must have found out long ago the misunderstandings that lurk in kisses, must know that, even though they may mean nothing to the man, he is generally convinced they mean the world and all to the girl? And when the man was a Midge—

"It's not that," she said. "It's—do you mean to say you can't see the idiot's in love with you?"

"That's why he wants to kiss me, I suppose."

Averil's mellow tones had given place to the clipped, hard voice she only used when she was angry. Her face had gone as cold and obstinate as a stone, and the deep sea eyes were clouded almost to black. Sally had never seen her just like that before, and she took, with one side of her mind, a purely detached pleasure in watching the transformation.

"You don't mean to marry him, of course, so it isn't fair. You're making him hope impossible things. Oh, you must see it!"

48

# SURPLUS

"Midge and I understand each other," said Averil, in the same cold voice. "It's our business."

"Don't you see it's my business, too?" pleaded Sally, at that. "Don't you see that everything you do affects me just as much as it does yourself? I can't believe we don't think alike about that sort of thing, when we do about everything else."

"Well, we evidently don't, if you think what I did just now was wrong."

"Not wrong, but—beneath you. Letting Midge think you're the sort of girl who can't live without love-making in dark corners——"

Averil turned away, as if the discussion were not worth continuance. But Sally, in the bitterness of her heart, could not leave it at that. Instead, she said the most foolish thing possible under the circumstances.

"Do you think your Midge, for all he's such an old friend, would have done what I did for you, this afternoon?"

She met the scorn in Averil's eyes, and looked away.

"If you want to know, Midge would have given me his last penny, and never mentioned that he wasn't a millionaire, instead of boasting about it."

So there was Sally, left with the heart of her cowering in a ditch, while her tongue still wanted to brazen it out against the beloved. She had never before seen Averil angry, and the shock of it thrilled while it scared her.

But she whirled about, crying—

"Of course, Midge is perfect, and I don't pretend to be. I'm off to bed."

Even then she paused a second, with the door in her hand, before shutting it. But Averil, by habit and instinct, was silent. She knew that when Sally said the room was hot, for instance, it was no use arguing the point, because Sally could prove it *was* hot. On the other hand, it was no use telling her to open the window, because sooner or later she would complain about the draught.

A queer creature, Sally, full of sudden twists and turns—it was she who had the artistic temperament, of course. Averil having had to do all her life with simple, downright natures—people who treated their loves and hates and fears as things not to be argued about, but accepted, as one accepts day and night —found that temperament a stimulating, delightful novelty. Occasionally, though, it might be trying, because so difficult to understand.

To-night—well, to-night it had caused her to lose her temper. A thing unheard of, a dreadful, scorching, terrifying thing. Averil thanked Heaven that it was over now. Of course, Sally would have come to her senses in the morning, would be her friendly self again.

She was really sleepier than usual, though she always did drop off the moment her head touched the pillow—

Upstairs, Sally lay staring through the uncurtained window on to a jungle of roof stacks. The moon had not yet risen, but enough light struck up from the street at the corner to give the illusion of monstrous height to those buildings. Up and up they towered, hiding the sky, almost. Near the top of the highest was a single lighted window, staring malevolently down. A woman was singing up there, and the thin, remote sound of it floated across to Sally.

She had been unkind to Averil, to the dream girl.

But of the things she had said, she had meant only that she was disappointed.

Knowing the perfect friend possessed innumerable virtues she herself lacked, she had—illogically—expected her to have only the faults she shared, and could therefore understand. Allowing herself to be kissed by the originals of those photographs—including this shambling, presumptuous young Midge, who would be unduly encouraged thereby, poor devil! It was out of character, somehow, like a stucco porch on a Georgian mansion. It would have put Averil more on a level with ordinary girls—if anything could do that.

Sally remembered with a stab that, for the first time, she had not said good-night to Averil. (A Kennion, left to herself, would no more have dreamt of saying "good-night," in so many words, to her housemates, than of curtseying to her elders. Both meaningless rituals. If you were fond of people, of course you wanted them to have a good night!)

She thought that the dark girl must be regretting her last taunt, by now—the accusation of "boasting." It had been a thing said in anger, and Sally knew from experience how much that meant. Probably she was wishing to goodness she had submitted to a little well-meant advice—after all, it had been only that—rather than turn and rend the giver. She would say so, to-morrow. But to-morrow would be a long time coming, with the minutes lasting as long as they were doing now—

Sally opened her door softly, and stole downstairs. Outside the studio door she paused, hearing her heart beats echo against the narrow walls, breathing in the smell of stale gas. She knew how disconcerting it was to have one's door opened, in the darkness, without a reassuring voice. So she called "Averil!" through the keyhole.

Averil was a light sleeper, and she answered almost at once.

"That's all right, old thing," she said, when Sally had finished talking, and the relief in her voice was open to no question.

But on the way upstairs again, a doubting devil whispered to Sally.

"Are you sure she wasn't asleep—asleep, when you cared so much?"

## CHAPTER VI

MIDGE achieved no more doorstep tender-
nesses, as far as Sally knew, and Averil
seemed to have forgotten the whole incident, washed it from her memory, leaving not a stain
behind.

True, she did not volunteer the information "Midge
*isn't* a more generous, unselfish friend than you are—
of course he isn't!" But that was not Averil's way.

Little, happy things helped Sally to believe that she
would have said it, if she had been asked. The way
she had of throwing her head back, looking up with
teasing, smiling eyes from her lowly seat on the floor,
when Sally had said something affectionate. The
care she took to remember Sally's tastes in sugar and
salt, and to make the tea exactly right. The number
of times she asked, and followed, Sally's advice as to
the best subjects for her specimen posters.—It was
clearly a waste of time to worry about Midge.

Then, ten days later, Averil got a letter from her
mother commanding her to return at once, or face
the prospect of never being invited again, and to stay
over Christmas. And, when she read that part of the
letter aloud—Sally was already at the door, on her way
to Sampson's—she was interrupted.

"Our first Christmas together? You don't want
to go? You simply can't!"

After which, Sally ran off to work, leaving Averil
to wonder what on earth she meant. Surely most
people—any one of the old Marchester coterie of cou-

sins, for instance—would have said at once that she ought to go home, would have tried to insist on her going, however much they personally wanted her to stay?

Sampson greeted Sally on arrival that morning.

"I've had an enquiry from a gentleman down Richmond way," he said. "I want you to take one of the light cars down to show him. If you manage like you did last time——"

It was not his first oblique, but meaning reference to the occasion when she had come back on such friendly terms with her first customer that he had sold her his machine for a mere song. Sally had taken care to explain that she had only bought it to sell again, so as not to give the impression that her private means were large, or indeed that she had any at all. She knew that nothing enrages the employer of labour, from the Government downwards, more than the mere suspicion that his women workers are not entirely dependent on their earnings for each mouthful of bread. Otherwise, are they not taking it out of the mouths of fathers?

Yet many a man, whose income already runs well into the thousands, is given a directorship worth several thousands more without a second's hesitation. Presumably, thought Sally, that he may be enabled to support thereon at least three extra wives and thirty children.

In this case, though, the explanation was apparently waste of breath. The only aspect of the case that had struck, and kept on striking Sampson, was the fact that she had "got on A1 with the gentleman," and it was because of that fact he was sending her down to Richmond to-day.

# SURPLUS

It was on the tip of Sally's tongue to refuse the errand, and if she had not thought of Averil, counselling prudence, she would probably have done so. She hated the idea that it was only because of her sex she was considered capable of bringing off a deal with a "gentleman," not because her methods of salesmanship showed promise, or in order to give her a sporting chance. But she considered, in time, that it would be idiotic to quarrel with the opportunity on such an account. If her sex did, in spite of herself, give her an advantage—and probably Sampson was right in assuming that it did—why not use it to gain a position in the trade, so high that expert knowledge alone would enable her to keep it? Sally was not the first woman who has used this specious argument.

As she swung down Holland Park Avenue in the wake of a taxi, she was thinking about Averil and Midge, and only incidentally about the morning's letter from Mrs. Kennion. That did not matter—Averil would not go, of course—but Midge might. Averil had given up saying good-night to him on the doorstep, but she had not attempted to hasten his departure when it pleased him to stay late. Did that mean that she was failing to keep him in his right place, which was of no account, compared to Sally's?

But that was absurd. Averil's eyes had looked so wistful that morning, like a dog's that is being called two ways at once. She would never have looked like that for anyone but Sally. Seeing how used she was to giving way to her mother unreasonably, on the score of "anything for peace," it would be splendid to go back to her and say she was to do just whatever she liked about going home (knowing all the time that she would stay).

55

# SURPLUS

On Hammersmith Bridge, a cheerful November sun glinted on the little gilded cupolas of the great arches that span the roadway at each end, making of this bridge a fitting gate into the country. Nowhere else in London is there a boundary that seems so sharp and definite. On the Hammersmith side, only a hundred yards back, a teeming cluster of thoroughfares, two Tube stations, multitudes of clanging trams and electric advertisements, screaming from the sky. And then, on the other side, a road that is no longer a street, with detached houses that are almost cottages, smothered in trees and shrubs—real, green, sappy-looking laurels and hollies, not like the blasé, suavely trimmed specimens in the parks. Even the motors seem to run more sweetly on the further side, with less harsh striving of frustrated effort. As to the horses, they prick their tired ears and step out faster, with a brave jingling of hoofs and harness, as if they suddenly remembered the long lost paddocks of their youth. Barnes and East Sheen lie ahead—how their very names smack of the country, after the iron grimness of Hammersmith.

Nearing East Sheen, on the blind corner where the road narrows and bears sharply to the left, Sally in her little car hugged the wall. Just behind her was a limousine, straining at the leash as it waited to pass. And in the middle of the bend, as usual, there was a No. 33 swinging up from Richmond, taking up three-quarters of the room. She noticed its deck was empty, except for a couple of men huddled in overcoats.

Then, without a second's warning, the steering wheel between her hands refused to function. A violent wrench to the left—the merest touch should have

56

been enough—left it immovable. The 'bus loomed right above her, gigantic, poised to swoop. She felt for the brakes.

There was no time to be afraid, to think of anything, except "Why doesn't that damned 'bus stop——why *won't* it stop——?"

.   .   .   .   .   .   .   .

That afternoon, Midge came to the house in Farthing Lane intent on forcing an issue with Averil. At least, he had been resolved, until he saw her in her old paint-stained overall, standing with her back to him before the easel. She had shut one eye, and was sketching an imaginary line with one strong brown finger. And Midge straightway became an inarticulate youth, with hair a little bit too long and an untidy mouth, and saw that the best thing he could do was to drape himself over a chair by the fire and watch her. As he had done last time, and the time before.

But that day, the issue forced itself. Averil was working on the poster of the "Modern Woman's Armour," which had been shamefully neglected.

"I've been so busy with the life classes," she said. "And getting two specimen miniatures ready for this new man of Sally's to see when he comes, that I've not had a minute to touch this lately."

"It's going to be good," said Midge. He would, of course, have said the same of anything else of hers.

"I don't know—yes, perhaps. But I must get Sally to give me another sitting. I simply can't get her expression."

Midge put another shovelful of coal on the fire, rejoicing that Sally was not there to reprove his recklessness. What an irritating habit she had, though, of creeping into the conversation! Lately it had become

57

impossible to be with Averil for five minutes on end without hearing her name. It was always Sally's opinions she quoted, Sally who was working so hard, Sally who would not like it if they did not come straight home after the theatre, because she was tired. Midge was all at once certain that it would get worse and worse, if he could not do something to prevent it. There would be simply none of Averil left for him.

"Supposing this man, whoever he is, never turns up?" he said suddenly.

"Right eyebrow wants to go a bit higher," mused Averil. "Oh, I expect he'll turn up all right. Sally seemed pretty certain."

That name again!

"Yes, but supposing he doesn't? There's nothing to make him, you know. He hasn't met you."

"Then he won't—that's all. What are you driving at, Midge?"

Averil came across the room to the fire. She leant one arm on the mantelpiece, and stirred the fire with her toe.

"And supposing you never get any more commissions than you're getting now?" pursued Midge. "You know that's not unlikely, Plums. And they say there's an awful lot of competition in the poster line, even when you've finished your training. The chances are you'll never make enough to be really independent."

"What an old croaker you are, this afternoon! It must be time for your tea," laughed Averil.

She was moving off to the cupboard when Midge, suddenly brave with desperation, caught her arm.

"You're not going to put me off like that. I want

58

to know—seriously—how long you're going to stick it out?"

"And I tell you—seriously—that I don't know. I've hardly started yet. Will that satisfy you?"

She stood looking down on him, in her eyes the lure of unconscious strength that Sally had seen there. It seemed that one word, one movement more must force her to reveal her secret heart, to cross the hair line between the passive state of loving, being loved, and the active state of loving. Midge thought, "It's now or never—she'll never be so near me again." And he put his head down, so to speak, and rushed his fence.

"No, it won't. You know how I feel about you. You know how many times I've asked you to marry me, at least I daresay you haven't bothered to count, but I know. Of course, it was all impossible in the old days, but now—there's some talk of an assistant managership that'll be vacant soon, and I've got a good chance for it—so there's nothing really against it, is there—Plums?"

"Only that I don't want to get married. My career's got to come first. Sally says I'm going to be a great artist."

She smiled at him, and he moved his fingers towards her wrist.

"That wretched girl!" he cried, goaded beyond bearing. "It's always the way, when two women get together on their own. Can't you see what she's doing to you?"

"What is she doing?"

Averil's tone was ominous, but the young man had gone too far to retract. Like most nervous people, when once his feelings had got the better of his shyness, there was no holding him.

59

"She's doing all she can to make you like herself. You never used to talk all this rot about your career coming first. That's what all these women say, and not one of them means it."

"Sally does, anyway," said Averil.

"Then she ought to be ashamed of herself. And there's no reason why you should copy her—*you* don't mean it—you may now, but you won't always. If you stay with that girl, she won't let you marry anybody. I know I'm not fearfully clever, but I can see that much. She's trying to get you in her power, and keep you all to herself."

Averil shook her head vigorously. It was true in a way, she knew, but not in that way. One of Sally's little eccentricities was that she preferred the evenings when the two of them were alone together, and Averil judged that the reason was that she had never been used to life with a large family party. She preferred to hold forth to an audience of one—and there were always so many things she had to talk about, bless her! But to say of her, "She won't let you marry anybody"! Midge did not understand Sally, that was all, and he had no right to criticise and abuse her. He was show-ing himself a prey to petty jealousy.

"You're all wrong about Sally. She's not as selfish as all that. If she thought I really wanted to get married, she wouldn't say a word against it."

"Well, if so—can't you possibly marry me?"

He had risen, and was standing over her. The short winter twilight had set in, and the grey window square behind him was growing momentarily more indistinct. But there was the fire glow to dance in the dark hair of his lady, to soften the curve of her firm brown throat, to pick out the unexpected dimple

60

SURPLUS

in the side of her round chin.  Unlike Sally, he saw
no hint of squareness about that chin.  To him, it did
not say, "I can take care of myself, and of you, too."
It said, "I *can* take care of myself—but I'd just as
soon you did it for me."

"You could go on with your work as much as you
liked.  We've always been good pals, haven't we?
Think what pals we could be if we got married!"

His hands were on hers, on her shoulders—she
could feel their trembling.

"Are you sure you don't care like that?" he whispered.

And Averil was not sure.  She had always loved
certain things about Midge Earnshaw—above all,
the real goodness of him, which she alone seemed to
be able to assess at its true value.  He was the most
truly unselfish person she knew, and unselfishness
was the quality in others that most appealed, perhaps,
to Averil.  In the old days he had never actually
proposed to her, she knew, because he did not think
it fair to ask her to wait.  Silently he had watched
her being sought by other men.

He was shy and *gauche,* but Averil understood and
sympathised with that.  He was so young still, only
a boy for all his tallness.  He might do great things
yet.  She had not tried to pull his hands away, and a
warm current flowed from them that the vitality in
her leapt up to meet.  There would be something so
simple and easy in doing what he wanted.

They neither of them heard footsteps on the stairs,
but they did hear a knock.  It was Mrs. Dunn,
puffing explosively, with a telegram for Averil.

"Miss Wraith injured motor accident, asking for
you."

# SURPLUS

If Midge had known what that little yellow envelope was going to do to him, he would have torn it from her hand and cast it to the flames. As it was, he merely said—

"What's up—darling?" waiting to finish the sentence till Mrs. Dunn had disappeared.

"It's Sally," answered Averil quickly. "She's had a smash. She's all alone in a hospital in East Sheen. The poor old thing, they don't say how bad she is——"

She was busy already, taking down her big coat from the peg behind the door. Midge stood where she had left him, following her with his eyes again.

"Answer before you go, Plums. Say you'll come to me?"

But Averil had her hand on the door knob.

"How can I, now this minute? Sally wants me."

She was slipping away from him again, and she had been so near. That time when he had kissed her good-night, it had been on her forehead only, the sort of salute a brother might have given. She had not seemed to care then, whether he felt it as that or not, But to-night he felt she would care—would see that they could not even pretend, in future, to be just pals.

"That's damned nonsense!"—he caught her wrist again. "You know I don't mean just at this minute, I mean for always. Don't go without answering, Plums—please!"

But Averil had altogether ceased to tremble, now.

"If you must have an answer this minute—though I don't see why you should—it'll be no," she said.

"You don't mean——"

# SURPLUS

"I do. I'm not going to desert Sally like that. We've only just started together; I must have time to think over it. Let me go, Midge, dear! We shan't even be friends, if you don't——"

He was left listening to her firm, quick footsteps—she did not run—and the shutting of the street door. On the floor lay the crumpled telegram, where she had thrown it. Mechanically he picked it up, smoothed it, and folded it neatly, again and again, into a tiny square.

He knew Averil well enough to know that hers was not an impulsive nature. She preferred to have a good long time in which to make up her mind, and to be left quite free during that time, at the end of which her decision was irrevocable. And she expected her friends to trust her to have their interests at heart, without any urging on their part. He remembered an occasion when he had wanted her to fix a day for an excursion, and she had said she couldn't, for fear she might have to let him down after all. But he had gone on pressing her, and in the end she had said she could not go at all.

It had been touch and go, that afternoon, he thought. If the telegram had not come just when it did. As it was, the balance had been tipped in Sally's favour, whether permanently or not remained to be seen. But Midge was afraid. He had waited so patiently during these last months of renewed intercourse, and now at the last, victory within sight, he had done the forbidden thing—he had pressed her to decide.

Already he regretted it. Also he cursed all the breed of bachelor girls, more particularly such as attempted to gain converts to their silly theories of independence, with a thoroughness that would have surprised and impressed Sally. During his sojourn in the East he had acquired proficiency in that art, if in nothing else.

## CHAPTER VII

THE position of Barton's Nursing Home was responsible for adding many guineas to its fees. It lay well back from the main road, and was surrounded by opulent looking gardens which, as a matter of fact, belonged to the neighbouring residences, but nobody was to know that until they had actually become inmates, and had attempted to explore beyond the narrow domain of Barton's proper.

Being a private institution, its outer aspect was a little more friendly than that of our excellent public hospitals. The windows were all curtained, so that one could not catch vague, sinister glimpses of starched white caps and meticulously trim blue uniforms, bulging only in the right places, moving soundlessly, like shadows of ill omen, on their mysterious business at the bedside. The windows themselves were opened to different widths, not all arranged on the same pattern, to admit the same prescribed amount of air. And on the sill of one of them lay a brush and comb, spread out to dry, just as if ordinary human beings, still occupied with the frivolities of living, had placed them there.

But the front door was obviously a hospital door, painted a sickly light green to match the gate posts, with the usual array of bells at the side, all so clean and shiny—shiny and efficient, like the surgeon's knife. Averil's breath quickened a little as she pressed the one marked "Visitors."

She had had time, during her hurried journey, to think a good deal about Sally. Though she might have a queer temper, she also had a fund of sympathy to counteract it. She could be such a dear, in her best moods, and she so badly wanted looking after! The sudden quixotism of the motor cycle purchase had been typical of her, too. Averil forgot the scorn that had possessed her when, so soon afterwards, Sally had asked, "Do you think Midge, for all he's such an old friend, would have done the same?"

Averil did not wonder whether that bid for first place in her gratitude had not been equally characteristic—it would have needed far too much sifting out of motives. The plain facts at present were that Sally was in trouble, through no fault of her own, and that she, Averil, was going to the rescue as fast as the 'bus would take her. (All the same, if the case had been reversed, Sally would have taken a taxi.)

She was lying propped with pillows when Averil entered.

"So you came at once—you brick! Did you find any bits of the car lying about in the road?"

"Did you think I should wait till to-morrow?" said Averil.

As always when she was moved at all, her voice was gruff, her manner detached to the point of hostility as she seated herself on the extreme edge of the bed foot. Sally, white beneath the brown, her eyes brilliant and smiling, was behaving in the jolly, careless way she best understood. This was how cousin Dina, for instance, would have taken a trifle like colliding with a 'bus.

"What happened, old thing?"

"The steering wheel jammed, goodness knows why,

and I couldn't stop in time. They say the 'bus pulled up in five yards, or I should have been finished. As it is, I'm only bruised and concussed a bit. But the car was smashed up."

Suddenly, thinking it over in order to describe it, Sally realised how bad she felt now. Her head ached and throbbed, the room swam round her dizzily, the hand she stretched out to clutch the counterpane would not close properly. And that was enough for Averil, whose warmest demonstration of affection was a smile, when you were well. She slipped from her perch and knelt, with her arm round Sally's shoulders.

"You wouldn't have cared if that 'bus hadn't stopped."

The words jumped from the very depths of a secret fear, and Sally did not try to hold them back. Why should she, seeing that the invalid, of all people, has licence to say just whatever she wants to? It was an opportunity to revel in.

"Of course, you know that's not true," Averil was muttering. "I should be—but why even think about it?"

"You've only known me such a little time, compared to your other friends."

"Yes. But I don't know—I feel as if we'd known each other for ages."

Sally turned sideways then, and looked up at the great grey violet eyes, in which so many hearts had drowned themselves in vain.

"D'you mean that? Don't say it, if it's not true."

"Of course. We're pals, Sally."

Anyone else would have left well alone, at that. But Sally, as usual, could not wait to find out whether this was the right moment for plunging to the heart of the matter.

"Not just casual, ordinary pals, but special ones? You may laugh, but I've never cared for anybody before this, not really. I've always known I should meet someone like you sooner or later, I suppose. If you leave me now, it'll be worse than before—are you going to leave me?"

Averil smiled at that.

"If you think I'm going to run off with Midge tomorrow, I can tell you I'm not."

"I never thought you'd be such a fool as to think of it, even," cried Sally. "It's only that having him around has made me frightened. Are you sure you're never going to leave me—for anybody else?"

There was silence for a moment in the little room, while from the corridor came the "whush, whush," of rubber heeled feet, the opening and shutting of a muffled door. Afterwards, Sally could always remember those sounds, and the cold, unwinking, sinister glow of the electric fire, that she could just see over the end of the bed.

"How can one tell for certain?" said Averil. "It's no good looking so far ahead. Let's be as happy as we can together now."

"But I can't—I'm afraid. Before Midge turned up, I thought you never even thought about the idea of getting married, any more than I do."

"Doesn't everyone think about it, now and again?"

"No," declared Sally. "Not when they've made up their mind that they're not suited for it, and when they've found that work and friendship's just as good. Haven't you made up your mind, too?"

Averil withdrew her arm.

## SURPLUS

"I'm not going to promise never to marry, if that's what you mean. How can I? Don't be such an idiot!" Then she added, "If you're friends with a person, you can trust them, and they can trust you, without any promises."

But Sally clutched her wrist with cold fingers.

"How can I trust you to stick to me, when you keep this man hanging round like this, on the chance of marrying you?"

Averil's silence was one of thought, but Sally put the worst construction on it.

"You mean you aren't going to stick to me," she cried. "You're going to leave me, sooner or later. All right, do it now, then—marry Midge, before I get so's I can't live without you!"

And she buried her head in the pillow, clenching her teeth on the sounds of her grief, but all the same reducing Averil to a state of terror that was partly mental and partly physical. Scenes of any sort—she had known very few—had always affected her as they are traditionally supposed to affect the male of the species. She would give or do almost anything to stop them. This one had come about so suddenly that she could not remember how it had started, but she gathered that the fault must in some way have been hers. At any rate, Sally must be pacified, and that at once.

"I'll send Midge right away, then. Will that do?"

"Not if you're going to wish you hadn't, after-wards," moaned Sally.

"What rot! I don't want to marry him."

"Or anybody else?"

"Or anybody else. And if I don't do it now, I'm pretty certain I never shall. I shall be too busy work-

69

ing. We'll end up single together, Sally, so cheer up!"

"But I don't want you to promise anything, or give up anything that'll make you happy, because of me— because you're sorry for me."

And Averil, the dream girl, the friend in a thousand, did not retort, "Why didn't you think of that earlier?" Instead, she said:

"I'm going to be happy, all right. So don't go on worrying about it. Isn't it about time you had supper? I'll call the nurse."

But Sally said:

"Let's shake hands on it."

So the short, square-tipped fingers closed over the long, thin ones. Through Sally's mind ran a text, strangely enough—a relic of the far off days when she had accompanied the family to church, and mumbled doubting prayers to a God she could never quite believe was listening. It was the cry of David over Jonathan—"Thy love for me was wonderful, passing the love of women."

This was a woman's friendship, and it should be— was already—a greater thing to both of them than the love of any man.

"You know I care, too," said Averil, then. "Only I can't talk about it, like you can. You'll just have to believe it."

"I'll try," promised Sally. "And I'll try not to talk about it either, after to-night. I know I'm inclined to drip with sentiment, but I'm going to stop up the leaks."

It ought to be easy, when the perfect friend had once said that she cared, too—she who so seldom showed her feelings. Sally tried to fix that fact in her

# SURPLUS

brain, so that she would remember it if ever in the future she should be tempted to feel afraid.

Back in Farthing Lane, Averil felt as if virtue had gone out of her. It was almost impossible to tire her physically, but a scene of any sort left her weak all over. Her hand was shaking as she began to write a letter—but no one would have guessed a thing like that of Averil.

As a matter of fact, an acceptance to an invitation would have taken just about as much careful thought before she could find the right words. Averil shared the awe of the savage or the solicitor for the written word. She had the feeling, always, that with each stroke of the pen she was committing herself irrevocably to a certain course of action, was giving some new power over herself to the recipient. And in this connection, the value of ambiguity did not occur to her. Unlike Sally, she had never said she would "come if it was fine," meaning if no more amusing invitation were to crop up in the meantime.

This letter was to Midge, and it told him that she could not do what he had asked that afternoon. It was short, and not effusive even for her, but she read it over twice and did not alter a word. Midge would understand; none of the "old crowd" had required long drawn out explanations. What good did explanations ever do, after all? Once one had made up one's mind, no amount of talking or thinking about it could make the slightest difference—all that had to be done beforehand, and the pros and cons carefully weighed.

Only sometimes, as in this case, one was hurried into a decision. Pity for Sally, who was taking everything so pluckily except the prospect of losing

71

SURPLUS

her, had forced her hand, and it was stronger than
her impulse, never anything but faint, to marry
Midge. The fact that it meant a ruthless cutting
short of the time wherein Midge might at least have
gone on hoping was unlucky for poor Midge, that
was all. Averil saw his point of view, and she was
sorry for him. But she felt certain that after the
first disappointment was over he would slip back into
his old niche of a valued friend, writing and coming
to see her as often as possible.

And even if he proved the exception to the rule,
and she lost his friendship altogether, there would
be no occasion to mention the fact to Sally. Averil,
when once she had decided to make any kind of sacrifice, could be relied on to pay the bill without grum-
bling when it turned out to be larger than she had
bargained for. That was in her bond of friendship.

So she went out and posted her letter in the new
scarlet box at the corner, and listened to the dull plop
as it dropped on top of the others—the bundles of
words that could never be recalled, that had travelled
all the way from to-day to yesterday, from the realm
of things still in the making to that of things un-
changeably accomplished, in their passage through that
capacious, ever open, sardonically grinning mouth.
And then, on the way back, she began to think of her
latest poster, "The Man Who Left his 'Page's Patent
Collar Stud' Behind," that she was doing for the sev-
enth lesson of the correspondence course.

She did not think, "Sally deliberately worked on
my pity, till she made me give her a promise I did not
want to give." Sally was her friend, and it would
have been an insult to suspect her of such a low-down
trick. To Averil, the corner stone of friendship and

SURPLUS

of love was that one should desire the greatest happiness of the other, always and inevitably, as the earth went round the sun. It followed that if Sally had been given reason to think that marriage with Midge was the thing she wanted most, there would have been no opposition.

Which conclusion on Averil's part proved that many love affairs cannot teach some people the infinite variety of love.

# CHAPTER VIII

SALLY was still feeling distinctly shaky when she went back to work, but she could not bear the thought of missing any more chances of commission on the orders she felt sure must have been flocking in, during her absence.

She found Mr. Sampson more blandly courteous than usual, and full of anxious enquiries as to her health. Asked as to the state of the wrecked car, he expressed the opinion that it was only fit for the scrap heap.

"A new car, too—such a thing has never happened to the firm before."

He had an air of speaking more in sorrow than in anger that surprised Sally.

"You can claim from the insurance people, of course?" she said. "The steering wheel—but I suppose you've heard what happened?"

He pulled at the lapels of his coat with great deliberation, but his eye did not meet Sally's.

"Miss Kennion told me what you said happened. "That is the claim I shall state," he said.

But there was an emphasis on the last word that a slower mind than Sally's could not have failed to notice.

"Do you mean you don't believe it?" she asked.

Sampson repudiated the bare idea of such a thing with a wave of the hands.

"Don't mistake me, please, Miss Wraith," he

begged. "I'm quite sure you *think* that's what happened. We all know how easy it is to lose one's nerve——"

"Lose one's nerve," cried Sally. "Do you think I haven't got more nerve than to drive straight into a 'bus for no reason at all, after all the experience I've had? How on earth d'you imagine I got through the war without a smash, then?"

As always, when she was angry, her voice had a shrill note in it that carried far. The red-haired youth who polished the cars had stopped his work and was frankly listening. Sampson reached behind her and shut the door of the hutch.

"Even the best drivers are liable to lose their heads occasionally," he said suavely.

"But I tell you I didn't lose my head!"—with the instinct of a trapped creature, Sally began to search her mind for a possible rescuer—"Ask anybody who saw the accident. Ask the police—one of them came to me for particulars, while I was in the hospital."

"Nobody seems to know exactly what happened, but they all agree that you looked very frightened, and that you gave the wheel a sudden wrench. Some say it was after that that the car swerved."

"The last lot are telling lies, then," declared Sally. "And as for looking frightened—wouldn't you, if you saw a 'bus right on top of you, and your steering wheel was jammed?"

Sampson passed a pale hand weakly over his brow. "Women," said the gesture, "oh, you women!"

"Look here, Miss Wraith, there is no occasion for either of us to lose our tempers," he said, with the irritating calmness of the man who means that he has no occasion to lose his, "I am quite prepared to accept your own account of how the accident occurred. But I'm afraid—I am really very sorry—we shall have to dispense with your services after this week."

Sally was so amazed and angry that she could scarcely speak at first. Then she said:

"You mean you're dismissing me because your car was faulty, and nearly killed me?"

The rabbit man registered pain at her language with renewed flapping of hands. It took a woman employee to accept dismissal with so little dignity, so much futile argument!

"Not at all, Miss Wraith. It was only a question of telling you now, or a little later. This—er—unfortunate accident has merely precipitated matters. The fact is, I am making other arrangements."

"Other arrangements?"

She might have been a bristling terrier, trying to bolt him from his corner.

"Yes. I—if you will have it, Miss Wraith, I find it causes great dissatisfaction among the other employees, having you put over their heads in such a position. If there are any commissions going, my foreman and mechanics naturally consider they are entitled to earn them. I think it will be better to employ an ordinary clerk for the duties you have hitherto carried out—admirably, I admit!"

"I don't believe you ever meant me to be anything but a clerk," cried Sally. "You had me here under false pretences, and just because I'm not a man, you thought I wouldn't dare to object."

She bit back the rest of her speech, and added with her best imitation of calmness.

"Very well, Mr. Sampson, I'll leave at once. I suppose you will give me a reference?"

"Certainly—oh, certainly!" he beamed. "A reference as a competent driver would do, I suppose? Competent driver—him, yes." ("What does it matter," he thought. "Her next employer—if she ever finds one—won't be able to come down on me for that.")

It was long past dinner time when Sally came slowly up the stairs of No. 17, after a dismal pilgrimage. All down Portland Street, Langham Place, South Audley Street—Martin was right, nobody wanted a woman in the motor trade.

"Back already—what's happened?" asked Averil, over her shoulder, from the easel.

Sally told her, adding, "What *shall* we do, Averil?"

Looking from the window into Farthing Lane, the greyness of it appalled her. Even the cat crouching on the doorstep opposite was grey and gaunt, a typical London cat, spending the hours in a trance of apathy till night restored to him his spiritual home upon the housetops.

Averil pulled her away from the window, into a chair.

"You poor old thing! I can see you haven't had any lunch—I'm going to get you some straight away."

As if lunch could help! Couldn't Averil see what it meant, that they would not be able to go on together, unless something turned up soon?

"Supposing I can't get another job?"

"But you will, surely," said Averil cheerfully.

"Not in the motor trade. I might as a clerk of some sort."

"But that would mean giving up your career altogether," objected Averil. "How can you think of such a thing?"

77

# SURPLUS

There she stood, very straight and square, the darling ends of her hair etched, fan-like, against the window. One had only to look at her to see that she would never be defeated by life. In the long run she would always get what she wanted, not by fighting for it, but by knowing how to wait for it. Also—and this most of all—because she had the priceless gift of wanting only the thing that was possible. If Averil should ever find herself running after a mirage, she would abandon the chase forthwith.

But here was Sally, having so far tried only one avenue of access to her chosen career, and willing, apparently, to give it up without more ado! Averil did not understand it.

"Why not try another place—Coventry or somewhere, where the big works are?"

"But that sort of place would be hopeless for your kind of work," said Sally.

"Well, I could carry on here."

Sally stared for a second, then sprang to her feet, upsetting her chair in the process.

"After all this time," Sally cried. "After what you said the other night in the hospital—you still don't see that we've got to stick together, whatever happens?"

"My dear old thing, I was only putting myself in your place. Don't you want to do the best for your career?"

"Not if it means leaving you. I'm keen enough on the motor business, but if it comes to choosing between it and you—and you talk as if you didn't mind a bit!"

"Of course I mind, for myself," said Averil. "I should hate you to go off and leave me, Sally, you know that. I was thinking what was best for you, that's all."

78

# SURPLUS

"Well, think again, then, and don't be so bally unselfish," growled Sally. Then shame took her, and she added, "It's I that ought to be thinking what's best for you—and I know you ought to leave me, for your own sake. I shall always have luck like this, and it'll mean that I shall drag you down too. I'm a failure, Averil —by a neck, every time."

But Averil shook her head.

"You're nothing of the sort. And as to dragging me down, that's all nonsense. We're going to succeed together. You said so yourself, not so long ago."

Sally could not speak just then, but she burrowed her head against the comforting shoulder. Then she strolled over to the window again, and stood idly looking out. The door of the motor shed, belonging to the shop opposite, was open now, and she could see the buff coloured outlines of Carnier's motor cycle, the one she had purchased and stored there such a long time ago— no, only the day before the accident. It looked quite imposing, from here.

Suddenly she thought, why not make use of that white elephant, run it as a motor cycle taxi? They were having a great success in some places—

At once, Sally was a being transformed. The room was not big enough to hold her and her plans as one by one she poured them forth to Averil, scarcely waiting for an answer, so anxious was she to get every detail settled at once.

"And you must come in as a sleeping partner," she added the final touch. "As soon as you've anything saved, you must put it into the firm. That is, if the thing succeeds, which it's going to!"

"I shouldn't wait for that," smiled Averil, "if I had the money now."

# SURPLUS

There remained the finding of a suitable place for the new venture, and here again it was Miss Landison who helped. For as soon as Averil had suggested Salter's Ridge, Sally thought of writing straight to "Turrets." And the answer, saying that as far as she knew there were only two taxi cabs in the place at present, and there should be room for another, was more satisfactory than Sally had dared to hope. Not only that, but Miss Landison mentioned there was a furnished cottage going cheap.

Not "rooms," but a whole cottage, where you had the place to yourself, where you could settle down! On that night of her life, Sally was an optimist, believing that all things work together for good—to the being who has found the perfect friend. Obviously, it was all owing to Averil, without whose existence the motor cycle would never have been purchased, nor experience patiently gained in the thralldom of Sampson. It was another case of the house that Jack built.

Averil herself was so delighted, too. Sally thought how glad she must be that she had promised to become a partner in the firm—glad for her own sake. Now that they were to have a home of their own, and sacrifices that Averil was making—in giving up the life classes she had started at the Art School, for instance —were more than equalised.

To Sally, that had always been the only inducement towards married life, with anybody but the Fairy Prince—a house of your own. It was so difficult to save enough, out of any feminine salary, to buy one! Which explained why she could understand a girl marrying almost anyone for that—just for the sake of being able to furnish the drawing-room to suit herself, even if the chairs and tables had to be made of packing cases.

The very patch of ground on which the house was built, she coveted.  Somewhere, far back in the Wraith ancestry—they came of a good old stock—there must have been a feudal lord who died defending his castle, when he could have saved himself by surrendering it. Perhaps, too, a trusty friend—his lady, or a brother baron—had stood with him on the battlements, and gone down beside him, laughing, into the darkness.

For a house that is not shared by the right person is as much like a home as a bowl of fresh water is to a whiting.

## CHAPTER IX

"MOSS COTTAGE" was, from the outside at least, a thing to dream of.

It was not, strictly speaking, a cottage at all, but a little L-shaped bungalow, with a steeply pointed roof that might have been mistaken for the second story. Its outer walls were of stone, grey and yellow and pink with weather, as all self-respecting cottage walls should be, but the roof was of slate instead of beautiful furry thatch. This disappointment, however, was made up for by its romantic situation, backed by the rising shoulder of the forest, fronting a wide common pock-marked with patches of black, sandy soil, where gorse bushes had been burnt down the summer before.

Its position was, in fact, a little too romantic in the opinion of Salter's Ridge, which accounted for its ridiculous rental. It belonged to the noble and absentee owner of the forest, whose father had originally built it as a shrine for his less reputable week-end devotions. It was two miles from the main road, three from the golf club and the famous "Tankard Hotel." Moreover, it was reputed to be so damp that it "came off the ceiling in patches."

It had a little garden, very much overgrown with thistles from the common, an open red brick fireplace, and a piano. These facts alone had been enough to send Sally into ecstasies, without counting the well at the bottom of the garden, and the quaint glazed porch, which was intended to keep the wind from the front door. But it was Sally who grumbled when, after the first day of their tenancy, they found that the wind ignored this barrier and came in uninvited, not content with cracks in the floors and the gaps in the window frames, so that the carpets bellied like a ship in full sail, and the china chinked and rattled in its wall cupboards.

As to the piano, only about one note in three would strike, and that was liable to stick if struck with any energy. The fireplace, too, was a snare and a delusion. Either it refused to draw, or else, when the wind was in the east, it burnt so fiercely that, for economy's sake, its eagerness had to be damped with coke—whereupon it gave forth clouds of evil-smelling smoke. And the water from the well had to be drawn up laboriously in a leaky bucket.

These drawbacks hit Sally hardest, because she had expected most. So she grumbled—though nothing would have induced her to leave Moss Cottage—and Averil set to work to improve matters.

"We've got it now, so what's the use of worrying?"

It was Averil who thought of a device of cushions for ensuring sleep of nights, although the mattresses resembled the Brighton Road in the matter of ridges and sudden potholes—if you avoided the former, you landed on the latter, there being no fairway between. It was Averil who had the piano tuned, and the leaky bucket mended.

These things accomplished, Sally settled down to love Moss Cottage. She brought back primrose roots from the forest and planted them round the porch, while Averil covered the window seat cushions afresh. Every evening they sat huddled in overcoats while the

SURPLUS

breeze played round them, and Sally, though she never
forgot to curse the cold, would not have exchanged it
for central heating in someone else's house. It was
like a perpetual camping out, only that the roof over
their heads was solid. But it was "getting a home
together."

So, on a February evening, Sally walked down the
path between the larch trees, and knew that she was
going home.

It had been a day of thick white mists, such as
Salter's Ridge delights in during the winter months—
mountain mist, it is proudly called. Now the sky was
clear and sparsely star spangled, but wisps of mist
still clung to the undergrowth, and to the piles of boul-
ders that lay on each side of the path, where the trees
were thinnest. At each step it seemed the bare
branches above her head rustled in friendly greeting,
though there was no wind. For that forest was never
damp and sodden and sleepy, as other forests are in
winter. It was filled to the last twig with keen, expec-
tant life, not supinely waiting, but holding itself back
on purpose from the first step towards greenness, so
that Spring, when it came, should be the more glorious
surprise.

Sally had just come from the Turret House, from
which she carried spoils in the shape of a couple of
books on loan. Averil declared that poor Miss Landison never saw them unless they wanted to borrow
something, and it was not far from the truth, thought
Sally ruefully. Miss Landison really was a brick, and
took such an interest in the taxi business.

This was progressing, though slowly. Engagements
were not too numerous as yet, Sally's vehicle being
under a grave disadvantage compared with the two
84

original taxis of Salter's Ridge, whose owners were both on the telephone.

Moreover, the motor cycle itself, being no longer in its first youth, challenged unfavourable comparison with those two up-to-date cars. "Georgina," so called because the proper name of her species was so dull and impersonal—consisting, as it did, of a series of letters that might have meant anything—was at her best a noisy brute. Each time she went over a bump there arose a protest from every nut and bolt, a creaking from the wicker sidecar, a rattling of accessories, from head lamp glass to back number plate.

Still, she ran cheaply, and several casual patrons had already become regulars. At first, they had looked on her with the usual suspicion. A taxi driver who was "by way of being a lady" would, they argued, be quite certain to take advantage of the fact. She would want to know them socially, would get herself called on, invited out to tea—and then how could one argue with her over the matter of an over-charged fare, or curse her for being late, or press 3d. into her palm when she had lifted one's suitcase down from the luggage grid?

But it soon appeared that Miss Wraith insisted firmly on remaining a taxi driver, and nothing else. She never opened her lips except when spoken to, and then her answers, though considerably more civil and well informed than the average taxi driver's, were impersonal to a degree. She accepted a tip with the same matter of course nod and smile from Mrs. Mc-Intyre, the coal merchant's widow, as from Claud Hennesy, who was the only eligible bachelor among the Residents, and very much aware of the fact. Which procedure, though mortifying to the latter gentleman, was all to the good as regarded her business chances. In fact, judging by her Residential reception, Sally began to have hopes of a golden harvest when the summer visitors should arrive.

She also felt that, since the Farthing Lane days, the perfect friendship had grown deeper, more indestructible. She and Averil knew each other better, and each had grown, in some subtle way, more like the other. Averil talked more, was a little more demonstrative, while Sally had a precarious hold on a certain amount of Averil's calmness. She no longer expected quite so much of the dream girl, but was content that she should have a different taste in friends, for instance. And it was her borrowed level-headedness that helped Sally towards such a reasonable conclusion.

"You caught Averil at an empty time in her life," it said to her. "She had lost sight of her old circle of friends, and had found no new ones to take their places. Now, when she meets any of them again, you mustn't show her you're jealous. After all, she's put you first—she's living with you, which is more than she did with any of them."

Midge, for example, had evidently not meant much in the scheme of things. Averil never mentioned his name now, never heard from him. He had been, indeed, a swiftly passing shadow—past and unregretted.

On this particular evening, as Sally neared the bottom of the path, a light flickered from the back of the cottage. It must be Averil, taking her turn at getting supper; Sally could hear her singing softly to herself, not anxious or worried about anything.

"That smells good!" called Sally.

Averil came out from the kitchen, a frying pan in her hand. She was wearing a brilliant striped apron,

86

a contrast to Sally's ancient, stained trench coat. But it was not worth while changing to a new coat, on a motor cycle. One only washed one's hands between trips, because, otherwise, the food would taste of petrol.

"I had such a stroke of luck to-day, I caught old General What's-his-name—you know, the one who's in the *Sussex Gazette*—coming out of the station. He was going to take Tyler's car, I think, but as soon as he saw me he changed his mind. Tyler was simply raging. He gave me a look that ought to have curdled my petrol."

"I knew you'd do well, as soon as you got properly started," said Averil. "But do take care not to fall foul of the other taxi drivers."

"They'd all of them cut my throat with pleasure, I know that. But I'm not in their power, like I was in Sampson's. Besides, it's all in the day's work."

She liked the careless attitude that last phrase conveyed, it was worthy of Averil herself.

They had finished supper when Averil announced that she had had a visit from Claud Hennesy, who had been introduced to her three weeks ago by the golf club secretary. He wanted her to play with him in the next foursomes competition, and she had said yes, so as to get rid of him quickly and go on working.

"Did you ask him to find a partner for me?" asked Sally quickly.

"Yes. But he said he didn't know of anyone."

"Oh, no one ever does want to play with me," said a bitter, frowning Sally.

"Silly! They would if you gave them a chance. But you're always so rude to them, they're afraid to come near you."

87

SURPLUS

This aspect of the matter pleased Sally, on the other's lips.  At the same time, she would have liked a partner, for the occasions when Averil had one.  She wanted, now, to be Averil's equal as far as possible, even in the power of attracting male homage without lifting a finger for it.  This, not for the sake of the homage itself, but because she could not rid her mind of the fear that Averil might despise her, just a little for lacking it.  Averil's love for her must also have in it something of admiration.  No longer would she, Sally, be the worshipper, and Averil the modest idol, forced willy-nilly on to a pedestal—perfect friendship does not lie that way, she had decided.  But it was so terribly hard to do or be anything that Averil could admire!

To-night, however, Averil evidently saw the right half of the truth, and Sally wanted to do all in her power to mark her gratitude.

"You'll play with him, and win it," she said.  "And I'll walk round with you."

"That'll be splendid," said Averil.

There was never any intentional sarcasm behind Averil's words, and she meant it.  Claud Hennesy had a magnificent drive, but otherwise he did not appeal to her in the least.  Sally's conversation was infinitely preferable.

"By the way," she added, "there's a friend of yours in the paper to-day."

She pointed to a photograph, headed by the caption, "New Breed of Cattle."  But the picture was recognisable as that of a man.

"Mr. Glen Carnier," ran the paragraph underneath, "part owner of a farm near Nairobi, who has produced a new and promising breed of cattle, a cross be-

tween the Highland variety and a native bred short-
horn——"

"So that's why he hasn't bothered to get you any
commissions!" commented Sally. "Though I wrote
to him, care of Sampson's, and sent him our new address. Too busy getting on himself—I might have
known it. I suppose he never bothered to call round
and tell me he was leaving the country, even."

"Oh, well, I don't blame him, if he had to go in a
hurry," said Averil. "It's a good thing you've got
some good out of his machine, anyhow."

Together they bent over the newspaper. Averil put
her finger over the lower part of the face, concealing
it.

"He's got rather jolly eyes."

"Think so? It's a pity he doesn't keep his word.
That would be worth a lot more. I've got no use for
a bargain breaker."

"He's a bit like Bobby Hepworth," remarked
Averil.

Sally looked up at the photographs over the fireplace. Yes, they both had what she called athletic
faces—rather broad, with that direct, calm gaze, and
muscular neck. Of course, this Carnier, too, would
have been Averil's sort—that is to say, he would wor-
ship her, and she would be a good pal to him and enjoy
getting his letters.

"If he'd seen you, he wouldn't have forgotten about
the commissions. He wouldn't have left in such a
hurry!"

"Nonsense. He was awfully interested in *you,*
Sally. Remember the way he told you his private
affairs, the very first time he met you."

Sally thought, "Yes, but that's as far as his interest

89

went. People always do tell me the history of their lives straight off—I don't know why."

Then she thought, "What does it matter, one way or the other?"

But Averil, her eyes dancing with mischief, had started to cut out the little picture.

"There—he must have a frame, poor dear. He can have that old one I used to keep Will Dowson's photo in. I know you can't be happy without a man hanging around."

"Cat!" laughed Sally. "People will think I go in for collecting actors' pictures out of the halfpenny press. You'd better let the wording show, anyhow—'New Breed of Cattle'—not a bad description, now I come to think of it!"

So Mr. Glen Carnier was duly installed between Bobby Hepworth and Dr. Barrington Hope, on the mantelpiece.

Like all regular old maids, as Sally put it, they kept a cat, an enormous tawny Tom, with the purr of a wild beast. It hung, that evening, over Sally's knee as she read aloud. The book was Conrad's *The Rescue,* and it filled the room, for her, with the quick smack of waves against planking, with furious creaking of masts and rigging, with scent of spices coming over a heaving, oily sea. She felt herself standing, Averil beside her, at the prow of an outbound vessel, pushing steadily onward into the night.

"We must travel together," she said.

"I've always longed to," sighed Averil, "but that's one of the things women can't do on their own without money."

"We could always go steerage, or get a passage on a merchant ship. That would be best of all."

# SURPLUS

"You'd have to sleep on a hard bunk, or a hammock. Think how you'd hate that!" teased Averil.

"I should hate it in a house. But on a ship—I don't care where I sleep, as long as it's an adventure. Do you?"

"Of course not. I can sleep anywhere. But I don't see why one shouldn't have a bed and adventure at the same time. And anyway I can't think of it now, I've got to do some work first."

"All right, we'll try and have beds thrown in, when the time comes," laughed Sally.

The crackling logs filled up the silence. Averil yawned, and gently poked the cat's ribs.

"Talking of beds——"

"You are—happy with me?" asked Sally suddenly, "Perfectly happy, I mean—never bored, or wanting anything else?"

"How could I be bored, with my work to think of always? And of course I'm happy. Why on earth d'you keep asking questions like that—do I look as if I was wasting away?"

"But perfectly happy means a lot, you know," said Sally. "I had my hand read, ages ago, and the woman told me I should never be really happy all my life. Cheering, wasn't it? But I am now, and I know it. That shows how miserable I must have been before. I keep telling myself, 'You've got what you were waiting for, when you felt you were never meant to get it—there must be a catch somewhere!"

Averil looked up with a caress in her eyes. But she said, "You've got heaps of things to make you happy—your work, and games, and music—everything I've got, only more, because you're cleverer."

"I'm afraid, sometimes," went on Sally, unheeding.

91

"I even say prayers about it, occasionally, on the chance. But I don't think anyone believes in prayers, since the war. You've only got to read the papers——"

"Perhaps the sort that still say their prayers don't get into the papers," put in Averil.

"Don't fool," cried Sally. "Seriously, do you ever say yours? D'you believe in that sort of God—in any sort?"

Averil went on playing with "Tins," her head bent over his delightful soft white waistcoat. Then she said:

"Not every night, like I used to as a kid. But I believe—oh, I don't know—one doesn't talk about such things, does one? But I suppose I believe in doing the best you can, and not waiting to find out first whether you're going to get rewarded for it."

It was impossible ever to get to the bottom of Averil, and that was part of her fascination for Sally. She seemed so simple, so direct, and yet there were always reserves, unsuspected opinions that one came upon suddenly, with caught breath, as on a jewel in an enchanted wood.

"Then you're not sure whether there's another life or not?" urged Sally.

"I haven't thought about it much, I can't see that it really matters much. If there is one, we've got to go through with it whatever it's like, and thinking about it won't make any difference. And if there isn't, then wanting it won't make it happen."

"But if someone you loved died? Supposing one of us died—wouldn't you want to make sure we should meet again?"

"What a ghoul you are, Sally! *Don't* be so wor-

ried about it. I hate you to be miserable like this."
The sympathy in her voice went to one's head like
wine. Sally wanted more of it.

"How can I help being worried? If I thought we
should be separated then——"

"As I say, I've never studied the subject. But I'm
pretty sure that we meet the people we've loved.
There wouldn't be any sense in life, otherwise," pronounced Averil.

But Sally said, "Supposing there isn't any sense
in it?"

On which Averil took her by the shoulders and
shook her, as one shakes a favourite child who wants
to put her fingers in the fire to see if it is hot.

"It's no good thinking about things like that. You
go round and round in a circle."

"But it's so damned hard not to!"

"I know—it's hard. I suppose I could do it myself, if I let myself go."

The bliss and safety of living with someone who had
the strength to think just as deeply as it was wise,
and then, of her own will, to stop thinking! Because
she was the perfect friend, she could be told all one's
own disordered fancies. There was no need to pause
and wonder how she would take it, whether she would
laugh when she ought to be serious, or mistake sarcasm for sentiment.

For Averil took a confidence in the only way it
ought to be taken. She took each thought that was
offered her and turned it round, before answering,
giving it back with something added—the finishing
touch, the sane touch. It was not that she resolved
one's doubts—and most of Sally's thoughts were
doubts—but that she took the sting from them.

93

# SURPLUS

"I don't know the answer," said Averil, in effect, "but I know it'll be all right. No, I don't know how I know—I just know."

And because she knew, Sally was comforted. But not before she had torn the subject to shreds in the fury of her doubting. With Averil—only with Averil—it was not necessary to stop at the beginning, as one had to with other people, because they were getting bored, or because it was so selfish, not to mention being bad form, to discuss gloomy, depressing topics like the soul and God. Averil was never bored, she never got tired of listening. It was her way of showing her delight in Sally's cleverness, her wonder at the swift, glancing movements of that mind so different in its methods from her own.

Now she did the thing of all others that Sally would have chosen at that moment. She went to the piano, and began to sing, in the small, haunting mezzo that was just what one would have expected from her speaking voice. Most of her songs were French—trifles, with an elusive, melancholy refrain, most of which were strangers to Sally. But she greeted them like long lost friends. They were the expression of the other part of Averil's nature, the wistfulness that was her Celtic heritage, but that she hid so carefully from the world.

> "Si vous n'avez rien a me dire,
> Pourquoi venez vous près de moi?
> Pourquoi me faire ce sourir,
> Qui tournerait la tête au roi?"

sang Averil. And though her own smile might well have turned a king's head, it was the tears in her voice that held the heart of Sally Wraith.

## CHAPTER X

IT was Miss Landison who introduced them to
Mavis Barron.

The winter was her worst time, and she lay on
her couch in the bay window day after day, all alone
among her bookshelves. It was a quaint, octagonal
room, beautiful even, with the atmosphere of slight
aloofness that characterised its inmate. As if she
wished the visitor, on entering, to perceive merely a
general effect of peace and order, and the smell of
leather bindings and of flowers—not a particular book
or blossom prominently displayed, not a fragrance peculiar to herself.

"I met a girl yesterday," she said once, when Sally
had come to borrow another book; "she walked
through my garden by mistake. She's training to be
a professional violinist, and her people can't afford to
pay her fees any longer. So she's come down here
to stay with her aunt out at Greenhurst, and is trying to
get a few pupils during the summer, so as to be able
to go back and finish. I told her about you two, and
she said she would so like to meet you."

Sally's thought was, "What do I want with other
girls, when I've got Averil?"

Miss Landison might have read it, for she said:

"It's just as well to make a few outside friends,
don't you think? One gets into a rut, sometimes, in
the country."

"You think Averil's bored?" said Sally quickly.
"But she isn't."

"No—I wasn't thinking of that," murmured Miss Landison.

In the end Mavis Barron was asked to tea, one day when Averil found time to make a cake. They wanted to entertain their first visitor in a style that should be worthy of Moss Cottage.

Sally had just come in from a station job when the strange girl arrived, and she was surprised to notice that a man accompanied her as far as the gate. She proved to be a tall, stately creature, with the face of a child who has not yet thought of growing up—skin a faintly flushed white, and hair that looked like the inside of a silver birch leaf. Sally admitted at once that her prettiness provided a delightful foil to Averil's dark beauty. In addition, she had a pretty, shy smile, utterly unlike anything in the nature of a professional musician that Sally had ever seen.

"I'm glad I let Mr. Gathorne show me the short way down through the woods," she said. "I'd never have found it by myself."

In response to their questions, she explained that St. John Gathorne was a Salter's Ridge resident and an artist, of all strange combinations. His wife had answered her advertisement, and she had just been arranging to give some lessons to his eldest little girl.

"He told me he'd often wanted to get inside this cottage, to see how much of a shock it would be after the outside. I believe he'd have come in just now, if I had let him!" she finished.

"What a pity you didn't. It would have been nice to meet a fellow artist," said Averil.

Whereupon Sally ran out at once, and came back breathless and triumphant, leading a wisp of a man by a cadaverously thin hand.

SURPLUS

"I never take tea," he was protesting querulously.
"Really, it's very kind of you—just for a minute,
then."

His hair was flattened back from a high, sallow
forehead, and his black eyes moved restlessly about
the room as he sat there, shoulders humped and head
thrust forward, in a position that reminded Sally of
a curious tortoise.

"Mr. Gathorne does those ripping full-page sketches
for "The Club Window" and "Mary," explained the
girl, and turning to him, "Miss Kennion is an artist,
too."

"Rotten stuff," he said at once. "If you're trying
to make a living out of art, Miss—Kennion?—let me
advise you to give it up. That is, unless you've got
a pull with the right people. Poster work? Even
that's too crowded to pay nowadays, unless you've got
a name."

He launched forth into a racy account of a man
he knew who had married the daughter of a Labour
M.P., and now did all the cartoons for a prominent
Liberal daily.

"Bilge, of course—all bilge," he finished, having
never raised his voice from its pitch of cold irritation.
"But it's the kind of thing they want. That's why I
do it myself. One has to live."

"Mr. Gathorne's been talking like that all the way
here, but I don't believe he really means it," commented Mavis Barron.

The man said nothing to that, but he looked across
at her and smiled. And for that moment his expression was eager and alert, almost charming. Then it
relapsed again into the expression of a discontented

97

and revengeful tortoise, who has been lured out of his shell on false pretences.

He evinced so little interest in Averil's work that Sally reluctantly gave up the attempt to make her show off, after a while. It was not that he found fault with it, but that each poster served merely to remind him of a man he knew who had made a hit with a rather similar subject, entirely owing to his judicious use of graft, back pull, undercut, and other strictly inartistic means. And these little stories, though piquant enough in themselves, were quite useless to Averil, whereas a few words of thoughtful criticism from an expert would have helped her enormously.

Miss Barron, on the other hand, was filled with joy and envy at each detail of their household arrangements.

"It's what I've always longed for," she said. "A cottage just like this. I loathe London, though, of course, I'm miserable away from it now. Two more years of training to go, and here I'm wasting the whole summer. My aunt says the rest will do me good, but I don't need it. I'm as strong as a horse."

She did not look delicate, in spite of the long hands, so white next to the other girls', and the crown of pale hair. There was none of the fine drawn virtuoso air about her that there is about so many amateurs. She did not have to be pressed to come again soon, and bring her violin.

Then Mr. Gathorne roused himself to say that he was going to ask his wife to call.

"But don't expect her for months," he warned them. "She never moves out of the house without the latest infant, and I expect this'll be too far for it, or too damp or something."

# SURPLUS

So they went away together up the dark forest
pathway, and Sally said:
"I rather hope she will come again, don't you?"
Which subtle method of finding out whether Averil
had really been ever so slightly bored by their solitude
was completely successful.
"As long as we have music," agreed Averil. "But
I can't stand aimless tea parties."
And that was the best hearing of the afternoon.
The girl with the silver hair kept her promise.
After that first meeting, she came on to Moss Cottage
nearly every time on the days when she had lessons
in Salter's Ridge. Sometimes she came alone, and
sometimes St. John Gathorne came with her—that
was when she had been teaching his little girl. He
told them that his wife had not yet been able to call,
but that she hoped they would go and see her, instead.
"She's lazy, that's the trouble with her," said Mavis;
"and so wrapped up in the children—she's got five
already—that she doesn't take the slightest interest
in his work, except to complain because it doesn't
bring in enough money. And he doesn't care much
about the children. I can see that. I think he'd
rather have had none—he's a queer creature."
"Why on earth couples like that get married, I can't
imagine," said Sally. "It must be too awful for
words, to live with someone who isn't interested in
your work."
"Pretty bad if they're bored with your children,
too," put in Averil.
"I'm sorry for them both," Mavis said. "One
can't help seeing how things are in that household,
they don't make any secret of it. They squabble most
of the time—she storms, and he just smiles and talks

99

over her head to me about music. It's awfully decent of her to be so nice to me, considering. I think she's a dear, really, but silly. She tells him he's a failure because he's not making a big income, though he gets such splendid notices in the papers. And he—well, I think he can't forgive her because he had to give up portrait painting when the kiddies started coming. That's what he's really keen on, he told me the other day."

On the whole, it was not surprising that Mr. Gathorne found the atmosphere of Moss Cottage soothing, after his wife's tongue. He would sit hunched up and silent by the hour, listening to the music and watching the performer through half closed lids. Mavis with her fiddle under her chin was an ever-changing spirit, rather than a human girl with a pink and white complexion. She went with the music into far places of bliss, of agony, of striving and redemption, madness and laughter. She was sanctimonious with Handel, sentimental with Beethoven, crazy with Debussy, tender and whimsical with Kreisler.

"Ought to go straight to the top of the ladder," declared Gathorne once. "But she won't, because she hasn't got a money bag tacked on to her. If she were a German Jew, now, or a Bolshevik, or even a Pole who'd shot her husband, she'd be the rage soon enough, rich or poor. But as she's only an English girl, there's no chance for her."

Whereat Mavis would smile and go on playing and presently he would leap to his feet and seize her hands and shake them up and down. His head only reached her shoulder, but it was not funny.

"You'll be famous, in spite of everything! Even the public has only got to hear you once——"

SURPLUS

He said "public" as one says "pigs," and Mavis
smiled again.

Then, one day a letter came for Averil.

"From Dina at last!"

She began to read the thin, crackling sheets, her
elbows propped.

"Oh—she's coming home next year, for good.
Isn't it splendid!"

"Splendid," agreed Sally, pulling on her driving
gauntlets with a vicious jerk. (You mustn't show
her you're jealous.)

"And she wants me to share a flat with her, in town.
Uncle's agreed to get a housekeeper. It's what we
always wanted!"

"You never told me that," said Sally.

"Didn't I? We used to talk about it at school,
even."

Averil was busy finishing the letter, and her expression was as full of sympathy as it had always been
over Sally's joys and troubles.

"Surely you've told her you're living with me?
Has she forgotten?"

At that, Averil looked up.

"Of course not. But wouldn't it be rather a good
idea if we three shared rooms together—that is, if
you could get another job in town? I expect you
could, by that time, if you've done well here."

The suddenness of it deprived Sally of speech,
so that she just stood there, fumbling with her gloves.
Then she said:

"You mean you'd leave Moss Cottage and bring in
an outsider, so we can never be alone or anything?"

Averil smoothed the letter in front of her with
maddening placidity.

101

"Why not? It would be just splendid, having you both. And it wouldn't be just yet, anyhow. Besides, she's not an outsider. She's my cousin, and the best friend I ever had."

"That——" Sally swallowed hurriedly. "And what about me, then? If she thinks that she's going to——"

"You don't know her, Sally. She's got a wonderful nature. I only gave up telling you about her because you didn't seem interested. At least, I thought that was it, but I'm beginning to wonder——"

But Sally had harked back to the main idea.

"If she's your best friend—if she comes first—then where do I come in?"

Averil could not help laughing at her tone.

"Of course, I care for you too, silly! You're an ordinary jolly good pal, but Dina—well, I shall never care for any other girl quite as I do for her. We were brought up together, almost."

"An ordinary friend"—the wind whistled it past Sally's ears as she rode, that morning. Meaning that the perfect friendship was not the best that could possibly happen, after all, but a trivial, common-place thing, such as her own with Cecily Winter of the old days. Just a person one liked a little better than the general run of acquaintances, so that one enjoyed meeting her occasionally—

Work finished, she walked out across the common towards a clump of pine trees that were a landmark in the middle of it, thinking what to say to Averil when she went in. It was so intensely quiet that she expected, against reason, to hear the whirring wings of a flight of starlings far overhead. Space and quiet and solitude are said to make one feel the insignificance of one's troubles, but they had the opposite effect on Sally.

"We are waiting," said the dark, sullen line of the forest on the other side of the common, and the ragged pine branches, and the oozing heather pads beneath her feet. "We are waiting to see what you will do."

And then came Averil's voice:

"Sally, Sally!"

Her apron made a patch of brilliant colour against the sombre background. She was life, she was strength and sanity—

"If you really care most for this Dina, you must live with her, I suppose." Sally got the words out quickly, but immediately withdrew them by adding, "Only then don't expect me to come too. I'm not going to be an ordinary acquaintance of yours. There are heaps of that kind about, if I wanted one."

Averil came closer, and Sally saw with amazement —and joy—that there were tears in her eyes.

"You don't understand. Sometimes you will take everything I say the wrong way, and I can't stop to think whether each word can have two meanings or not. I didn't mean 'ordinary' in that sense. I meant one of the dearest friends I've got. Isn't that enough?"

"No!" cried Sally. "I want to be the best of all, the same as you are to me. And you tell me Dina is that."

"I don't do sums in arithmetic about my friends. I love them all for different reasons, or for no reason at all. There's no question of putting one before the others."

Sally sprang to her feet to answer that.

"Don't you remember that night when I had my smash? You said then there was something special about our friendship—you know you did."

"If I did—and we said such a lot, that night, I really don't remember—I meant that I've lived with you, and not with them, and that makes a difference. Do stop this and be reasonable."

She put a hand on Sally's arm, but it was shaken off.

"Tell me the honest truth. Do you want to live with this Dina more than you do with me?"

For a moment, Averil made no answer. Then she said:

"I should like to see something of her, of course. If you look at it from her point of view, it's hard luck to come back, after all our plans, and find I've fixed up with another girl."

"Now listen to my point of view," said Sally. "If you go with her, I shan't be able to let you go without me, when it comes to the point. But I should be utterly miserable, and so would you. I should feel you'd only let me come out of pity, and that I was the unwanted third, in the way. So, I know you wouldn't remind me I was second, but I shouldn't be able to forget it. It would spoil everything, I tell you."

There was the die cast, and both of them knew it.

"You wouldn't be my friend any more—is that it?" asked Averil.

"I'd rather have nothing than—second best."

The absurdity of the whole thing would have struck Averil at another moment, but just then something in Sally forced her to take it seriously. Why was Sally so intense, so un-jolly?

"You're making me choose again," she said.

"Can't you leave it alone, and see what happens when the time comes?"

Sally noticed that word "again," but it never occurred to her that Averil could be alluding to the affair of Midge. So far as she knew, no choice had been involved there. She decided that "again" must be another word with a perfectly harmless second meaning.

"I can't live with that hanging over me," she said more calmly. "Don't you see? It's you that don't understand, and you always have, up till to-day!"

Averil turned to face Moss Cottage.

"I must have a little time to think it over. I —I'll go home for a fortnight. I ought to have gone before, mother's furious with me."

"A fortnight! Make it a week," begged Sally.

"I'll try. Come on in now. And whatever happens, don't let's fight. When I come back I'll let you know—if I *must* decide."

The sun came out from behind a cloud as they walked back, and the smoke from their own chimney made friendly spirals against the sky. The victory was hers already, Sally felt. After all, she was on the spot, and the other girl was still eight thousand miles away.

As it turned out, Averil stayed away ten days, and they were the longest Sally could remember. Directly she was alone, she began to be afraid again. Averil had gone into the middle of the enemy's camp, would be subjected daily to the urgings of Mrs. Kennion, who would be certain to prefer that her daughter, if she lived away from home at all, should do so in company with cousin Dina rather than an outsider. The Kennions would hold together, of course.

"Besides, I know she's jealous because Averil chose to come with me. She blames me for enticing her away."

Her own attitude towards that unknown quantity, Averil's mother, was easily defined. She wished the lady well, as long as she could be made to realise that Averil's future lay, not in marriage, but in work with another girl, whose name was Sally Wraith. But when it appeared that Mrs. Kennion not only wanted Averil to marry, but had even, in the past, urged the claims of more than one totally unsuitable suitor, her claims to consideration—which meant to possession of Averil—dwindled to nothing in Sally's eyes. With all her passionate sympathy for loneliness in any shape, she had none for the woman who wanted her daughter to leave her for a man—almost any man— yet grudged her to another woman.

It seemed so inconsistent. You either wanted your child's happiness more than your own, in which case all was well with Averil, who was perfectly happy. Or else you wanted to keep her with you at any price. Either of these viewpoints Sally could have understood—especially the latter—but Mrs. Kennion's baffled and irritated her.

To be on the safe side, she wrote a long letter, imploring Averil not to listen to her mother, but to make up her mind quite independently. And Averil did not answer it.

"There wasn't anything to say," she explained, on her return. "You know what ages it takes me to write a letter."

"You might have told me what you've decided— whether you're going to stick to me!"

# SURPLUS

Averil looked tired, for a wonder, and there were dark smudges under the wonderful eyes.

"If you still mean what you said about our friendship being finished if we share with Dina—do you, by the way?"

"Yes," said Sally, greatly daring, telling herself that she did.

"Then I'll explain to Dina that I can't go with her. She'll understand. She'll go on being my friend, whether I live with her or not."

Sally would have had the grace to feel sorry for Dina, if she could. But had not Dina a father who worshipped her, not to mention the crowd of other men who were always buzzing round her, according to Averil? Sally told herself that it was probably no exaggeration. Dina very likely did not photograph well, had not really a cruel expression and an aggressive nose. Sally was willing to credit her with all the graces, so she renounced her claim to Averil. Surely, Dina had enough love in her life already.

So the victory was to Sally, the girl on the spot. The fruits of it tasted so sweet that she could afford to ignore the bitter core.

## CHAPTER XI

JUNE came round again, with her hazy, shimmering noons and long, pine-scented evenings, when bats and midges are abroad. Sally had her hands full now with the visitors, running them from station to golf course, or down to Brighton for the day.

Occasionally, on slack week ends, the partners packed a tooth-brush and a comb apiece, and went out along the twisty lanes and sand-yellow forest-bordered roads to see what they could see. They would sleep in a farmhouse, in the village inn, under a hedge, if nothing else was handy. Supper-teas of eggs and rindy bacon, cider from the cask, slices of spongy bread and jam—the stars to watch, and the scent of cooling grass, and stealthy scrabbling things in the hedge behind them. It was all adventure— just a foretaste of the day when they two would stand together at the prow of a questing ship. Adventure, just to call out that it was a gorgeous night, and to hear her low voice answering "Rather!"

For Sally knew now that the secret heart of love was looking forward together—to everything, even pain, so it was shared. That was a time of more perfect understanding between them than any that had gone before. There seemed no more dark corners to be revealed in Averil. The worst was known, and, matched with those old half loves and still remaining friendships, Sally's star stood steadfast and serene.

# SURPLUS

Dina's name was never mentioned at Moss Cottage now. Sally had made up her mind to bide her time, till Averil should be forced to realise that the comparatively new, but preordained friendship was a greater thing than the old had ever been. To realise even though she might never admit it.

For the Kennions never admitted, in so many words, that they had made a mistake. That, again, was part of their code. If a Kennion said the time was four o'clock when the clock said five, then it was always the clock that lied.

This was a characteristic Sally was beginning to allow for. Also, by slow and hard degrees, she was learning the wisdom of at least feigning contentment with seven-eighths of a loaf, when there was every chance of getting the whole loaf later on. It was only a question of patience.

At the same time, she saw to it that Averil had as much gaiety as was possible under the circumstances. Every evening, when work allowed, they went together to the tennis club, and Sally revelled in the attention the other girl excited—the more or less veiled glances from the male visitors, the discreet enquiries from the matrons. Visitors to Moss Cottage, for bridge or music, were encouraged, and evenings *a deux* were no longer the unbroken rule. Averil must have as many new friends as she wanted—friends who were newer than Sally, and therefore had no prior claims.

As it happened, the beautiful artist who had buried herself "away on the common" with a female taxi driver appealed to the imagination of Salter's Ridge, which immediately scented a romance gone wrong on the part of the former. Nothing less than an unfortunate love affair in the recent past could account, to their minds, for so pretty a girl choosing such a place of residence. So Averil could easily have become the fashion among the élite—had she bestirred herself to that end.

Instead, to Sally's joy, she played fast and loose with her opportunities—refused invitations because she was too busy, or because Sally could not come too, missed appointments on the tennis court because it looked like rain, and generally gave the impression that popularity was wasted on her. And after every excursion into the outside world, she joined with Sally in laughter, always good humoured on her part, oftener caustic on Sally's, over the little foibles and eccentricities of its denizens. So that the best part of those adventures was the coming home.

Young Mavis Barron was still their only constant visitor. Once she brought with her Mrs. Gathorne, a large brunette with handsome, somnolent eyes, who apologised profusely for not having called before.

"Miss Barron is doing wonders with my Dorothy," she said. "The child used to loathe practising, but now she seems to love it."

Questioned as to what Dorothy was learning, she was quite unable to say without Mavis's assistance.

"I don't know one note of music from the other," she admitted, cheerfully. "But I want her to be able to play for people when she's asked. It's so useful for a girl. I'm having Joan taught to paint."

"You've got a teacher on the spot for that, anyway," suggested Sally.

"St. John, you mean? Oh, he wouldn't be bothered with her. And if he would, she shouldn't learn from him. I want her to paint cheerful pictures, that you

can hang up in the drawing-room, and he'd teach her
to do the awful skinny sort of portrait he used to do
himself.  I know he would."

"But he's a great artist, all the same," said Mavis,
laughing.

"It's a good thing some people think so, my dear,"
said his wife, with a snap in her voice that was unmistakable.

"Quite a decent sort," Averil pronounced, when she
had departed.

"A cow as to the eyes, but a devil about the chin,"
amended Sally.

Perfect, this mutual forming of opinions about
places and people new to them both!  It was so long,
now, since anyone belonging to Averil's past life had
crossed the threshold—or even sent a projection of
themselves in the pages of a letter—to trouble the
peace of Moss Cottage with their grasping demands on
her.  There was no more need, Sally judged, even to
think of the past.  Only the future counted, now, that
they were to make together.

Then, on a hot, windy afternoon, Sally came home
to tea to find a car blocking the lane outside.  It was
a four-seater with a solid reputation, not particularly
noted for speed.  Enough brass fittings to please the
eye, but not enough to dazzle.  A comfortably off,
even modestly opulent car, but not extravagant.  It
was painted dark green, a colour Sally hated, and
its coating of dust showed that it had travelled
far.

Sally slunk in by the back door because she knew
her face was tomato coloured, except for the patches
round her eyes left by her goggles.  She felt disin-
clined for visitors, just then.

SURPLUS

"Hullo, Sally!" called Averil. "Here's Dr. Barrington Hope—you know who I mean—he's just come from town to look me up."

Sally shook hands.

"If you've heard as much about me as I have about you this afternoon, you must know quite a lot," said the man genially.

Genial was an adjective that seemed to have been made for him. He was thickset and very little taller than Averil, with an almost completely round face, in which were set a pair of small, very twinkling dark eyes. His hair was turning grey at the edges, and Sally noticed, as he turned, the bald spot on the top. There was an effect of well-kept breadth about him, increased by the broad cordiality of his smile. It was constantly in use, that smile, and it had left permanent creases in the plump cheeks. At least, the smile fitted the creases.

He had the air of a moderately successful retired business man, who did not ask too much of life, but took his pleasures where he found them, and found them all good. Somewhere about fifty, Sally judged —a safe age.

"I was just beginning to wonder whether my young friend Rill was still kicking her heels up, or whether she'd kicked them up once too often and come a cropper," he said with a comfortable chuckle, in which Averil joined. "So I ran down to Hinstead this morning, and Mrs. Kennion sent me on here. I had no idea the Little'un had left the maternal nest. She never wrote to me."

"Well, you didn't to me," said Averil, this being her first contribution to the conversation.

"I did, for a year after I left the Army. And then

112

your answers took so long coming, and I was so busy,
that I gave it up as a bad job."

"He's very busy now," said Averil, looking at him
with the proud, somehow maternal interest that she
had always ready for the achievements of her friends.
"He's turned into *the* great authority on mental dis-
eases since I saw him last."

"Hold on, Little'un, I never said that!" cried Dr.
Hope. "I do my best, but it doesn't go as far as
that."

"Are you a specialist, then?" asked Sally, with a
nervous smile.

She knew, by now, that Averil liked her to amuse
and interest any new guests, to draw them out as she,
Averil, could not do, however old her acquaintance-
ship with them might be. For this purpose, it was
necessary to get each one on to his own particular
subject. But doctors were so touchy about their rank
and title, and to Sally the ramifications of the medical
profession were as an uncharted sea.

"Not an ordinary alienist, no. I practise chiefly
in the funny thing nobody can spell—psychotherapy.
Since the war I've been treating shell shock cases in a
big hospital in Manchester—too far off for week-
ending in these parts, you see—but now I'm looking
about for a place to start a home of my own. When
I find it, I'm going to try some new ideas that'll make
you all sit up and take notice."

"Tell Sally about them, I know she'll be interested,"
prompted Averil.

But Sally said:

"I haven't had tea yet."

Instantly Averil jumped up in dismay. The heat
had taken a little of the colour from her cheeks, so

113

that her eyes shone out a deeper shade than ever, dominating her sapphire dress.

"You must be tired out," she said, "I'll get it for you."

Dr. Hope sent one of his broadest smiles after her as she vanished. He had risen, and began to examine the photographs, going from one to the other with a comment on each that showed he had seen them before. Of course, Averil must have had them with her in the old days, when he had first met her.

"Mr. Glen Carnier—h'm, a new flame of hers, I suppose."

Sally did not contradict him. She was waiting for him to ask further questions, watching for the first sign of anything like jealousy on his part. But Dr. Hope had already passed on to the next photograph, which was his own.

"Hullo, she's still got that! I was a bit of a swell in those days, wasn't I?"

"I suppose you saw a lot of Averil?" Sally said, thinking how callous it sounded to allude to the war merely in connection with one's uniform. Forgetting that herself had once been sorry the war was over.

"Oh, we had some fine times! She did more work than all the other drivers put together, or what she called work. So we had to have a little rest and refreshment sometimes. Eh, Little'un?"

Averil, coming in with the tea, nodded and smiled.

"You never did any work, though," she said. "You were a perfect slug for laziness, and you know it."

He made a playful lunge at her, which she evaded behind a chair. Then he put his hands on her shoulders, in fatherly fashion, and propelled her towards the studio corner.

"I haven't seen your works of art yet. How's it progressing—R.A. standard yet?"

He examined all the exhibits minutely, holding the miniatures out at arm's length and screwing his eyes up, in the manner of the expert. Finally he picked out "The Armour of the Modern Woman" as his favourite among the posters.

"But you must finish her face," he said. "Whatever she lacks in real life, it's not face."

"I know I ought to," agreed Averil. "But Sally's been my model for it, and I can't make it come alive at all. I feel I'll never do any good with it, now."

"Better try another model. And give her a pair of breeks instead of that tunic thing, while you are about it. She'd sell like hot cakes, in breeks."

Sally thought of the beautiful limbs with the winged heels enclosed in breeks, and shuddered.

"It's supposed to be allegorical, you know," she put in.

"Yes, I'd rather gathered that"—his amused voice made her feel how smug hers must have sounded— "But the trousers would be allegorical, too, wouldn't they? That's the way to tackle the good old B.P. anyhow, and if Averil's going to make good, that's what she's got to do."

And Averil laughed, and expected he was right.

Later, when plans for the evening were discussed, it turned out that he had been hoping they would both do him the honour of dining with him at the "Tankard," in the village. He looked from one to the other with a beaming smile when he gave the invitation, but Sally shook her head.

"I've got to meet the last train to-night," she said. "But don't worry about me. You go."

"No, we wouldn't think of it. Would we, Barry?" said Averil.

"Most certainly not. We'll have a picnic here instead. And while you're getting it ready, I'll take the old bus up to the village and bring back some extras. I know how awkward it is, having a guest descend on you without warning like this."

He brought back, among other delicacies, a bottle of Australian burgundy, and a half bottle of port.

"The best I could get," he explained. "I expect it's as sour as vinegar, but knowing your little weakness, Rill, I thought it would be better than nothing."

They all laughed, and Sally wondered why she had not found out before that Averil had a weakness of that description.

"To our next merry meeting," he pledged Averil, after the meal was finished. And, turning to Sally, "Here's the best of luck to 'Georgina' and her driver."

Sally was pleased with him then, for including her of his own accord in the toast. He evidently did not agree with the people who said it was mere waste of time for a girl to go into the motor business.

It appeared that he was fond of music, too. In response to his request, Averil sang one of Sally's favourites. And when the last wailing chords had crashed into silence—there were no lingering chords on that piano—Dr. Hope settled himself more deeply in his chair, and took another cigar.

"Very nice. You've come on a lot since I heard you last. How about something cheerful now, eh?"

So the concert ended with the shouting of a revue

chorus, the sound of it pouring through the open window into the listening forest.

"How long is he going to stay?" asked Sally, when he drove off.

"Only till to-morrow night. But he's going to try and get down occasionally for week ends, he says. Isn't he rather a dear old thing?"

"Very jolly," said Sally. "But I shouldn't have thought he was a bit clever. Rather a fool, in fact."

"Wait till you know him better. It's only his ragging that makes you think so, he always does it."

"I've been trying to think what he reminds me of," said Sally, "and I know now. That advertisement for 'Monkey Brand'—he's the living image of it."

"So he is!" laughed Averil. "I must tell him that, he'll love it."

Next morning, Dr. Hope had a golf bag slung over his shoulder.

"Who's for a round?" he called from the doorway, with the sun behind him showing up the frayed patches on the carpet, and the stain on the ceiling where the lamp had smoked. He looked slightly taller in tweeds, but the pudginess of his short fingers betrayed the indoor man.

He drove Averil out to the Southbeach course, where Sally, by his special request, managed to join them; and on the first tee he explained that he was terribly out of practice. He then proceeded, without taking breath, to raise his driver negligently to the level of his waist—the way the ordinary player takes a short mashie shot—bring it straight down on top of the ball, and smite it out of sight along the fairway.

Sally gasped. It was such a drive as she, in months

of practising the correct method, could never have achieved.

"I never swing," explained the doctor, "it's just a knack with the wrists—there—like that. Golf consists solely of knack, except as regards the actual length of the drive, where strength is a factor. You people who swing your arms about are simply wasting yours, before you get near the ball. After all, what you're out for is to hit it, not to pose for the pictures!"

To Sally, the little lecture was worse than useless. The course was strange to her, and its heat shimmering smoothness, broken by artificial bunkers in every direction, was deceptive after the moorland stretches and natural ravines of Salter's Ridge. Added to which, she had just seen an exceptional drive brought off with the same ease, and much the same action, as if the club had been a duster and the ball a fly on the window pane. Consequently, she missed the ball completely.

"Ah, you *thought* you were going to miss that," said Dr. Hope, with his jolly smile. "I saw you making a mental picture of yourself missing it—another example of the power of the subconscious!"

After that, Sally could do nothing right. She got into every bunker within reach, and mostly into those that belonged to other holes than the one she was playing. Halfway round the course:

"You both ought to give me two strokes at least," she said, in a voice of ice.

But when Averil, laughing this to scorn, suggested that they might try giving her half a stroke, say, just till she was on her game again, she refused.

"I might as well carry on. You people must enjoy

feeling how brilliant you are, next to a duffer like
me."

At the tenth, hitting at random, she happened to
catch her ball on the right spot, and sent it flying over
a boundary wall into a patch of gorse.

"That finishes it," she said. "It's no good looking
for that ball, and the only other one I've got is a new
one. I'm not going to hack that about just to amuse
you!"

She laughed in a stifled way. But Barry appeared
to take it for granted that his own hearty laugh fitted
the occasion.

"Cheer up, Miss Sally! You'll soon get your eye
in again. Bring out the last ewe lamb, and let's see
you slaughter it."

"I tell you I can't afford to go wasting balls like
that."

She was looking away from him, or she would have
caught the sudden flash of his eyes on her face.

"Use this one, then," he said at once, dropping a
ball at her feet. "I've got more than I've room for,
and it's only a re-paint."

"No, thanks," snapped Sally. "I don't want to lose
your balls. Besides—I can see it's a new one."

"The price of one ball more or less won't break
me," he said pleasantly, "but if you'd rather not, let's
get on with the business. You can be umpire between
Rill and me, and see we don't cheat."

Not a word about ingratitude, mind you—just an
easy passing over the whole incident. He began to
tell them about a tournament he had once played in,
and won, by the merest fluke, from a plus three opponent. But Sally, lagging behind, was feeling that
she had shown herself as a petty, bad-tempered, un-

sporting little fool, in contrast to the calm magnanimity of a man. She, who had once pointed out to Averil what a mistake it was to suppose that there were more real sports among men than among the frailer sex! Yet the thing seemed to have happened of itself, somehow. If only she could have held her tongue, laughed at defeat as Averil would have done, as she was doing now, while she bandied gay insults with her opponent.

They were old friends, those two—

That night she said:

"You two were pretty close together chatting away, while I was trailing round after you. Having a good laugh at me, I suppose?"

"You're imagining things as usual!" said Averil. "As it happens, Barry was telling me how mother behaved this morning. She pretty well gave him to understand she'd finished with me."

"And it's all my fault!" cried Sally, at that. "I'm making you quarrel with your family, because you've stuck to me. And I wanted you to be so happy, to have everything——"

Averil could not long resist her in her moods of self-abasement.

"It's not your fault that you existed, is it? We met, and I wanted to come away and work, and now I'm going on working. It's my fault, if it's anybody's."

## CHAPTER XII

THE occasional week-end visits continued, and Sally was beginning rather to enjoy them. After that first unlucky day there was no more golf, and in other amusements she could hold her own. And Dr. Hope, unlike Midge, never showed her that he did not want her, never attempted to leave her out of any programme. On the contrary, he made her feel that the party would not be complete without her.

So, on Sally's free afternoons, his car conveyed them both to Southbeach or Linden Gap, where he lunched and dined them at the best hotel in the place. Everything of the best was always forthcoming at his request, too, from the most comfortable chairs in the lounge to the best table in the dining-room. A little discreet badinage with the waitress, or a chat with the manager as from one man of the world to another ensured these essentials to a successful visit.

In fact, an aura of success surrounded him, and that is the spell that is hardest to resist. Even Sally was not proof against it, though she called him a conceited little windbag whenever he started explaining exactly how anything under discussion should be done, from fixing a collar stud to fitting new gears to a motor cycle, ignoring her assurances that she could do it quite well already. She laughed at him, but indulgently; at least, he was not a callow youth of Midge's stamp, he had a little more excuse for thinking he knew.

He seemed to like giving them accounts, detailed but always with the omission of names and dates, of many strange cases that had come under his treatment.

"Do you ever hypnotise them?" asked Sally, once.

"Very rarely. I don't consider it either necessary or desirable, except in special cases. I find it easy enough to diagnose without that, as a rule. You just say to yourself, it's either *that* big complex, or it's *that*"—he demonstrated with two forks on the pattern of the table cloth—"and when you've eliminated one, you just probe away at the other till you've got what you want."

"Poor devil of a patient!" said Sally, with a laugh at the transfixed table cloth.

After all, she found she could not take Dr. Hope's profession very seriously. To begin with, he was behind the times. His was the last creed but one— it had reached the stage where the worshippers lose their first ecstatic faith and begin to ask awkward questions. As a mere matter of policy, he should have left it behind, and followed after a newer one, urging his patients to repeat their little hymn of "day by day we grow better and better." Instead of which he stayed on in the comparatively old paths of psychotherapy, probably, thought Sally, because he had learnt one set of catch words and could not be bothered to learn another. Or, more probably still, because he found it paid—this occurred to her a little later on. What Dr. Hope wanted was a tastefully furnished, solid nursing home, full of wealthy private patients who had a natural horror of the newest fangled experiments as applied to their disorders—not a horde of shrieking fanatics besieging his front door, and for·

getting to deposit their cheques in their excitement.

In any case, as the phenomenally gifted, miraculous healer of sick minds, he neither looked nor acted the part. He seemed to her so entirely the *bon camarade*, the lover of a good vintage, the fatherly admirer of pretty girls *en masse*, and Averil (because she happened to be available at the moment) in particular.

"I can't imagine his hypnotising anybody," she said to Averil once, "or making them answer questions they didn't want to. With those little twinkly eyes of his! I believe he's pulling our legs."

"Then how d'you think he managed to get on the staff of the biggest hospital in Manchester?"

"Lord knows—there are lots of fools about. I bet you anything you like he couldn't hypnotise me, anyhow."

"Why don't you ask him to, next time he comes down?" suggested Averil.

Next time was an evening towards the end of September. Averil had prepared a dainty supper table, with dessert and white wine and a small bottle of *crême de menthe*, "because it seems such a shame to let him go out and buy it every time."

A little card table he had brought them stood folded in a corner, and on the piano top another gift of his, a pot of exotic chrysanthemums, snaky petalled, scarlet and orange in the soft oil light. The whole room looked different, somehow—more sophisticated, less of a log cabin in the wilderness.

Sally noticed the difference, but could not put it down to any particular item, unless it were the clothes they wore themselves. It was the first time they had "dressed" for a meal at Moss Cottage. Averil was in a soft, square necked black gown, that showed some of the whiteness of her neck and shoulders, instead of only the usual glowing brown V. Sally, to keep her company, had put on a little amber coloured dress with quaint gold panels. She went to the side window and leaned out, looking up into the maze of slender trunks, faintly illumined by the drawing back of the curtain. It was as if the forest were hanging over her, peering past her into the room, waiting for something to happen.

"Come and listen to this owl!" she called. "He's got a lot to say to-night."

But Averil was at the porch.

"I hear the car," she said.

Dr. Hope wore a bowler, slightly on the back of his head, that made him look more than ever the business man. And he had a little black bag, reminiscent of a solicitor, perhaps, rather than a doctor—a wrinkled, slightly worn, man-of-the-world bag, with no shiny mystery about it.

"Case sheets," he explained, adding, "I've got some good news for a good girl, Little'un!"

"About the 'Tinkers' Tackproof Tyres' poster?" cried Averil. "Good man! I am glad I let you take it back with you."

"You were afraid I'd forget about it, weren't you, Miss Averil? but I never forget, when it's a question of helping a pal along. I did just what I told you I would, spoke to that man I know on the advertising staff of Tinkers'. And he said he thought they might be able to use it, if you could alter it a bit. He wants you to go up and see him about it."

"You brick. Barry!" said Averil.

And Sally stifled a stab of envy that it was he, and

not herself, who had been instrumental in selling
Averil's first poster for her.

The supper thus auspiciously begun was one of the
gayest Sally could remember. Barry kept them laughing with his sidelights on the mannerisms and eccentricities of his nameless patients. He compli-
mented Sally on her dress—"So you know what colours you look best in, Mademoiselle!" Then he
branched off into a description of one of his many
trips abroad.

"My choice is the Riviera every time," he said.
"Perfect climate, perfect food, jolly people—and the
Casino in the evenings. Monte, that's the place.
The three times I've been there I've paid all my hotel
expenses out of my winnings. There's a system I
know—very simple and safe. I just set myself to win
a certain amount clear each day, and I go on till I've
made it. Then I stop at once—that's the secret."

"Teach us," commanded Averil.

Her eyes were eager, and reflections shone and
danced in them from the green liquid in the bottom
of her glass, which was a common tumbler.

"Not much good here. I'll take you out there,
one day—take you both, if you like. I could get my
brother's wife to look after you girls, just to please
old Mrs. Grundy."

"That would be a good idea," said Averil. "I've
always longed to go abroad, especially somewhere
warm. I love the sun so."

"And a gamble, too, eh?" he chuckled. "I know
you women!"

Sally said nothing. She had suddenly remembered
the last occasion on which Averil had admitted to a
longing for travel. Then, there had been the sighing

of wind in the rigging, the impenetrable darkness of
the open sea at night, and two adventurers, only two,
at the prow.

"What shall we do to amuse ourselves to-night?"
Barry was saying. "Suppose you give us a concert,
Little'un—or we can play cut-throat if you like, I've
got plenty of pennies."

He jingled them in his pocket.

"I've been wondering," said Sally, suddenly, "how
do you hypnotise people, really? Could you do it now,
for instance, to one of us?"

"Oh, yes, Sally wants you to give a demonstration,
Barry. She doesn't think you look the part," laughed
Averil.

He looked quickly from one to the other, still smiling, perfectly at ease.

"I can't hypnotise people who deliberately set themselves against it. Nobody can."

"I——" began Sally.

"You'd be a bad subject, Sally. You'd fight against
it, all the time, even if you tried not to. But Averil—
she'd be good."

"There, Averil, he thinks you've got a weaker will
than I have," scoffed Sally.

"On the contrary, it's only the strong-willed people
who can let themselves go properly," said the little doctor drily. "So there, Miss Sally!"

"All right, do it to her, then."

He looked at Averil, who nodded.

"You want me to, really? Very well."

Still smiling, with the air of a parent indulging a
couple of children, he settled Averil in the arm chair,
her face to the light, and himself sat down facing
her.

"Now look at me," he ordered quietly. "And think of nothing—nothing at all."

He fixed his eyes on her. After a moment, he leaned forward and began to wave his hands gently back and forth, close to her face. And Sally, watching, saw her eyes cloud and darken, and the fixed, luminous pupils gradually disappear under the heavy fringe of her lashes. Then, with a little tired sigh, she dropped her head sideways on to the chair back.

"Call her," said Barry, and Sally called, but there was no answer. Averil lay there asleep, yet not asleep —the shell of her, from which the spirit had been sent forth, wandering. And at that moment the cat, stretched at her feet, leapt up and fled with a screech for the window.

"Wake her up," cried Sally. "Wake her up— quickly!" and there was agonised fear in her voice.

Dr. Hope's smile broadened, but he bent forward obediently and made another pass. And almost at once Averil opened her eyes, staring round the room vacantly at first, then with full consciousness.

"Aren't I a good patient?" she said slowly.

"So good that you've frightened Sally nearly into a fit."

"Sorry I was such an idiot," said Sally shortly. "It was the yell 'Tins' let out. My nerves aren't too good these days—too much driving, I suppose. That's quite a good parlour trick of yours, but, of course, it must be pretty easy. Nearly everybody can do it if they try."

He glanced round at her, and said:

"Cats are extraordinarily sensitive to anything at all supernormal that is taking place near them. 'Tins' wasn't frightened of me, you know. He's very fond of me."

Sally felt herself blushing, because he had read her thoughts so exactly. There must be something objectionable about a man from whom an animal fled. Yet it was true, she knew, that "Tins" had hitherto made a favourite of the little doctor, and preferred his lap to theirs, uncomfortable though it was.

His calmness irritated her. For some obscure reason, the incident struck her, wholly unjustly, as an insolent exhibition of his power over Averil. A power greater than any she possessed, that he could use when he would, without asking her permission. Absurd, of course, since there was no reason why he should want to use power of any sort over Averil, his friend. She looked at him again—yes, he was exactly the same as before, the same little twinkly eyes, the same bald patch on the top of his head. Suddenly she felt she wanted to challenge him. If he had real brains, not just knowledge of a few childish passes, let him prove it.

"Now let's hear how you set about your precious analysis business," she said. "Imagine I've come to you to be cured of something queer—oh, a habit of picking up stones in the road, or something equally absurd."

"I could analyse you without making up any symptoms, my dear girl," he said. "But I don't think you'd like it."

"Look out, Sally!" teased Averil. "He's going to give you a bad character."

She still spoke slowly, but her beauty shone out all the more clearly because of the slight languidness.

"I don't care," said Sally. "If I've got anything

the matter with me I might as well know. Come on then—out with it!"

"It's nothing very terrible," he said, laughing again. "Lots of women have it in various forms, especially nowadays. Just a repressed emotion—unconsciously repressed, usually—forming a complex."

"Cutting out the technical stuff, what exactly do you mean?"

Sally was not laughing at all.

"Well"—he put the tips of his fingers together, in the gesture that no man can resist when he is about to dispense wisdom—"the two great instincts that give rise to all human emotions are self-preservation and self-perpetuation. Anyone who drives either of these instincts inwards—represses it, in fact—becomes an abnormal person. That's why a soldier——"

"Oh, we know all about that shell-shocked soldier, and the way he bottled up his fear in the firing line, and it comes out in all sorts of funny symptoms," interrupted Sally. "Don't you suppose we ever read the papers? I show my fear as soon as I feel it, so that's all right, anyhow."

"You certainly do," he agreed.

"Then I suppose you mean the other thing's repressed in me—self-perpetuation. And if by that you mean that I'm not yearning to get married and have a family, I certainly am not," she said, looking him full in the face. "I expect I've said so in front of you, before now. There's no secret about it."

"Certainly not—why should there be? I said the instinct was unconsciously suppressed. Probably something that happened in your early childhood. But you never told me—I just saw it. How? Oh, by several little signs," he added evasively.

"Guessed, you mean," she cried. "It must have been quite easy. But you're all wrong about its being suppressed—I simply haven't got that instinct. Why should I have? Do you mean to say you're such an early Victorian that you still think the only thing women exist for is to have families?"

"Not the only thing, but the chief thing. It's what we're all here for. How would the race go on, otherwise?"

"If you're going to begin maundering about the race—" Sally shrugged her shoulders. "Personally, I shouldn't care if it stopped to-morrow. Perhaps you would—but is that any reason why I should have a family? Will you tell me that?"

Sally thought she had caught him rather neatly there. She wanted Averil to see how well she could keep her end up, even on the subject of offspring, on which she did not profess to be an expert.

"The normal woman, Sally, feels it her greatest privilege," he said.

"How do you know? Do they all tell you whether they have children because they want to, or because their husbands want to, or because it's the thing to do—or just because the children happen along?"

Sally's voice had risen now, her hands were strained across her knee. He did not need to look at her to know it.

"It's all simply a sign of that complex of yours," he said. "But there's no occasion to get angry about it, is there? I only told you because you would have it. Nothing to be ashamed of, as you say."

"But you think there is!" she thrust.

"No, I'm sorry, that's all. It means you're bound to have a more or less uncomfortable time through life

—abnormal people always do, people who aren't running straight on nature's lines."

"Heaps of women don't want children," declared Sally.

"Only the abnormal ones. And even they do, right down underneath. Only their conscious minds take charge and persuade them that, as there aren't enough men to go round, they had better not waste their time wanting what they can't get. So they go about saying men are contemptible animals, and that having a kiddy is rather a shocking proceeding than otherwise."

"Shut up, Barry!" said Averil, the peacemaker; "I know you're only teasing Sally, but she hates it."

But Sally thrust the effort aside.

"Do you mean that if I let you treat me, as you call it, you could make me want to have children?" she asked bluntly.

"I certainly could."

"Well, you certainly won't have the chance, anyway. Not that I believe it—I don't—but I wouldn't put myself in the power of a person with your ideas for anything. I'd rather die!"

"Now I'm in for it," he smiled at Averil. "Sally's finished with me. But it wasn't me that started the discussion."

"Why don't you stick up for me, Averil?" asked Sally. "You don't want to get married, either."

"Averil hasn't met the right man—that's why," he broke in, before she could answer. "I didn't say I could make a girl of character want to marry the first man who came along."

Sally reminded herself that he was only trying to get a rise out of her, had been trying all along. So

# SURPLUS

far she had risen beautifully, but she was not going to do it any more.

"What do you say to that, Averil?" she asked, and her mouth smiled resolutely.

Averill still lay back in her chair. A scarlet petal from one of the chrysanthemums had fallen on her lap and lay there, motionless, against the black of her dress.

"I love listening to you two. *I* don't know what instincts I've got, I've never thought about it. He'll say they're unconscious, though. That's a grand loophole of yours, Barry."

"Yes," cried Sally triumphantly. "That's what it is, a loophole."

She propped her elbows on the table, bringing her face nearer to his.

"If I was a girl of character, as you call it, I'd put my tongue out at you. I suppose you make out that love's only that instinct?"

"At bottom," he corrected. "Though civilisation is always inventing pretty words to wrap it up in. Just at present, we like to call ourselves 'in tune'—the other day it was 'soul mates.' As if the instinct itself weren't more beautiful than anything else could be!"

"Then how do you explain the kind of love that isn't between the sexes?" demanded Sally.

"Friendship? That's a different thing. It really springs from our old friend 'self-preservation.' Savages chose the stronger warriors for their friends. We choose the people who possess some quality we lack in ourselves—courage, tenderness, common sense. The same instinct is often present in love, but it is the other—always—that dominates."

132

# SURPLUS

"Friendship" and "love"—he said the words as a surgeon says "bone" and "muscle." Sally could not help admiring his admirably detached attitude. The power of stating an opinion as if it were simply the truth, take it or leave it—the speaker having no personal interest one way or the other—was a thing that aroused envy in her, as well as irritation. Like all sceptics, she had moments when she coveted any sort of belief, so long as it was calm and certain.

But in this belief she meant to shake him, if it was humanly possible, and Averil was to see the shaking done.

"And all the other qualities, love of beauty, self-sacrifice—the soul qualities? How do you account for them, or are they instincts too?"

"The soul—aren't we getting rather too serious, girls?" he said. "Let's have another drink all round, and talk about something else."

He poured just the right amount into the three glasses on the table. Then he struck a match, and put it to each glass in turn, watching the tiny blue flames lick across the surface of the emerald liquid. It reminded Sally of the stage setting in "The Little Mermaid" ballet, or of the posters of the Cornish Riviera on the Underground, that Averil was always wishing she could emulate. It made the stains on the ceiling much more apparent, and turned Sally's dress from amber to a dirty pale brown. But it could not take the colour from the scarlet petal on Averil's lap.

"As we've gone so far I'd like to hear your theories on the subject," Sally said.

"Well, it's a word I don't use myself—soul. Many serious scientists don't nowadays, you know. We say 'mind' instead. A little bit of the great mind force, life force—nature—call it God, if you like."

"It seems to me you might as well call it the soul and have done with it!"

"Not if you mean the sort of soul the Spiritualists mean," he said. "It has no separate life of its own, apart from the body. Our minds are only different because our brains are different. When the brain dies, the force inside it goes back to the universal Force, like an electric current to the earth."

He had almost forgotten his audience now in his subject, and Sally began to realise what a hopeless task she had set herself. His theories, all of them, she had come across before, in books. But to read about theories, and to meet someone who actually holds them, are two very different things. Sally was thrown off her balance, and caught at a straw.

"Spiritualism—yes, what about that? Lots of cleverer men than you believe in it."

"It's not a question of cleverness," he smiled. "It's a question of keeping both eyes open, instead of one, of not believing a thing because you want to believe it, and therefore it's the easiest thing to do."

"You've never studied it," she risked.

"My dear girl, I went into the whole subject soon after the war ended, when the craze was at its height. I was perfectly ready to be convinced, as I am of anything—I had no personal bias one way or the other. I went to numbers of séances, and every single thing I heard and saw could be explained by mind—subconscious mind, when the medium was honest. All that the 'spirits' said came out of the minds of the people at the séance, little things they had forgotten they ever knew, but that their subconscious mind had stored up.

# SURPLUS

The medium's sensitive mind simply caught up these memories and put them into words."

"How the dickens could you know all that?" said Sally.

He was insufferably conceited, after all. He assumed to himself the prerogative of the Almighty, knowledge of all the secrets of men's hearts.

"I put several of the sitters under hypnosis afterwards. And it all came out—the day when He apologised for giving Her a bunch of flowers that were faded, or when they met an ugly woman in the street, and He said that her teeth were like Aunt Jane's. All the trivial details that sound so new, so fresh, and so 'exactly like Him,' when a spirit repeats them."

Sally was silent. She saw, now, that this little man with a pretty taste in wines and a jolly smile had powers of argument that at least equalled hers. And he had studied the subject scientifically, while she had not. Because of that, he would end by twisting her round his short, broad finger, making a fool of her in front of Averil. It was that she minded most. But she had a few more bolts left in her armoury.

"You're just a common or garden materialist—'Eat and drink, for to-morrow we die'—no future life—it's as old as the hills, that stuff!"

"On the contrary," he said, "I've been talking about mind, not matter. There's all the difference in the world. And as to a future life, there's life that goes on for ever in the universal Mind, always showing itself in new forms."

"Is that all?"

"Isn't that enough? But if we want our own little individualities, or brains, to survive, we can pass them

135

on to our children. Self-perpetuation—see the idea now, Sally?"

Sally winced at the word, like a horse flicked on the raw.

"It's not my idea of a future life," she said.

Then she cursed that unruly tongue of hers, that had delivered her naked into the hand of the enemy. For the man looked at her with genuine pity in his eyes, the pity of the strong for the weak and ignorant.

"Did you want to have a harp and sit on a cloud with the other little cherubs, or what?" he asked gently. "Personal survival *must* be through one's children, anything else is simply unthinkable. Imagine each separate flea that ever existed going on living for ever! Because you can't draw the line at humanity, you know—all the ancient religions saw that, and even Christians insist on including their favourite dogs and horses, nowadays. If a dog, why not a flea? Why not a lump of jelly fish?"

"Well, why not?" retorted Sally desperately. "At least, why shouldn't the flea climb higher in the scale, from one life to another?"

"Ah, there you're coming to another subject altogether," he assured her. "Evolution's sound enough, right up to Shaw's superman, probably. But surely you can see there's nothing personal in that? When the flea becomes a dog, has he got the same mind— the same soul, if you prefer the word—as he started with? Here's 'Tins,' now," he patted his knee, and the cat jumped up. "I say, Tins, d'you remember the days when you were a little bit of jelly fish?"

The tawny beauty kneaded hard, his purring mingled, as usual, with the tiny shrill cries that were his idea of conversation.

"Tins says he'd rather I didn't mention it. He hates the very idea of living in water, now."

"Well, you're wrong, anyway," said Sally. "I don't know enough to prove it here and now, but I could. I know you're wrong."

"I know it," he repeated, smiling at her. "What about the people who swore the earth was flat? They knew it, too."

He lifted the cat gently down.

"Splendid—go on thinking I'm wrong, it'll probably be much better for you. And now I must be off, girls. Why, it's nearly one— See you to-morrow!"

When they had watched his head lights go swinging down the lane, cutting a path for him through the blackness, Averil locked up behind him. Any ill-intentioned person could, without the smallest trouble, have climbed through the open bedroom windows, but the front door was always carefully locked. It is a British characteristic. From our foreign policies to our divorce laws, we lock the door and leave the window open.

Sally walked slowly to the table and sat down.

"I hope you've enjoyed the evening," she said lightly. Then she put her head down on her arms and began to cry.

"Sally, my dear old thing!" Averil was bending over her at once. "You've not been taking him seriously? Barry always plays up like that, when anyone draws him on. You simply asked for it."

Sally shook her bent head.

"He meant it, every word."

"He may have meant some, but not all," persisted Averil. "And even if he did, what does it matter?

Can't you go on believing what you did before? You said yourself he was wrong."

"Don't you *know* I always take the opposite side, when anyone's as certain of themselves as he is? I've done it with you often enough, just for the sake of argument."

"Your arguments may begin like that, but they sometimes end in fights all the same," said Averil, moving a little further away. "Then if you believe what he says, what's all the trouble about?"

"Oh, believe," cried Sally. "I don't believe in anything, for certain. How can I—how can anyone—these days? Till I was about fifteen, I believed more or less in Christianity, going to church and all that. After that, I began to think—and read. And then all these new schemes came along, at least they were new to me—Christian science, spiritualism, psychotherapy, self-suggestion, monkey glands. They all sound true, while I'm reading them, but one can't believe them all. They've taken away all the faith I ever had—which wasn't too much—and given me nothing in exchange."

"One can just go on feeling in oneself that things are going to turn out all right," said Averil softly.

Sally clutched her hand.

"You can, you mean. And that's all that matters to me, now. I don't care whether we snuff out altogether or not, as long as we do it together. It's not that I'm worrying about, it's—oh, the beastly things he said about instincts, I suppose."

"That 'self-perpetuation'?"

"Yes. If he's right, you've got that instinct and I

138

haven't. That means you're different. Sooner or later, you'll want to get married."

"Far as I remember, he had the sense to add that I wouldn't, unless I met the right man. I never have, and I never shall. I'm too particular—too civilised, I suppose he'd call it. How many more times d'you want me to say it?" . .

"I'll try not to mention it again," said Sally gratefully.

She got up, shaking her shoulders, as though they had been freed from a burden.

"As to that idea of a future life only in one's children, that's too absurd for words. How can you live in all of them, supposing you have lots? Thirteen little bits of oneself—ugh! loathsome thought! I'd rather go back to the universal what's-its-name, and be done with it."

"I don't know," said Averil slowly. "I'd never thought of it like that before."

But Sally was at the window, and did not catch the words. A young moon was up now, and the trees stood straight and aloof, communing with themselves, taking no further interest in Moss Cottage. Perhaps they had lost hope that anything would happen in that room.

## CHAPTER XIII

SALLY found it impossible, after that evening, to look on Dr. Hope with the same amused, slightly contemptuous eyes.

From being merely an incident in their life, a man who had reached a sensible age, and amused himself by giving a good time to a couple of girls, with no ulterior motive, he had become a force to be reckoned with. And it was, she felt definitely now, a hostile force. He had declared himself on the side of the accepted order of things—the maid to the man, and failing that a more or less wasted life for both of them.

Hitherto he had entered so thoroughly into the spirit of the thing at Moss Cottage. He had suggested little improvements on the domestic side, as if he recognised it for a permanent home. He had tried to find commissions for Averil, helped Sally with repairs to "Georgina," and never by word or look suggested that the life of two working girls on their own together was not as fine and desirable as any other life they could have found. But now—he had as good as said that Averil, at least, was made for a better one.

"She's not yet found the right man, that's all."

Anybody who could say a thing like that was an enemy of Sally's, to be classed with Midge, and Mrs. Kennion, and Dina—the list was growing. Dr. Hope, though he was not trying to take Averil away for himself and was therefore relatively unimportant, was in league with those other disturbers of the peace in theory.

140

Sally did not want to seem to put objections in the way of his visits—but one week-end she found she needed a rest after a particularly heavy week. The next, she wanted Averil to go for a drive with her, so it would be no good his coming down that Sunday.

Then, when at last the little doctor came again, she met his pallishness with extreme politeness, and watched him like a cat with a mouse. So that even Averil noticed.

"You don't seem to like Barry any more," she said. "And I thought you were getting on so beautifully! Now—he's just the same to you, but you're not nearly so nice to him."

"I've changed my mind, I suppose," said Sally. "I —I don't like his ideas."

"You're the most contrary creature!" declared Averil. "You wouldn't believe me when I told you he wasn't a fool, at first. And now when he takes you seriously, and has a friendly argument with you, you blame him because his opinions aren't the same as yours."

"He's clever enough in his way. I quite admit that. It's—well, every time I open my mouth, I wonder what sort of nasty instinct he's going to read into my words. The other day he told me that the reason I'd dreamt I was flying was because I was suffering from thwarted ambition!"

"Only because you asked him first," smiled Averil.

"But he would have thought it all the same. Fancy having to live with a man like that! It would drive me mad."

"Well, he's not asking you to live with him. Besides, think how decent he's been to us both."

Sally could not deny it.

# SURPLUS

Financial matters, about that time, demanded considerable thought. With the end of summer the visitors, in the course of nature, took their departure. But there seemed also to be fewer resident clients than the winter before, and custom was falling off. People were beginning to buy their own cars in greater numbers, and there was an influx of tiny, three-wheeled vehicles with their engines sticking out at odd angles, immature and impertinent, like untidy flappers.

By a coincidence, the cause of Sally's first open breach with Dr. Hope was also financial—not, this time, a "friendly argument" over big issues, but a trivial, sordid, vulgar affair.

It happened in public, too. Barry had insisted on taking them for a whole week-end—his last—to a certain Southbeach hotel, owned by a retired fellow officer, whose wife could play chaperone. Sally had done her best to veto the idea, which involved allowing him to pay for her, perforce. But Averil seemed keen on it, and as he pointed out that the difference between accepting the cost of a night's lodging and the cost of a meal at his hands was extremely remote, there seemed no sensible reason to refuse.

And on the first night they sat down to bridge with a stranger, picked up by Barry in the lounge, as the fourth. Sally was half asleep already, in the tobacco fumed air of that padded, pile carpeted room, and against Averil and Barry—both experts—she and the stranger had never a chance. Obstinately, she refused to cut again, and all the time she lost and lost. They were playing for threepence a hundred—nothing to Barry—and the risks he took were stupendous, and they all came off.

142

# SURPLUS

"It's quits for you and me, I suppose?" she said to Averil, at the end.

She was thinking of a private arrangement, made some time ago, that they should not take money from each other. Averil had said it wasn't fair, since Sally always lost—through sheer bad luck, of course—and she could so ill afford it.

At the words, Dr. Hope turned to her, smiling broadly.

"That won't do, Sally. One must pay up in this game!"

"We—arranged beforehand," she said quickly, icily.

"Poor Rill! You'd have had to pay if you'd lost, something tells me."

Averil answered his bantering tone in kind.

"It tells you wrong, then," she said.

That was all. No furious defence of Sally, not even a confirmation of her statement about the pre-arrangement not to pay.

The rest of that evening was spoilt for one of the trio. Sally would scarcely answer Dr. Hope's remarks, not even when he chaffed her on her silence. Yet she had a suspicion, so strong it amounted to a certainty, that she was playing into his hands by sulking, that it was exactly what he had intended—to make her feel small and look small. If cornered he would say, of course, that he had been "only ragging"—how idiotic of her to take offence! But he had known it was the sort of thing she would be most likely to take offence at—a nasty, underhanded accusation of meanness, impossible to refute—as far as he knew—difficult to ignore. Too difficult, for Sally. It takes a strong mixture of patience (my turn next!), self-control and self-conceit, to keep a sweet smile pinned above a raging heart.

"Now I hope you see what your friend's like," she said, as soon as there was a chance of a talk with Averil alone.

"Like—what do you mean?"

"He's accused me in so many words of being a cad and trying to get out of paying my card debts."

Averil turned away.

"Surely even you couldn't have taken him seriously *that* time?"

"He meant to be nasty," repeated Sally. "And he's got to apologise. If he doesn't do it of his accord, you must tell him so."

"I certainly won't do anything of the kind," Averil flared. Her faults were growing more like Sally's, there was no doubt of that. It took considerably less, these days, to make her exhibit the fact that she had a temper hidden away somewhere.

"If you can't take the least bit of ragging without making a tragedy of it, I can't help you. I don't understand it."

"Then you won't stick up for me—when I've been insulted, I tell you?" cried Sally.

But the door was—not slammed, but firmly shut.

A trifle, the whole thing. But to Sally it meant that Averil, for the first time, had failed to take her part in a crisis. Averil, who had stood with her against an unjust employer, against the tyranny of competition in her job, against her own mother and cousin—against the world.

For it was obvious that this time, at least, Averil had meant what she said when she was angry. She was sweet and yielding in everything else, next morning, but she would not ask him to apologise. And he had evidently no thought of it. He was just charming to Sally, and the more charming he was, the more ungrateful appeared the unresponsiveness of the girl who was, after all, his guest.

But it was his last visit for a long time. The new nursing home had been bought at last, and he had to be on hand to superintend the furnishing. It was going to be a big thing, he said. But he would write, of course.

"Write away, as long as you stay away," muttered Sally to herself.

And directly he was gone, she decided that it had been only Averil's exaggerated ideas of loyalty that had made her take his part—only because Sally had started abusing him, not because she really sympathised with him.

Mavis Barron was going, too, having by now saved up enough to finish her training. She came to say good-bye on the day after the St. Martin's summer ended, wearing a close-fitting grey fur cap, against the upturned brim of which twinkled the silver of her hair. Sally thought she looked tired, and wondered whether she minded leaving Salter's Ridge because of St. John Gathorne. Perhaps she was thinking she would miss his admiration? It must be rather intoxicating to have a man, who was surly to everyone else, leap up and shake your hands and tell you you were wonderful!

Sally knew that in Mrs. Gathorne's place she would have been jealous, but Mrs. Gathorne did not seem to mind. They had met her once or twice walking with Mavis, who had a child on either arm—all children adored Mavis, and the little Gathornes were ap-

parently allowed to do so unchecked. Sally told herself that, of course, artists always struck up friendships
like that with each other, and sensible wives and
husbands approved. It was a natural rushing together of their respective geniuses, akin to Sally's own
rapturous recognition of any passenger who happened
to have driven a machine of the same type as
"Georgina."

Mavis admitted she was glad at the prospect of getting back to work, serious work.

"You've got all the luck," said Sally. "Once you've
made your début, you're all right. Slumps can't touch
you, and you don't have to depend on tips for your
profit, or live from hand to mouth like us. I envy
you."

"Do you?" said Mavis, smiling faintly. Then she
saw that Sally had turned from her to Averil again.
"I don't see why you should," she finished.

She had to leave early, as Gathorne was calling for
her and taking her back to Greenhurst.

"He'll miss you," said Averil, having arrived at the
other end of Sally's thought.

Averil's day trip to town, for the purpose of inter-
viewing the "Tinkers' Tackproof Tyre" people,
followed shortly afterwards. And it was a complete
success, as Sally knew the moment she saw her radiant
face. It appeared that Barry had made them promise
to consider a series of her posters.

"Oh, you saw him?"

"Of course, he took me round and introduced me."

"Hope he sent me his love," said Sally.

"He did. He said he hoped you were going as
strong as ever," Averil assured her, with mock
solemnity.

SURPLUS

And such was Sally's perversity that she was sorry
he had not forgotten to send her a message at all, so
that she might have had something to complain of.

Next day was a slack morning, an all too frequent
occurrence nowadays. She was putting in a much
needed hour's repair work in the cycle shed when
Averil came out to her, and at once began to help.

"Have you ever been proposed to in a railway
station?" she asked, in the middle of a silence.

"Only twice all told, and they were both in a ball-
room," replied Sally literally. She had never talked
much about her early imitation love affairs to Averil.
There were so many more worth while subjects to
discuss.

"In the refreshment room, with the train starting
in five minutes," pursued Averil. "That's where
Barry tried his luck last night."

"Barry——"

Sally broke into a helpless peal of laughter. The
idea of that little cock sparrow thinking he was grand
and magnificent enough to propose marrying Averil
was so ludicrous that she could not believe it.

"You're ragging again," she said when she could
speak.

"Not a bit of it," said Averil, laughing too. "He
told me he'd wanted to all along, from the first time
we met, when I was driving. Only he had no money
to speak of then. And after the war he took up this
psychotherapy business and didn't know at first
whether it was going to pay or not. But now he's doing so well that there's no longer any doubt."

Sally was silent with amazement.

"I can't imagine how he had the nerve," she said at
last. "Did you squash him, Averil? No, you prob-

147

ably let him down so gently he didn't know he was falling. You would."

"I said no, anyway, as loud as I could. But he wouldn't take it. He said I was to think it over well, and he didn't mind how long it took. I told him it was no good waiting, but he said he was going to wait all the same."

"So you left it like that?"

"What else could I do? It's a free country—if he likes to wait, nobody can stop him. He's doing it at his own risk."

"He must be crazy," mused Sally. "Why, all these months he's been acting the heavy uncle to us both, and now to burst out like this! I expect it's old age coming on. He thinks he'll have a final fling."

"You can't call him old, exactly."

"Middle aged, then. Besides, you two haven't got a single taste in common, barring golf and bridge. He's not musical, he doesn't care a bit for art except in breeches—and he's got those awful 'instinct' theories—he *must* be crazy! You're not going to let him go on worrying you?"

"He won't worry me," said Averil. "He promised not to mention the subject again unless I brought it up. Said he'd put the thing before me, now, and I can just make up my own mind. He'll go on being friends with me, whatever happens."

"It won't need much thinking over, that's certain."

Averil put her arm across Sally's shoulder.

"Not much," she agreed. "Come in to lunch now, my child."

Coming home that afternoon, Sally found her sorting through a bundle of old posters, among them the long neglected "Armour of the Modern Woman."

# SURPLUS

"Why don't you have another go at it?" asked Sally.

I shall never make anything of it now," said Averil thoughtfully. "I've tried long enough. I must think of another idea for the soap."

"Give up one of the best things you ever started?" cried Sally. "You can't!"

But Averil had decided. Neither entreaties nor threats could ever induce her to go on with anything she had made up her mind was a failure. She had put her best efforts into this poster, and she had failed, and that was all there was to it. No occasion for vain laments, but no sense in keeping on with it. She had already started to tear the sheet when Sally snatched it from her.

"If you don't want it, I'll have it! I've always wanted you to do something for me. And it is like me—in parts."

She did not know exactly why she wanted it. Perhaps because it was such a familiar feature in the room. It had come with them to Moss Cottage and hung there all the time, advancing by fits and starts towards completion. Sometimes the debonair girl warrior had possessed a face for a whole hour, till Averil in disgust had wiped it off again. She belonged, that featureless lady, to the partnership—she was something in the nature of a mascot.

So Sally, heedless of Averil's laughter, carried the defaced thing into her room. When she came back, she had remembered a different subject.

"Do you truly mean to say Barry's wanted to marry you ever since he met you, and you didn't guess? Not that one would. Barry in love——!"

"He says so," Averil spoke without removing the

149

long green holder. "He didn't go into raptures, but
I think he meant it. He does care."

"You ought to know," admitted Sally. "You've
had enough experience." She added, "It's all your
fault! You will lead these poor wretches on—at
least, not exactly that, but you won't choke them off
properly. It's Midge over again."

"Considering you've been with us pretty well every
minute of the time, you ought to know how I've treated
him."

They looked at each other, and it was Sally's eyes
that registered contrition.

"All right then, it wasn't your fault. But you must
take action now. We don't want the creature round
here any more."

"I've told you he's not going to worry me," said
Averil at that. "I shan't see him for months, anyhow, and he's promised not to mention a word of it
in his letters. Can't I go on being friends with him,
Sally, because he's offended you?"

"Of course," said Sally hurriedly.

"You mayn't like him now—you did at first, remember—but I do, in lots of ways. This isn't going
to make the slightest difference to the way he treats
me, things will go on just as they were before."

And Sally understood. Here was one more enemy
who had declared himself, only to meet with defeat—
a poor foolish enemy, this, who had never had a chance
from the beginning. Sally was filled with surprise
that a man with Dr. Hope's mental equipment—for
she never forgot, now, to grant him brains of a sort—
should have fooled himself into imagining that a girl
like Averil would seriously consider such a proposition. Couldn't he see she was only letting him love

her, as she had let so many better men before him, because she was too kind hearted to stop him? Also, since she had warned him now, she would not be to blame whatever happened in the future. Probably Dr. Barrington Hope, like the other silly moths, was obsessed with the conviction that any man could in the long run marry any girl, provided there was no one else in view. It was the natural corollary, after all, to his creed of all powerful, all prevailing instincts.

It was not Averil's fault that in her case the theory did not work.

# CHAPTER XIV

O N New Year's Eve, Sally took "Georgina" down to meet the last train from London. Cousin Dina had arrived back in England sooner than expected, and Averil had been up for the day to meet her. She had told Sally to expect her by this train; but the other passengers swept past her to their waiting cabs and were driven away, chattering to their friends, and there was never a sign of Averil's unassuming little black hat.

Sally drove back to her lonely supper, laid for two, in a mood of depression. But it did not last. What had she to grumble about, waiting another day? She was the home maker for Averil now, as Averil was for her. There must be a perfectly good reason why she had missed that train, and she would catch the first one to-morrow. She had never yet willingly delayed.

At long last, Sally was beginning to trust her out of her sight, though she had not yet said so even to herself. Perfect faith that nothing in the world could ever permanently break their life together was the last certainty left for Averil to bring out of a world of shifting shadows. But it was done now. Sally could look back pityingly at the old unreal figure of herself —the queer girl, with her loneliness, her brooding over books, her universal doubting. For she had found one person in whom she could believe.

So she sat by the fire and dreamed, and studied "Tins," who slept heavily in the chair opposite. He

SURPLUS

had been very unsociable lately. To-night, when Sally
picked him up because she wanted company, his body
lay inert and soft in her grasp. Suddenly, though,
he sat up on her knee, fixing her with his round, unwinking eyes, while his tawny tail threshed the air.
Then he leapt down, and silently, with deliberate
purpose in every curve, bounded across the room and
out through the half open window.

"So he's off again," commented Sally, with resigna-
tion.

They had long ago given up worrying about "Tins,"
who was an inveterate night prowler but had never
yet been shot or trapped in the woods.

Averil did not catch the first train next day, nor the
second. By dusk, Sally had begun to be afraid, in
spite of her common sense, borrowed from Averil.
Something must have happened, and it had been too
late to send a wire. But no wire came next day, nor
the day after that.

It was not till the third evening that the truant
arrived. And the first thing Sally noticed was that
she wore a smart new feathered hat, of a blue that
toned with her eyes.

"You forgot the day, I suppose?" said Sally, cold
and collected.

"Rather not. But they wanted me to stay over the
New Year and go to a show last night, and I knew
it wouldn't matter."

"And you couldn't let me know? Do you realise
how many times I've been down to the station to meet
you, and waited there in the cold? Oh, no, you didn't
think! You never do."

"All right, have it that way if you like," said
Averil.

153

"Just because you've met this Dina again, you can't think of anything else."

Averil's eyes were flawed sapphires set in bronze.

"I wish you were more like her. She wouldn't dream of greeting me as you have!"

"If you'd only just said you were sorry for not letting me know——"

"Dina wouldn't have wanted apologies. She'd have been only too glad I was having a good time."

"Oh, Dina!"

Sally shrugged her shoulders, her contrition nipped in the bud.

"She behaves like a real friend, Sally, and you—don't."

Sally stared at her. What had happened to make Averil break out like this when for once she was so obviously and entirely in the wrong? Even the mildest tempered person—and Sally never professed to be that—would have taken exception to Averil's behaviour on this occasion. There had been no cross word between them for a long time now, but surely no one could have helped saying a few little words about it? If they had grown into more than a few, it was Averil's doing.

"I'm beginning to see 'friend' means a different thing to you and me," Averil was saying. "And I can't alter myself to suit you. I've tried, but I can't."

"You've tried? It's me—" Sally stuttered because she could not get the words out quick enough— "It's me that's taught myself to put up with your—your casualness!"

Averil rose, looking out of the window over Sally's head.

154

"All right, that settles it. You agree that we don't get on together, and never shall. Well, I've promised Barry to think over his proposal again, seriously this time. I won't think any more. I'll let him know to-morrow."

The little doctor—the most despised of Sally's rivals, the only one she had never seriously reckoned with. A grotesque figure, surely, that at the mention of his name, in that new tone of Averil's, all her castle of security should crumble into dust.

"I suppose you think he broke his promise, and wrote and worried me about it? But I only saw him by accident, as it were. I thought—we both did—that he'd be away in Manchester all the week, but he managed to get back early, and he took me over his new home. Such a lovely place, Sally!"

Then Sally produced the most amazing travesty of a laugh that ever ruined an actress's reputation. It started low, and ended on a quavering top note.

"I know you don't mean it, but don't make a joke like that. I was a beast when you came in, but I'd been so worried when you didn't turn up. Awfully sorry."

But Averil said:

"It's not a joke. I've been thinking it over in a kind of way, of course, ever since he suggested it. But this last week I've begun to feel it's now or never, if I'm going to get married at all. I'm very nearly thirty, you know."

And you'd marry even that man—to get away from me!"

Averil's arms went out to that despairing cry.

"*Don't* take it like that. It's not settled yet, anyway. Nobody else knows a word about it, not even

Dina. I only told you because I knew you'd rather I warned you there was a chance."

"How big a chance?" said Sally.

Then it dawned on her that Averil was simply over-tired, and hardly knew what she was saying.

"Say you didn't mean a word of it!"

But Averil did not turn to her.

"It's awfully late. Do let's talk it over to-morrow."

"You said you were never—never going to get married."

"Not till I'd met the right man. Oh, Sally, do leave it alone."

"And is he the right man? That—to take you away from me?"

Sally bent down over her.

"You're not in love with him, you couldn't be. Averil, are you in love with him?"

At last the deep-sea eyes met hers full.

"If you mean the passionate kind—no. I'm very fond of him."

Sally straightened herself again.

"Then what's the idea? Are you getting tired of me, or what?"

"Of course not"—Averil put out a weary hand—"But we couldn't expect to go on living together all our lives, surely?"

She said it as if it were quite an ordinary statement, and it was too much for Sally.

"We are going on together—I thought it was to be for always and so did you," she cried. "We belong together. Promise you won't leave me, promise! You're the only creature I really care for in the world, you can't leave me alone. I want you too much."

# SURPLUS

"But, my dear old thing, Barry wants me too," said Averil.

And Sally explained that it couldn't matter to him as it did to her. He was a man, and he could never be as lonely as a woman is when she's got nobody. He would still have his nursing home to play about with, money, success, a big career. He was used to enjoying these things alone—did he look the kind of man to stop enjoying them, because Averil was denied him? He wanted her as the crown of his achievements; as a kind of rare and expensive liqueur, that puts the finishing touch to a good dinner. If he lost her, he would still have plenty left—whereas she, Sally, would have nothing.

"I can't think how you can talk like that," said Averil. "You've got a home, and people—don't they mean something?"

"You know I was always miserable at home. It's all like a bad dream to me now, that life? D'you want to drive me back to it, for good?"

The room was in half darkness, lit only by a candle, guttering in Sally's shaking hand. She had picked it up at the sound of Averil at the door, and forgotten to put it down.

"I don't want to drive you anywhere, silly! But I don't see why you shouldn't make yourself happy in Leamingham, or any other place. One always can, if one tries." ("You can, perhaps," muttered Sally.) "And it's not fair to make me responsible like this. Am I never to be free even to think of getting married, because of you? I've given up Midge already—no, I didn't tell you that was why I turned him down so finally, and never heard from him again. But it was

157

because of you—and he was a great friend of mine, too."

"You'd never have married him!"

"Perhaps not, but I should have thought it over a lot more carefully. No, that wasn't your fault, you didn't know what you were doing—but you did know Dina wanted me to live with her, and I wanted it too. But you made me give that up, because you said you wouldn't go on being my friend otherwise."

The flickering, candle-cast shadow made the dream girl's face look very stern as she sat there, delivering judgment. There was yet another count to add to the indictment—Averil had started, and she was going to finish this time.

"It wasn't your fault that I left home with you in the first place. But you didn't want mother to have anything of me at all, if you could help it. You forgot she's got much more right than you."

"Then she's got more than Dr. Hope!" broke in Sally.

In vain Averil reminded her that one's people never felt the same, when it was a question of marriage. Sally said one's people simply felt everybody else ought to marry because *they* had done it, and that was why they were always more or less against their girls having careers, even nowadays. That didn't prove they were right. They were the old generation—they still couldn't see there was anything for women but marriage, and children. But Averil must know they were wrong. Hadn't she a life work of her own already, and a home that was far more truly hers than any a man could give her, because she had earned it herself?

"I won't marry to please them. I promise you that,"

said Averil, clinging to fact amid the stormy sea of theories.

Sally stood up, shielding the candle from the window.

"I suppose you realise that, if you married, you wouldn't ever see me again?"

"And why on earth not?"

Averil stifled a yawn. She was used, by now, to dear old Sally's funny, dramatic ultimatums.

"Because I couldn't bear it. Haven't you noticed what happens between friends, when one of them marries—how they drift apart?"

"I've got lots of friends who are married, and we've been just as good pals afterwards," said Averil.

Did she really not know how maddening she was, or was she saying these things on purpose? The candle shook in Sally's hand as she answered:

"That's because you were such 'ordinary' sort of friends to start with. You'd never lived with those girls, or worked with them. After that, the idea of seeing each other only occasionally is—oh, it's impossible. Besides, what should I do alone?"

Whereat Averil laughed, then held out a penitent hand.

"Cheer up, old thing—I shall very likely decide against it, after all. And do hurry off and get warm. You'll catch your death of cold."

Death of cold—as if that mattered, in comparison to the catastrophe that threatened! Sally went back to her room and threw the window wide.

The trees were in a savage mood, that night. They fought each other with the roar of cannon and the patter of machine guns, with here and there the crack of a revolver shot above the clamour. Yet it was not of their own will, that battle. It was the wind that

SURPLUS

was the cause of all the trouble, and they were puppets
in its grip, from the tallest of the larches to the saplings by the path, yielding gracefully because there was
no choice—they had to.

But Sally thought of the things Averil had said, and
wondered whether they were justified. Had she, then,
failed Averil, made life at Moss Cottage a thing of
such doubtful attractions that life with a Barrington
Hope was preferable? She went over in her mind the
incidents Averil had complained of. Every one of
them had been brought about by the same fear—that
Averil would leave her. Was that kind of jealousy,
then, a fault unforgivable—jealousy that arose simply
from too much love? Averil had praised Dina's unselfishness, because she did not claim her friend as a
life companion. That simply proved, to Sally's mind,
that Dina cared less. At any rate, it is impossible to
choose with what degree and kind of feeling one will
love. As well try to harness the wind that harasses
the tree tops.

"I'll behave as if nothing had happened, to-morrow,"
she decided. "It'll blow over, this new scheme,
probably it was only seeing Dina again that made her
think she wanted a change from the life here. She'll
settle down again, if I don't worry her. She loves it
here as much as I do, really, and she'll go on loving it.
I'm going to follow her own advice and take things
for granted—take it for granted that she'll stick to me."

And to-morrow, Averil announced that she must go
back to London to stay—"for a bit, anyhow." Her
father had written again, stating that if she refused to
follow his wishes and go home to look after her mother,
she ought at least to justify her refusal by making
good in her career, and finishing her course at the Art

160

School. If she continued to refuse, he warned her that he would be reluctantly compelled to discontinue her allowance.

"He wrote to you like that before, then? You never told me."

"What was the use of worrying you for nothing? I'd refused," said Averil.

She went on to hope that Sally would be sensible and agree that London *was* the best place for an artist with her way to make? She herself had known it all along. Hotly questioned on this point, she admitted that she had agreed to come to Salter's Ridge, in the first place, because it had been the best plan for Sally. Also, she had hoped it might be possible for herself.

For once Sally, the waverer, made up her mind without hesitation.

"All right, if you must go, I'll come too, and chance getting another job."

She glanced up, waiting for a glad assent. But Averil said:

"I meant—alone. Do let me finish, old thing! It'll only be for a couple of months or so, I expect. But I must have absolute peace and quiet, if I'm to work really hard."

"I'm not going to stop your working, am I?" Sally's voice was getting out of her control again— "Haven't I always been keener on your career than I was on my own?"

"It's not only that," said Averil at last, "it's that I've got to decide about this other thing now—getting married. You won't give me a minute's peace to think it over calmly, if you're there. Honestly, now, will you?"

Then Sally cried that it needed no thinking over,

thereby rendering an answer to Averil's last question superfluous. And to cut short the other things she wanted to say—a tired *rechauffé* of last night's arguments, with all the original fiery seasoning gone stale —she rushed out to "Georgina."

When she came back, there was a green cabin trunk with neat brass fittings on the floor, already packed. Averil had decided to go at once.

Sally did not know which objection to begin with. How could she bear it, being left alone like that in suspense, not knowing when her partner was coming back, or whether she was coming at all? Averil would have Dr. Hope round her all day long, pleading his absurd suit, with Dina probably backing him up. Neither of them would spend a second in considering Sally's point of view. It wasn't fair!

"Well, isn't it Barry's turn to have the field to himself?" asked Averil. She hated saying a conceited thing like that, but one somehow couldn't help it, with Sally. "You've been always with me, up till now. But he's not going to mention it again till I have my answer ready."

"Don't you believe it—he'll do just as much persuading as he thinks you need," Sally clung to her. "He'll get you in his power, I believe he's started already. He'll make you forget all about me and Moss Cottage!"

"Nonsense," said Averil softly, "I'm more likely to miss the splendid times we've had here, if you let me go quietly now. And don't worry me while I'm away, just leave me absolutely alone for the present. Don't you see, the sooner I go, the sooner I'll be back, perhaps? But I must keep a clear head this time, to think it all out."

# SURPLUS

Afterwards, Sally could never imagine how it was that she had let Averil go at all. She remembered vaguely that Averil had done all the talking, on the way down to the station, explaining that she must get one of the village girls to sleep in the cottage at nights, if she found it lonely. But the art course only lasted two months, no time, after all.

Then two things vividly—Averil's arms going round her swiftly, as the train came in, Averil saying "I expect I'll soon be back. And I *do* care— always shall, whether you believe it or not!"

And then, jumping on to the footboard of the moving train, and being pulled back by a porter. There was such a lot of important arguments she had had no time to mention—but the train had gathered speed remorselessly, and the last thing she saw was Averil leaning out, holding on to the new blue hat, calling, "Take care of yourself!"

So the only thing to do was to write at once, while the arguments were still fresh in one's mind, and before the opposition could get a word in. Sally wrote that letter in the cold, deserted waiting room, lit by a swinging gas lamp, only half turned on, that threw strange greenish shadows on the wall.

"I can't let you go like this, without telling you I do understand how you feel about my having worried you. I *did* try to keep you to myself, at first, because I was so afraid one of your old friends would take you away. But lately I've begun to trust you just as you want me to—truly I have, though I didn't tell you so. I won't be jealous ever again, when you come back."

"But you must come back, because I want you more than anybody else could. I'm not the sort that can

163

ever succeed by themselves, you ought to know me well enough to know that. I'm an awful coward, really. But as long as you stick to the old firm——"

That was it, a note of cheery optimism to finish up with. Sally flattered herself, as she addressed it to the old number in Farthing Lane, that it was just the sort of letter to appeal to Averil. In it, sentiment was discounted, and the claims of work were insisted on. Surely Averil could not show herself less keen for the advancement of Sally's career, than she had expected Sally to be for her own?

Coming home, she had the impulse to go and pour out her trouble to Miss Landison, who was the only creature left in Salter's Ridge with whom it was possible to talk in any way intimately. Not that Miss Landison ever seemed to invite confidences, but one felt she was there, ready and willing to receive them when offered, and in her turn to give advice—when asked. And it is only people with imaginary grievances who prefer to be pressed to disburden themselves.

The octagonal room was unlighted, its windows all open to the breath of the forest, pouring in, keen and riotous, disdaining invalidism. And the dim shape on the rug-piled couch was motionless.

"I—I'm afraid you're worse," stammered Sally. "If I'd known—did I wake you up, coming so late?"

"I wasn't asleep," said Miss Landison softly. "If people only knew what they missed, snoring all night! It's when one's thoughts come alive—if they're bad, they're very very bad, so bad they're almost beautiful. And if they're good, they're too wonderful to be believed, any other time."

Then she put a hand on Sally's arm.

"Something's happened," she said.

# SURPLUS

And Sally stood silent. She longed to be told that she was worrying over nothing, that of course Averil would come back. But that would have meant an admission of weakness. Averil would never go round seeking comfort and caresses when she was hurt—she would nurse her own wounds in silence.

"Nothing's happened—at least, nothing bad. Averil's gone up to town for a little, to finish her training. Good idea, isn't it?"

Then she went away. She had lived up, for once, to Averil's code.

## CHAPTER XV

HOW many of us can lie still, unbound, beneath the sword of Damocles?

Sally spent the time that followed Averil's departure in watching out for the postman, whenever she was not actually engaged on a job. Averil had said, to be sure, that she wanted to be left quite alone and not worried. But if she would not answer even the most cheerful, reasonable letters, such as the one composed in the station waiting room, what was one to do?

She might conceivably be planning to come straight back and explain in person that everything was going to be all right—only that Averil never did things like that, on impulse, except in the one matter of her leaving Moss Cottage. It occurred to Sally that that had been all arranged and accomplished in a single day, a miracle, surely, of impulsiveness? Just one of those very occasional inconsistencies that cropped up in her nature, Sally thought, thereby saving her from the dead level of perfection.

So, when the days went by and neither Averil herself nor any news of her appeared, Sally wrote again, sitting breeched and booted before a fire that would not flame, lacking Averil's magic touch with the poker. The whole room had an oddly uncared for appearance, for the matter of that. Dust lay thick on the piano top, the table cloth was stained (Sally could not be bothered to hunt out a clean one), and tools lay about on the floor, whence Averil would have summarily

ejected them.   Also a forlorn saucer of milk, waiting
for "Tins," who never came to claim it.

No one came to the cottage now, except for St.
Gathorne, who called once to enquire whether they
had heard from Mavis lately?   On being answered
in the negative, he had gone away, refusing to come
in, for which Sally was glad, though he would have
been someone to talk to.   He belonged to a four that
was now broken up, and she did not want to entertain
him until her partner, at least, should be present once
again.

When at last Averil wrote, she said she was far too
busy with her classes to have time for a proper letter.
But if Sally was already tired of waiting for her decision about coming back, couldn't she find someone
else to share the cottage with her, some other girl
to live with?

"It wouldn't be fair of me to make you miss a chance
of getting someone who could promise to stay with
you, just because my own plans are so uncertain at
present."

It wouldn't be fair—!

.     .     .     .     .     .     .

A table in one of the more obscure establishments
of Messrs. Lyons, bearing upon its flaccid marble top
a couple of thick cups—one with its contents un-
touched, the other emptied—But a table across which
many a drama had been acted out, in its time, and
many a battle waged.

Sally had decided that if she could only see Averil
again for an hour, ten minutes even, more could be
accomplished than in a dozen letters.   Letters were so
cold, so limited in their powers of explanation, especially Averil's.   And it was absurd to suppose that

Averil would not be glad to see her when she was actually on the spot.

So Sally, taking no chances, had presented herself without warning at the street door of the Dallington School of Arts, just as the students were coming out to lunch. And Averil had said:

"Sally! Is anything wrong? Why on earth didn't you tell me you were coming?"

It appeared that Averil had only a quarter of an hour to spare for lunch. So there they sat, and the precious minutes slipped past while Sally tried to remember exactly what she had come to say. It had all seemed so simple in the quiet of Moss Cottage, but here, in the turmoil that accompanies the consumption of the greatest possible amount of food in the shortest possible time, it seemed impossible. What had this busy, fiercely practical world to do with a friendship passing the love of men, or any other ideal that did not pay?

Averil herself seemed, even in those few weeks, to have changed slightly. Her sudden, charming smile was less frequent, the squareness of her little chin was subtly emphasised. She wore a new painting overall, gaily patterned, instead of the old, stained garment. Nobody gave it a second glance, since the art students often patronised that restaurant. But Sally thought how much better the old one had suited her.

"You must know I was only thinking of you," Averil was saying. "I don't want to feel I'm sacrificing you, because I can't decide yet. You know it was only that, not because I 'wanted to get rid of you.' No, I *can't* promise anything till the end of this course. And I shall be miserable all the time if you keep worrying me, Sally," she added piteously.

# SURPLUS

"It's all very well for you—you don't lie awake at nights, wondering if you're going to be left stranded. Didn't you read my letters at all?"

"Of course," said Averil. "But they're all full of the same sort of thing. Asking me to forget everything else, and think of you only—and I can't do it, so there's nothing more to say. I've got father to consider now, and Barry—and myself. Don't you *want* me to think of myself at all?"

The nearest groups were beginning to look round, and Averil, red with embarrassment, signalled a waitress to take their bill. But Sally, heedless of who saw or what they thought, leant across the table.

"Can't you be happy with me again, like we were before? I haven't changed——"

Then the waitress was beside them, and Averil was explaining that she had to hurry off. But why didn't Sally stay and finish her lunch comfortably? Whereat Sally followed her out, and took her arm as she hurried down the street.

"They're turning you against me, Dr. Hope and Dina. You weren't a bit glad to see me."

"Well, considering I especially asked you not to come. I knew it would only mean trouble, if you did. And Dina and Barry haven't mentioned your name, as far as I can remember. We've had such lots to talk about."

"Out of sight, out of mind. I said so!" cried Sally, as Dallington's came in sight again.

"I'm not like that, I tell you," said Averil quickly. "If I weren't thinking so much about you, I should be getting through a lot more work."

They were at the door.

"Look here, I must see you again, somewhere where

169

we can talk. What time d'you get off? I'll meet you."

"My dear, Barry's taking me to dinner at his club this evening. I shall have just time to get back to Farthing Lane and change. If we'd only known you were coming!"

"Can't you put him off?" begged Sally, still holding her arm.

But Averil had no idea where to find him at that hour. Besides, wouldn't it be rather hard luck on him, after ordering a special dinner and everything? She appealed to Sally's common sense.

"That's all you care about now, upsetting his two-penny dinner parties! I believe you're afraid of him. Have you promised him—anything yet?"

The other students were casting curious glances, as they passed in at the doorway and up the wide stone steps.

"I must fly," said Averil. "Of course I've not promised him anything. I'll let you know the minute I have. Don't keep worrying over it, Sally—please don't! Can't you get anyone—well, not if you don't want to, of course. Yes, write—I love your letters— if only you'll tell me all the news, and give this one subject a rest!"

Then, with a wave of the hand, she was running up the stairs, where Sally could not possibly follow her.

.      .      .      .      .      .      .      .

Nothing had been accomplished, after all. Sally went back to Moss Cottage repeating to herself all the things she had meant to say, and had not said. Well, they must go in a letter—letters were better than talking, in many ways. One could say what one wanted to calmly, without losing one's temper, being betrayed into side issues.

The whole terrible break had come so suddenly that Sally was still unable to think coherently. One moment, she wished she had been willing from the first to share Averil with her other friends, even to share her permanently with cousin Dina. That would have been bad enough, but better—so it seemed now—than the risk of losing her altogether. Or again, was the explanation simply that Averil was being hypnotised, slowly and subtly, this time without her knowledge?

For Sally was convinced that, apart from supernormal compulsion, nothing but the sudden flowering of a long standing grievance against herself could account for the fact that Averil contemplated, however remotely, marriage with the little doctor as an alternative to life with her. And she was certain that the barrier between them could be easily removed, if only one knew exactly where it lay, and even Dr. Hope's fell practices counteracted. In any case, the change could not be in Averil herself—in these short weeks, from the perfect friend to a stranger.

With all her mind on these questions, Sally's business did not benefit. There came a day when she caused two of her passengers to miss their trains through confusing their orders, and another when she forgot an order altogether. Georgina was growing shabby, too. She must be repainted, when Averil came home. There would be small chance of buying a new machine that summer, after all, as the savings were nearly gone.

Then, one blowy March morning, she met Mrs. St. John Gathorne, and found herself greeting the once seen face with an eagerness that was the measure of

her loneliness—but at once she noticed that the lady's
chin was very much in evidence. It even appeared she
would have preferred to avoid the meeting. However, she smiled frostily.

"So your friend's in town, is she? I'm not surprised, she must have been a regular fish out of
water down here. I suppose you'll be leaving soon,
too?"

She went off, not waiting for an answer. Sally told
herself that she must expect such treatment, while
Averil was away. Without her beautiful partner, she
was a mere uninteresting taxi driver, considered from
the residents' point of view. And this Mrs. Gathorne
thought Averil had gone for good, so she did not mind
snubbing a too effusive Sally. That was about the
size of it.

.        .        .        .        .        .        .

How hostile the house lookeu, with no light in the
first floor windows!

Sally had broken her promise again, and taken a
day off to come up to London and see Averil, choosing
Farthing Lane this time. Mrs. Dunn, at any rate, had
been delighted to see her.

"Miss Kennion 'aint back yet, Miss. She do work
hard, these times, the room upstairs is chock full of
legs and arms like, what she's made drawings of for
her posters, all round the walls. Talking of arms,
Miss, you never saw the likes of the one I've had on
me since Christmas——"

Sally shut the door on her at last, promising to set
a match to the gas herself. But she left the room half
lit from the street lamp over the way. It had a cosy,
lived in look, but the arrangement of the furniture had
been altered. No more camp beds, no more packing

case stands. Instead, there was a new easel, with a cunning little extension table for the accommodation of paints and brushes. And the studies hanging on the walls—Sally stood a long time looking at them. It hurt to think that Averil had gained so much precision of line, so much improvement in her detail figure work, without her knowledge—without a word of praise from her.

A half empty box of chocolates lay on the table, and a crumpled theatre programme. Sally noticed it was a revue programme, Barry's choice, of course—Averil had always hated revues.

Then footsteps on the stairs, firm and clear, easy to pick out among a thousand others.

"Who's that?" called Averil sharply from the shadowed doorway.

"It's only me—Sally." (Her nerves weren't so good since she had been in London on her own—no wonder!)

"If only I'd known you were coming——" the old protest, in the old caressing tone. "You can't have had any supper, child?"

"I don't want any. I've come to say—I can't stand it any longer. You must make up your mind. You haven't answered one of my letters lately."

Averil said that Dina and Barry were calling for her almost at once, and going on to a show. Wouldn't Sally come too?

"Put them off for once, my dear," begged Sally. "No, I'm not being unreasonable. If I'd let you know I was coming, you'd have been out."

It had come to her suddenly that the breach between them was wide enough, now, for even that to be possible. But Averil said:

SURPLUS

"What nonsense! However—I must send a note, that's all."

When she had finished writing it, Sally was still in the same position.

"You must have realised by now what a crazy idea that was, of marrying Dr. Hope. You're just keeping me in suspense out of pure cussedness, because you won't admit I was right. Isn't that it?"

Averil stood up then, seeming almost tall in her tailored silver grey costume with its collar of silver fox.

"I told you I couldn't decide till I've finished my training. But if you must know now, Sally—I suppose it'll be for him."

Sally said—repeated, in different keys—that it was impossible. Surely everyone else, Dina for instance, must agree how impossible it was?

"Do come and sit down like a sensible person," said Averil. "All Dina says about it is that I must please myself, of course."

"Then I suppose she thinks I'm perfectly dreadful for trying to stop you—I imagine you've told her I have tried? She's jealous, that's what it is, because you chose to live with me and not with her."

"I didn't tell her," Averil declared. "She found out, when I was so upset after the last time you came up. If you must know, she does think you're being selfish, and she can't understand it. I'd always told her you were such a wonderful person. But as to being jealous of you—Dina's not so small as that."

So Averil *had* discussed, picked to pieces her character with a third person—the bitterness of it!

"She'd understand fast enough if she were in my

174

place, faced with my future," cried Sally. "Besides,
I want you to be happy, too."

"In your own way, Sally."

"Not anybody's way—just happy. You admit
we've been happy up to date, and there's no earthly
reason we shouldn't go on. I haven't changed, I tell
you, except that I care more than I did at first, even."

Averil was looking out of the window, challengingly
silent, and Sally came close to her.

"What can that fat bundle of instincts give you that
I can't? I can give you more real love than he ever
could. I saved all mine up for you, and he's given his
to lots of other things—and people. I can give you
more real companionship, because you and I've got
every taste in common, and you and he haven't. He
may give you money, but what's that, compared with
being happy?"

"Nothing," said Averil, very low.

"It's the one worth while thing he can give you that
I can't—except children, of course."

Sally paused, considering this exception, so casually
mentioned. It had always been there, at the back of
her mind, but only at this moment had it struck her
with its full, stunning force.

"Oh, Averil, is it that you want—so much you don't
mind who their father is, and don't mind breaking me
and throwing away the bits?"

It sounded so absurdly bald, put like that—but the
dark girl did not answer the question. She sat still,
the soft fur falling away from her soft brown throat,
the line of her lashes curved downwards.

"I'm beginning to feel I never knew you properly,"
she said slowly. "So mother and Midge were right—
you're determined I shan't ever marry?"

"Not the wrong man," cried Sally.

"You wouldn't think any man was right."

"Perhaps not. But if you were so wildly in love with him you couldn't live without him, it would be different. Liking to go to theatres and play golf with him isn't enough, not even if you had—children. He's simply not your sort. You'd be miserable——"

"I'm the best judge of that," interrupted Averil.

"Or, if you weren't, it would only be because you can make yourself happy anywhere, as you said the other day. Don't you see it works both ways? I'm not asking you to give up happiness, only to choose between two different kinds. And you ought to choose the kind that means least suffering to the other person. Where's your precious unselfishness that you talk so much about?"

Then Averil lost her calm, for once, and declared that Sally had no right to talk about love. To try and stop your best friend from marrying, just because you wanted to keep her for yourself! And Sally said:

"I wish I'd never met you—you're going to spoil my life all right." And then: "No, that's not true. It's a wonderful thing, our friendship, it's not a failure. It can't be."

She held out her hands to the other girl, who took them.

"Don't, Sally. You know I don't want to stop being friends with you, if I marry. I should want you to come and stay with me often—not just week-ends, but long visits, whenever you could get away. It's your own fault if you can't go on caring after I'm married. I never can understand it."

"Of course, I should still care, whatever you did." (Would nothing make her see the obvious?) "But

176

SURPLUS

I should have to try and forget there'd ever been such
a person as you. Can't you see it would be the only
hope for me, if I'm to be left alone again?"
After thought, Averil shook her head.
"I can't see it. You talk as if there was nothing
but me in the world." The tender note crept into her
voice again. "I wish you didn't feel like that!"
"I daresay you do, but it's no use wishing. I can't
help it."
"And you'll have your career."
Sally envisaged "Georgina," torn and travel stained,
tottering on her wheels.
"I told you. I shan't have the pluck to go on without you. You make all the difference. And if it
comes to that," she added, "what about your own
career, if you marry?"
"Barry will let me go on with it, of course. I
wouldn't think of marrying anyone who wouldn't.
He can help me a lot, too—he knows so many useful
people."
She talked as though the pros and cons were all
weighed, the total already added up in favour of matri-
mony. But she smiled as she said it, as if warning
her hearer not to take her too seriously.
"Try and forget the awful things you've found out
about me," whispered Sally. "My selfishness and all
that—though goodness knows I never tried to hide
them. And give Moss Cottage another trial—if you
don't want to, you needn't stick to it."
"I'll go on thinking it over," said Averil. "That's
all I can promise. You know I do consider your side
of it, and I'm sorry."
"I don't want your pity," cried the hastily resur-
rected pride in Sally.

"Then you want everything else of me, Sally! But —I've got my own life to think about, too."

So, in one of those subtly profound remarks that seemed, on Averil's lips, to be happy accidents, the final words on the subject were said. Sally spent the rest of the evening trying to prolong the discussion, but Averil had nothing more to add. It came to that —she had to think about her own life, too.

.     .     .     .     .     .     .     .

Speed—a panting engine under you, chafing to be free, leaping ahead at a touch, keeping pace with desire. Passing placid fields and houses, donkey carts, stooping men on bicycles, clattering lorries, long-nosed, smug limousines—spurning them all behind you to go on fighting your way against a gale in calm weather. Here is an unfailing anodyne for every kind of mental trouble. Only, like other drugs, its effects pass speedily too.

Sally was on her way to London, on "Georgina" this time, and the end of the waiting had come. She might as well have taken the train; better, in fact, if time saving were her object.

But she wanted to keep moving all the time. A train had to be waited for, it had to stop at intermediate stations, while you sat in the carriage with your hands folded, feeling you were getting nowhere.

The last month had been the hardest to bear. She had forced herself to obey orders, and maintain unbroken silence towards Averil, on the principle of better late than never. But in the nights, when there was nothing to do but think over the way Averil was behaving, and try to figure out whether that traitorous new attitude of hers towards the partnership was really what it seemed, or whether it was assumed in order to

178

assert her right to decide any question so personal as her own marriage without advice or interference—it was in the nights that waiting was so hard. But Sally told herself that no news was good news, when no word came from town. She was doing exactly what Averil had asked her, now, allowing time for the memory of their past happiness to prevail over every other consideration.

One day the charwoman brought a particularly tasty bit of gossip.

"Isn't it terrible about Mr. Gathorne, Miss? You didn't know? I thought not. I said to Mrs. Cazalet's cook, you and that Miss Kennion hadn't no more to do with it than a couple of babies, when she started going on at me. 'No more'n a couple of innocent babies' was the words I made use of. There was others 'eard me say it!"

It eventually transpired that St. John Gathorne had, only the other day, slipped the domestic coils and caught the fastest train (having no "Georgina") to London and Mavis Barron. And that he had left a note to say he was not coming back. And that his wife, who had expected some such development for some time past, had already publicly announced that she had no intention of divorcing him. Also, she made no secret of her opinion that the inmates of Moss Cottage were accessories after the fact.

It was rumoured at the club in the High Street, where the feminine élite of Salter's Ridge went up and down with shopping baskets on their arms, that the guilty pair had held their stolen meetings in Moss Cottage. It was not to be supposed that two women in possession of their eyesight had deduced nothing suspicious from an attractive young vampire of their own sex being constantly accompanied by a married man. An obviously adoring married man, too, a fact that was all the more significant from his general reputation for surliness. Of course, Miss K. and her taxi friend must have seen all along there was "something up." And the fact that the meetings had gone on up to the very night of Mavis's departure showed that they approved. Decently disposed persons would have warned his poor wife long ago, and she with three children and all.

When she was convinced that the thing was true—which was only after Mrs. Gathorne had cut her dead in the street—it was not what Salter's Ridge thought that worried Sally, but the besmirching of Moss Cottage. Those two had been favoured guests in paradise, and they had fouled its portals with their sordid intrigues and deceits. Mavis had seemed to appreciate the honour; and all the time she had come down the forest pathway not for love of an afternoon's music with congenial spirits, but for love of a man to whom she had no right.

Sally had no particular concern for what are commonly called the moral issues in such a case, and her apprehensive sympathies were more for Mavis than for the deserted wife, who struck her as eminently capable of getting along without any husband, and more especially without St. John. If Mavis had taken them into her confidence at all, given them any inkling of the true state of affairs—Sally was too occupied with other matters to consider whether there had not been inklings, after all. She saw only that there had been treachery to the atmosphere of Moss Cottage, and could not forgive it.

Of course, it would happen when Averil was away.

# SURPLUS

Averil's absence was the signal for the outside world to break in on her, forcing her to make contact with its petty nastiness. Only when Averil came back would these things recede again into the place where they belonged, like mud to the bottom of a clear pool.

When Averil's last letter had come, Sally stood looking at it for some seconds after the postman gave it her. When she ripped it open, the sheets were torn.

After enquiring after Sally's work, Averil wrote:

"That reminds me, Barry has fixed up for Dina and me to go and stay with his sister in Devonshire next week. I suppose there's no chance you could spare a week-end and run down? It would be lovely if you could. We shall probably get married in the early autumn, though this is quite unofficial as yet. We've asked father to wire his consent."

She added that if Sally decided, as she hoped would be the case, to go home to her people in Leamingham, Dina would take over "Moss Cottage," as she wanted a country holiday—which would fit in nicely.

That was the way of it—and here was Sally, going up to battle once more. She was in such a hurry that she shouted out to each carter who obstructed her progress, glaring at him, when leisurely he drew in to let her pass, as if she were a madwoman. Cross roads were miraculously devoid of danger, traffic blocks gave way before her where it seemed they must have swallowed up a sane rider. But she was not sane that morning, any more than is the miser whose only treasure has been stolen. Her perfect friend had left her—worst of all, had left her joyfully, without a single word of regret.

The street door of No. 17, Farthing Lane, was a

chink open, so Sally walked up the stairs unannounced and paused on the first floor, listening to the voices that came through the sitting-room door. Averil's low murmur, Barry's throaty chuckle, and a strange woman's voice, rather loud (Dina, of course).

The three of them were bending over the table, their heads close together over the cards. Dr. Hope was evidently saying something funny about a trick he had made, because his words were followed by a burst of laughter, the strange girl's drowning the others. It sounded to Sally like a machine gun at short range, a series of sharp noises on a steady note. Then Averil looked towards the door, and stopped laughing.

"Why, here's Sally!" cried Dr. Hope. "Splendid, we wanted a fourth." He seated himself on the edge of the table, and pointed to his chair. "Get your three-pences ready—you'll want a lot. I've just made a grand slam for the third time running."

But Sally was not listening to him.

"Averil," she said, very quietly, "I want to see you for a minute. I can't stop long."

Averil had risen, made a step towards her. Now she exclaimed at her tired look, offered to make her a cup of tea at once.

"I don't want tea," said Sally patiently. "Come upstairs with me, will you?"

"I don't expect you feel too energetic, Plums," struck in Dina. She still sat at the table, and her eyes were fixed on Sally, though she spoke to the other girl. They were alive and snapping with intelligence.

"We had a late night last night, and there's another show on to-night," she explained.

"Has Averil told you to answer for her?" asked Sally quickly.

Dina's laugh rattled out again, then was stifled with an audible effort.

"I thought you were ragging," she said. "Is it anything serious, shall Barry and I go away, Plums?"

Her voice matched her laugh in its hard, staccato definition. A voice that would never be blurred with pity for the weakling, the undeserving. A voice whose owner had firmly made up her mind that life was full of jolly things, and that everybody's duty, whatever their private troubles, was to be funny as loudly and as often as they could in public. And Sally thought of it as the arch enemy, without whose influence Averil would never have thought twice of marriage with the little man who leant back, thumbs in buttonholes, saying, "Now, girls, what's the trouble?" like a bantam cock among his squabbling hens.

"All right, if you must see me alone, we'll go upstairs," said Averil wearily.

No one could have deluded themselves into believing she spoke in anger or in a hurry, as she sat on the bed asserting, in answer to Sally's questions, that she had meant what she said in her letter, and that she could not change her mind now.

"My dear old thing, of course I'm sorry, but it's no use my saying so, because you call it pity, and get furious. Besides, what's the good of rubbing a sore spot? If we've got to part, the less we talk about it the better. We've got a good time together to look back on—why spoil it?"

"Got to part! It's all very well for you to be so calm about it, and tell me not to worry. You'll have Dr. Hope and the excitement of getting married—though that won't last long—and money, and a house of your own, and children, perhaps. What shall I have? Just loneliness and counting grey hairs, and making enough to live on, with not a penny over, out of typing—if I'm lucky. The motor business was going to be for us two, it wasn't a one man business. It might have succeeded, if you'd stuck to me. Don't do it, Averil—don't leave 'Georgina' and me!"

And at that moment, Dina tapped at the door and entered, to fetch her handkerchief, she said.

She had taken it and was going out, when Sally intercepted her.

"You've persuaded her into believing she wasn't happy with me, and she was—until you came! It's all happened since you came home. Ours was the biggest friendship, bigger than anything you've ever imagined. And now you've deliberately spoilt it. I hope you're pleased with yourself."

Once more Dina laughed. She was a tall girl, and could easily have looked over Sally's head if she had chosen.

"I never attempted to put Plums against you, and you know it. She's made up her mind she wants to get married, and, of course, I've not said a word against it—that's all. As a matter of fact, now I've seen the way you go on, I should be proud if I *had* 'taken her away' from you. Instead of being glad she's going to be happy, you come up here and try your best to prevent it. If you want to know, I think she's well rid of you. You asked for it, or I shouldn't have said all this."

She was halfway down the stairs before anybody spoke. Then Averil murmured:

"Things aren't like that, of course."

And Sally stood still, staring at the perfect friend,

who had stayed with her all this time out of pity, who was now escaping from the toils. It seemed to her that the brown cheeks were pinker now, the low forehead whiter, the smile conscious of a secret expectancy she could not share. Averil had passed away from her into the great majority—she belonged, now, to the world wherein friendship pales into nothing beside marriage.

"You let her say it, you didn't interrupt her. It's all over, then. I was a fool, I ought to have known this would happen, from the first. I—I shan't see you again."

As it happened, it was in the street that they said good-bye. Averil had not wanted to come even that far, had pleaded that supper was to be early, because of the show, and if Sally wouldn't come with them— well, there would only just be time to dress, as it was. ("Come with them"—as if the hangman should suggest a friendly game with his victim, before releasing the drop!)

Sally had hoped she might lose that awful sense of impotence if she could get Averil away from walls, out in the fresh air, where they both belonged. But it was worse, in the street. Dina sat with her back to the window right above them, ready, presumably, to come to Averil's rescue if required. And inside the room sat Dr. Hope, too certain of his betrothed to take the smallest interest in the ending of her friendship with another woman.

"Come home with me, just for a little! I ought to have another chance."

"How can I possibly? While you feel like this about my getting married, it would be hopeless. If you'd only be sensible, Sally."

"You don't know what you're doing," said a chalky
faced Sally. You're going to marry a man who
doesn't believe in—souls. Oh no, he doesn't, whatever he says now. He'll make you into what he is
himself, just a chubby, good tempered animal, and
nothing else. You've changed already. You don't
care what you do to me, because I'm only another
girl. You're taking away the only faith I had in the
world."

Averil put a warm hand on her shoulder.

"My dear, you know that isn't true."

"I'm going now," said Sally slowly. She was already in the saddle.

"I don't think, I honestly don't, that you'll be any
happier with him than you were with me. You don't
love him as you did me, as you would again. But
you've chosen, and you must be happy. You won't
be, if you think about me—so you must forget me, do
you hear?"

A heroic speech for such a pitiable figure, with the
old stained trench coat flapping about her knees.

"I never shall," declared Averil. "And we're going
to meet often again, quite soon, I expect. I'll get
Barry to run me down to Salter's Ridge one day before
you leave. There are several things of mine I haven't
brought with me, I find. There's——"

"I shan't see you again, I tell you. Don't you understand—I shan't see you again?"

Averil was bending close to her to catch the words.
And her eyes were like a deep, cloud mirroring sea,
with a light far down in them that flickered faintly
now. Yet they were the same true-till-death eyes of
that dream friend who had come alive on an April
morning so long ago—or was it only two years ago?

# SURPLUS

Two years of happiness! It wasn't much, out of a lifetime.

"Don't look like that, Sally—dear——"

Then Dina put her head out of the window. she called.

"I say, Plums, it's nearly seven, we shall be late!"

And Averil turned, to wave up at the window, instead of finishing her sentence. And Sally let the devil in her heart leap to her mouth.

"You'd better take care of your happiness, when you get it. It'll have cost a lot—only the cost will be paid by another girl."

That, wiping out all the beautiful self-sacrifice, the dignity of farewell. She rode ten yards down the street, slowly, then turned to see how Averil was taking it.

But the door of No. 17 was already closing.

## CHAPTER XVI

SPEED makes it easy to believe in miracles.

On the way back, Sally thought that Averil would change her mind in time, before the end of the summer. Or Dr. Hope's nursing home would fail, and he would be unable to support a wife.

Or, failing that, the miracle would happen to herself instead. She would meet the way out now, quickly, before there was time to realise she was alone. The blinding headlights of each approaching car were eyes of death, peering for his prey. How easy to keep the middle of the road and steer straight on—but it was not easy. Always, at the last second, on the inner edge of the margin of safety, there was the invisible tug, forcing her to swerve, to let death thunder past her impotent. If only one did not know so exactly where that safety margin lay!

A fine rain had begun to fall by the time she reached the last hill, up the eastern shoulder of the ridge. Close on each side the forest stood, drinking in new life for its delicious, tender business of putting on a new spring mantle. But "Georgina" had been mercilessly pressed, and no amount of rain could cool the fever of her inner parts. Her even throb had long ago given place to an agonised clanking, that her rider had disregarded.

She had done her best, and now she could do no more. Half way up that hill she gave up the struggle, quite suddenly, without waste of words. "Finished," said the last clank.

# SURPLUS

Then Sally was walking up the hill, with never a look behind at "Georgina," whose day was done. She wanted to get home. "Moss Cottage" showed grey against a dark shroud. The posts of the garden shelter they had been going to finish stood naked, waiting the roof that would never come now, unless a stranger built it. There were the close folded buds of the primroses in the border by the door, and the rambler rose they had planted together last autumn, so as to make a real "artist's property" of the porch. It was just beginning to put out shoots—in a year, two years perhaps, it would be all over the front door. But Averil would not see its flowering.

The red bricks of the hearth were swept clean and bare, none of Averil's cigarette ends lying on it. Sally stood looking down at it for a long time. Then she looked up at the mantelpiece, where the row of photographs still stood.

Soon Averil would take them away. There would be only one left—the picture of a stranger cut from a newspaper—not good enough or real enough for Averil. Not the sort of thing she would want in her rooms, in the new home.

She would leave that behind, to be company for Sally, to take her place. In the old home, that was not a home any more.

# PART II.

## CHAPTER XVII

THE road that leads away from Paradise is stony, but it does not wind uphill. On the contrary, it is very straight and flat. Mile after mile it is bordered with tall, pointed trees, in whose drooping branches no wind rustles, no bird nests.

A fog hangs over it, so that it is impossible to see whether there is any bourne ahead. Sometimes, however, the fog lifts for a moment on the lighted windows of Zion left behind, and then the traveller stops to look back. A foolish proceeding, because the stones seem sharper afterwards.

On this road, there is never a fellow traveller to be met with. Thousands pass along it, so close they could touch each other if they tried. But each is hidden from the others in the fog.

. . . . . . . . .

Sally, back in Leamingham, made acquaintance for the first time with an interesting pathological fact. She found out that heartache is not merely a poetic simile, but an actual physical pain under the breast, persistent and sharp, like the pain of breathing with congested lungs. And age-long nights of considera-tion failed to reveal a cure for it.

She got to know what the window facing her bed looked like under every condition, how the moon, quarter risen, would slant a beam to touch a certain picture on the wall, or from her zenith would throw a, white radiance on the sill. She knew the different kinds of rattling the curtain rings made in a wind, and how the curtains themselves would belly inwards, leaving exposed a strip of sky, with perhaps a couple of stars. And while she noted these little things, her mind was busy writing and re-writing letters to Averil, all the time.

Some were letters of fury, some of helpless appeal. Doubtless they would have interested Dr. Hope as the evidences of her need of his treatment, and the thought of his indulgent, understanding chuckle nearly drove Sally into the crowning folly of addressing one to him. But not quite. He would have torn it up and forgotten it within the hour—and her bitterness was not against him, after all. He had broken no promises, betrayed no faith, stepped off no pedestal. Simply he had acted like every other man, in that he had gone straight for the woman he wanted, taking it as a foregone conclusion that such a non-essential state of affairs as a feminine partnership must be instantly dissolved at his coming. He had regarded her, Sally, not as an adversary, but as an anachronism, unworthy of serious consideration. And was there a single male creature who would have acted differently, under the circumstances? Sally admitted to herself that there was not.

She even grudgingly admitted that he had understood and allowed for a trait in Averil's nature that she herself had not allowed for. He had not rushed her. Instead, he had allowed her all the time she wanted to think over his proposal. He had never worried her, but had made it clear that though he

wanted her as a wife, his friendship would not cease
with her refusal. He had never grovelled—while Sally
had been, and always would be, abject before the
prospect of losing the partnership which meant so
infinitely much to her. Consequently, it had been a
case of "He that hath not, from him shall be taken
away even that which he hath." (Saying as true to
life as it is directly opposed to the common conception
of Christianity, for all the twistings and turnings of
its expounders.)

But Averil herself? Sally writhed, thinking of that
proud dark head caressed by his plump fingers, that
sword-keen glance matched with his fruity twinkle.
To give Averil up to a prince among men would have
been hard enough, but she told herself that it would
have been easier than this.

Her driven thoughts flew to her own character again.
Had it been, indeed, her own fault? If she had held
Averil lightly on a silken leash, instead of trying to
grapple her with links of steel, would the leash have
held? If she had been able to say, "Go when and
where you please—I want you to be happy in your
own way," and to resist retracting it immediately
afterwards, would Averil then have stayed?

Then, generally in the hour before dawn, when for
a little while the restless thoughts cease turning over
and over against each other and stand still, all bruised
and dishevelled, in the cold grey light, Sally knew
that such speculations were vain. Even if a picture
of her present fate had been held before her eyes in
timely warning, she could not have behaved differently,
because she could not have felt differently. And Sally
was the world's worst actress.

In the Leamingham household, two years had

brought no change at all. The house was irritatingly the same thin, tall maisonette with an art tiled roof, still filled with self-conscious superiority, standing back a little further than its neighbours from the road, in that delightful residential neighbourhood Sally had always called a tenth rate imitation of Golder's Green. Her father was the same. Not a hair of his head or his long, drooping moustache was greyer, and his erect, rather imposing carriage had developed no suspicion of a stoop. As of old, he was quite unable to refrain from saying, "I told you so." He added:

"What can you expect, if you try to settle down with an attractive girl, as this Miss Kennion apparently was?"

Sally tried, once or twice, to explain the magnitude of her loss to him.

"Can't you understand—can't you?" she cried, in his study that was so orderly and restrained, with its smell of stuffy leather, with the heads of the golf clubs shining from their bag in the far corner. But he drooped his moustache at her, and said:

"My dear child, what did you expect? It's only natural."

As a fact, Colonel Wraith was puzzled, even a little worried, by her face after a succession of sleepless nights. It occurred to him that her mother would have been able to deal with the situation, perhaps. Her sympathy had always been easy to arouse for the dissatisfied, the rebels, the square pegs in round holes—she might have understood what was the matter with Sally. Not understanding, he himself could only leave the girl alone for the present, to get over it. For which mercy Sally would have been duly grateful, if she had been in a state to notice it at all.

193

# SURPLUS

He even stated that he would have advanced her the money to buy a new motor cycle, ill as he could spare it, if he had not heard on all hands that the taxi driving business was a hopeless proposition for a woman. He could not afford to risk capital like that, with her brother still out of a job.

And for once Sally did not contradict him, though she still believed that, given a good partner and a sufficient stock of pluck and determination, there was as much chance for a woman in that business as in any other, of which man had until recently held the monopoly. But her partner had absconded, and taken the stock with her, so Sally had no use for a new "Georgina."

It had been necessary to explain that fact to Miss Landison, on her last morning in Salter's Ridge. The whole story had needed so few words—just, "Averil's going to get married, and I've lost my job."

Miss Landison had received the first part of the news without comment, only asking whether she could help with the job. And Sally had explained that nobody could help. The old machine was worthless scrap-iron, and even the gift of a new one would have been useless, not because the competition in Salter's Ridge was now too keen, but because she had no courage left to start afresh anywhere else.

"A girl wants a lot of push and bluff if she's going to succeed in a job like that, and I haven't any," was the way she put it.

"You must find another job, then. Whatever happens, don't sit down and do nothing," said Miss Landison.

Then, because Sally turned away with a quivering face at the sharpness in her tone, she added:

# SURPLUS

"Of course you think I don't understand at all. You'd go on thinking so, no matter what I said. And you'd be right in a way—not one of us ever truly understands another, Sally. We've just got to do without it, being understood. Don't you like having something private at the bottom of your heart, that nobody can pry into, whether they're friend or foe? Even if it's a trouble?"

"I—I don't feel like that."

"Not now, but you will."

The woman on the couch stretched out a hand and Sally came close to her.

"I didn't always feel like that, but I learnt to stand alone, in the end."

"I'm not going to be alone. Averil's not married yet," cried Sally.

She wanted to run out of the room, holding her head high. And at the same time she wanted to fling herself down beside the couch and beg to be allowed to stay in the Turret House, as companion, garden girl, anything so that she might bury herself in this quiet haven, with only the books for company, books that were constant friends, never going off to get married.

But in the end she did neither, because she had a feeling that Miss Landison would refuse the request, gently, but with contempt in her eyes. Miss Landison did not approve of people who asked for favours, that much was obvious. She did not ask, herself, for pity or kindness (though you would have thought she needed them enough), and she gave of her own pity and kindness only to those who did not ask her. So there you were.

Sally promised to send news of herself when she

195

could, and to remember that Miss Landison was her friend, if she ever needed one. Then she went away, thinking bitterly that good advice was cheap, and that the test of friendship, in which Averil had already failed, was to be not an absent, but a very present help in time of trouble.

"Not one of us ever truly understands another"— it was true. She, in the vanity of her heart, had thought she understood several people. Yet she had never glimpsed the possibility that Mavis Barron, following her career with such a single heart, should step aside from the path to listen to the wooing of another woman's husband. It had not occurred to her that Dr. Hope should change, suddenly, from the fatherly friend to the suitor. At least, had the change been sudden, or had she herself been blind all along— blind to his real nature, and to Averil's? Had she understood Averil at all?

When the torture of that thought became too insistent to be borne in silence any longer, she actually wrote and posted an expurgated edition of one of the midnight letters. She begged Averil to come down to Leamingham for a week-end, a day, a few hours even. "Because I must see you alone, just once more."

She did not mention the fate of "Georgina." That would have been an appeal for pity, and with Averil in her present mood would be foredoomed to failure. But if Averil would only come and see with her own eyes how matters stood, she might just conceivably begin to wish she had remained a partner of the firm which had so obviously and immediately gone to smash without her. It was a forlorn hope, Sally knew, but it was better than inaction. Surely even Dr. Hope and Dina could see nothing so very selfish

SURPLUS

and abnormal in asking for a farewell interview away
from their prying eyes.

But Averil evidently thought there was. After a
week's delay she wrote explaining that she was far
too busy with her trousseau and her classes ("He's
letting me go on up to the last minute"), to spare a
day away from town. The ceremony was fixed for
July 10th, and Averil wished it was all over. They
were treating themselves to a honeymoon on the
Riviera, but after that they'd probably settle in a flat
in town. Sally must let them know when she was
passing through. And, in a postscript:

"I hope the taxi business is going strong. Dina
and I went down to Moss Cottage the other day, and
she thinks it'll suit her nicely. There's a spanner
you left behind. Shall she send it on?"

So "we" was no longer Averil and Sally, but Averil
and her man, and there was no time to spare from
the trousseau to hold out even one finger to the partner left alone. Sally read that letter through many
times, but the neat, beautiful writing was fatally clear.
She could see the writer bending over it, choosing each
word deliberately, so that it should express exactly
what she meant. So Averil, who seemed to understand and sympathise with every smallest dream, now
could not realise that such a letter, written not as to a
once loved enemy, but as to a stranger who had never
been anything else, was the worst betrayal.

"If she'd meant it as a punishment, because I tried
to stop this marriage—but she didn't. She writes
like that because she never really cared a bit."

Yet there were nights when Sally remembered, in-
credulously, their pact in the hospital—Averil's strong
fingers on her wrist—and again, the train coming

197

SURPLUS

into Salter's Ridge station, on the day when Averil
went away. Then she had said, "I *do* care—always
shall, whether you believe it or not."

Pity—was that all there had been on Averil's side?
And then she told herself that it did not matter,
either way. Averil was gone, and it was no use calling her. But she did, under her breath—

"Averil, come back to me—come back! You don't
know how I need you, I've told you, but you've not
believed it. You think I'll forget, but how can I?
It's my life you're taking, I tell you."

Surely a cry like that must reach her, in the midst
of her trousseau buying? They had so often put
each other's thoughts into words, about the little things
that had not mattered. To Sally, that had been one of
the many signs of the uniqueness of their friendship.
Had the sign no significance, then?

Mrs. Rickaby would have laughed at the idea. And
she was a widow of some social standing, who had
been for the last year a near neighbour of the Wraiths',
and withal a thoroughly sensible, motherly person for
whom the Colonel had developed a sincere re-
spect.

As the days went on, and Sally still went about the
house like a homeless ghost, he began to feel that
something ought to be done about it. True, she spent
half her mornings scanning the advertisement columns
as of old, and the rest of the day she was to be found
helping the mechanics in a certain motor works, whose
manager, being temporarily short-handed, had very
kindly said she might give a hand whenever she cared
to come down. So, having sufficient occupation, she
should have begun to settle down again, her father
argued. When she failed to do so, he saw the ad-

visability of having an expert opinion on the case, and consulted Mrs. Rickaby.

That good lady was delighted to oblige. She had only one quarrel with the world, none the less real because unexpressed, which was that she had been sent into it a century too late. If she could have lived in an age when unmarried women were considered to be, and often were, entirely ignorant of what she termed "the deeper mysteries of life," and were thus fit subjects for guidance and instruction from the matron, her happiness would have been complete. It was an unfailing regret to her that such was not the case, nowadays. Her own daughters, reaching the age when their womanhood should have just "begun to flower" (her favourite phrase), had stared at her in pitying amazement when she tried to break gently to them facts which they already took as a matter of course. The matron's legitimate province was so sadly restricted. Nobody now believed that babies were a present from the stork.

Here, however, was a girl who stood in obvious need of a motherly word in the ear. All this to-do because a girl friend had left her to get married! She did not look peculiar, either—Mrs. Rickaby knew that some people considered it a pretty face, though she herself did not admire that brown skin and thinness. Her father had said she was clever, too, which made it all the more remarkable that at her age, and girls being what they were nowadays, she did not know better. Well, poor thing, her own mother had died young.

"My dear, I know how you must miss your friend. Partings are always so trying, but life is made up of partings. You'll realise that, when you come to my age," she began, ever so tactfully, putting a hand on

Sally's shoulder.   Sympathy always unlocked the doors
of the heart.

"Quite," said Sally briefly.

Evidently her lock was a little rusty, or else that
key did not fit.  Mrs. Rickaby tried another.

"Are you worrying because you're afraid your
friend won't take any interest in you, after she's
married?  Then I can tell you something to comfort
you.  Though girlish friendships may never be *quite*
the same after one of them has married, you will find
that she'll have room in her heart for you again, after
a couple of years or so.  At first, she may be entirely
wrapped up in her husband, and you will feel an
intruder—it's only natural!  But afterwards, you'll
see——"

There, that was the sort of faintly flavoured cynical
remark that was calculated to appeal to the younger
generation.  If this girl had any of the modern spirit
in her, she would react to it.

But Sally shook her head.  She did not want to
make the forlorn effort of explaining herself, but old
habit held.  Whether the opposition was worth arguing with or not, she must always state her case.

"It's not that, Mrs. Rickaby.  I—it's my home I've
lost, you see."

"My dear child!  Isn't this your home?"

"No, it's father's.  And I'm not exactly a child,
I'm nearly thirty.  I want a home of my own, where
I can choose my own furniture and make a mess of my
own cooking.  And I want someone to share it with."

"But that's what we women marry for—at least,
that's one of the reasons," protested Mrs. Rickaby,
eyes snapping.

"Do we?  Well, I didn't."

# SURPLUS

Sally was walking up and down the room, trying not to let her voice break. Of all things, she did not want to give way in front of this blithering old humbug, who would certainly proceed to talk it all over with her father. The whole interview was obviously a put up job between them.

Mrs. Rickaby, seeing the agitated walk, drew her own conclusions. Now was the time for an appeal to the girl's better nature.

"My dear, the fonder you were of this friend of yours, the more you must want her to be happy. Surely you don't want her to miss the greatest thing in life?"

"I suppose you mean marriage, and children?" said Sally.

She was sitting down now, leaning towards the older woman. Mrs. Rickaby, nodding assent, thought she had never seen so confiding and innocent a face. A dear girl, this!

"But you see I don't think that *is* the greatest thing—always. I don't think it was for her. I think she's letting herself down almost as badly as she is me."

Across the faded, art green carpet they stared at each other, the two generations, with scarcely a thought or feeling in common, in spite of their shared sex.

"You mean he's not good enough for her, my dear? But as to that, we must each judge for ourselves. As long as he makes her happy——"

Sally shrugged her shoulders. It was really not worth contesting for the last word. Not in a thousand years could Mrs. Rickaby have been brought to understand that a woman, otherwise sane, might consider a good friendship better than a mediocre mar-

riage. After all, in her young days marriage was the
only career. How could one expect her to think
differently?

So Sally went back to her nightly imaginary letter
writing, and let the thought that Averil was not married yet absorb her. If thought were so all powerful
as the new schools said, could not the force of her desire bring to pass a miracle, even now? If the power
of thought meant anything at all, it should be capable
of drawing Averil away from a Barry Hope. (Only,
unfortunately, we are only promised that it can make
us "better and better"—not that it can give us a beautiful nose, or a sweet singing voice, or anything else
we particularly want.)

Her father was too distressed at the failure of Mrs.
Rickaby's intervention not to show it. The poor man
had certainly some cause for annoyance. Here was
the daughter whom he had thought at least permanently, if not entirely satisfactorily, provided with an
occupation, thrown back upon his hands again, minus a
job. Minus, also, the desire for one, or so it appeared
from her behaviour.

"You're simply making yourself ill, brooding over
this wretched girl. Can't you make up your mind to
it that she's gone, and think of something else? Go
about more, and meet people. It's not natural, the way
you're shutting yourself up."

"Oh, for goodness sake leave me alone!" she choked
then, and fled from him.

There was nothing else to think of, even if one tried.
That miserable, ill-fated career of hers was no longer
interesting. She had lost all desire to see herself
as a motor magnate, owning a fleet of impeccable
"Georginas" and their four-wheeled peers. That goal

was too far off ever to be reached alone, so why go on dreaming of it?

She continued her daily visits to the workshop in the town, more for the sake of occupation than for the work itself. Engines were still interesting, and Sally still loved them, but with a cold, detached shadow of her former enthusiasm. Instead of longing to take every car she saw out on the road, to try its paces and tune it to the highest possible level of speed and economy, she was content to sit about in the workshop, doing odd jobs of cleaning and filing. She did not want to do anything that demanded imagination and initiative, in those days—she wanted just to come back in the evenings so physically tired that she would have a chance of sleeping. Tiredness gave her a sort of vague, glowing feeling that things were coming right. There might be a letter from Averil on the hall table, or the girl herself might be there, round the next corner. She would have the old tender, teasing light in her eyes, and say:

"Of course you didn't trust me, you thought I'd gone away for good. Just like you, Sally!"

Towards the end of July, Cecily Winter, who had been a fellow driver in the war, and now was Mrs. John Torrow, came back to her people in Leamingham on a visit. Hearing that the Wraith girl was at home, but not going about at all—and Mrs. Rickaby, the only person who seemed to have talked to her, declared that she was in a very queer state—Cecily decided to investigate.

She chose the evening when Sally had just received, by the last post, an invitation to Averil's wedding. It was a formal card with, on the back, "Mind you come to this Show." To open an envelope addressed in the well-known writing and find that, had roused in Sally a rage that was all the more violent because her father, catching sight of the card, remarked:

"That's all right, then, you're friends again. Nice of her to ask you. Now I hope you'll cheer up, my dear."

Nice, to be given an opportunity of watching one's dream in flight, to sit quietly in a corner of the church behind Dina and Mrs. Kennion and their friends while Averil tied herself for life to a Barry Hope. Nice, of all debased, detestable words in the language——

Cecily found her in her bedroom, which was an index of her state of mind. In common with hotel apartments, it had that soul-deadening atmosphere of impermanence that defies analysis. The dressing-table carried a rather sparse array of toilet instruments, strewn untidily, as if they had just been unpacked and were awaiting re-packing on the morrow. Trunks and a cardboard hat-box in a corner heightened this illusion. Sally was living in her boxes, evidently. She had put no photographs about, no sketches on the walls, no ribboned, scented sachets such as embellished Cecily's own room. Yet she had had time enough to make it homelike.

Cecily had always been a merry, good-tempered creature, but there was a sleek bloom on her face that had not been there five years ago, when they had last met.

"What's up with you, Sally?" she asked unexpectedly. "You're looking off colour."

And the desire to tell someone overmastered Sally. Here at least was a girl of her own age, a good sort, a sport, who surely ought to be able to see two sides of a question, if anybody could.

SURPLUS

"But that always happens," she said, when she had
listened to an outline of the facts, "when two women
start living together. If she wants to marry, you
couldn't expect her to give it up, to stay with you.
It would be jolly selfish of you if you did."

"Not even if I knew the man wasn't good enough—
not if I knew she'd been perfectly happy with me, and
would be again, if he could be got rid of? Because
she didn't really love the man, any more than she'd
loved a dozen others."

"How could you be sure of that? And anyway, if
she wanted to get married——"

It might have been Mrs. Rickaby over again!

"Then you believe in marriage for its own sake, too?
Oh, Cecily, I shouldn't have thought it of you! Is
that why you married Jim?"

Cecily considered, swinging the tip of one perfectly
polished shoe. The colour had deepened a little in
her clear cheeks.

"One marries for lots of reasons. Kiddies, for one.
I was very fond of Jim, though nothing like as keen
as I am now. We're a perfect laughing stock of a
couple, you know."

"For the sake of having kiddies," Sally caught her
up. "Giving them any father who happens to strike
you as a kind, obliging sort of man—you think a girl's
right to leave her friend to go to smash, without even
saying she's sorry?"

"You're a queer, cold-blooded person!" laughed
Cecily. "Of course it's right—it's natural."

"Natural—right—I don't see that it follows. Unless the idea is for us all to be as like the original monkeys as we can."

Sally's face was flaming, and tears—that came so
205

SURPLUS

readily now—stood in her eyes. Watching her, the
other woman shifted uneasily in her chair. Cecily
had none of Mrs. Rickaby's excited curiosity, con-
fronted with such a situation.

"Monkeys," she said; "what are you raving about?"

"I'm sick of being told how 'natural' it is," cried
Sally. "You and Mrs. Rickaby and father—oh, and
all the rest of the world, I suppose—you none of you
waste one second's sympathy on me. It doesn't matter
if I and every other girl in the same position—and I
expect there are others, though they daren't complain—
it doesn't matter what happens to us, as long as you
people can follow your instincts. You put 'instincts'
before truth, and honour, and kindness, and so do the
animals. And you do it consciously, you're proud of
yourselves. Yet when a man gives way to his instincts for killing, and doesn't stop at human beings,
you hang him. In peace time, that is."

"Sally—that's a wrong instinct! You can't compare them," protested Cecily.

"I don't compare them. I'm merely pointing out
what happens when you carry this idea of putting
'instincts' in front of everything else right through.
Besides, it's pretty hard to say just when they begin
to be wrong. What about me, for instance? I've got
an instinct for friendship. I want love every bit as
much as you do, only it's not the same kind. I'm
*not* cold blooded—do I look it?" she cried, stamping
her foot.

"It can't be—as strong, that feeling."

"Of course you say it can't, because you haven't
got it. It's the strongest I know, anyway. I tell you
that losing this friend means as much to me as losing
your child or husband would mean to you. And yet

206

you all curse me for selfishness, because I fight to the
last breath to keep her. Wouldn't you fight to keep
Jim, even if you saw he was falling in love with another woman, and wanted to go? Or would you sit
still and say you wanted his happiness, and not your
own?"

"I don't know," said Cecily. "I should try. No
—I don't think I could do that."

"Exactly. And I can't, either. I know I ought
to, but I can't."

Cecily had no words with which to meet this on-
slaught. She told herself she had always known Sally
Wraith was queer, but not as queer as this.

"But it's absolutely different, you and your friend,
and me and Jim," she said at last, with a little laugh.

"Because of the sex part, you mean? Can't you
even imagine a love that hasn't any sex? Just being
with the person you love, working and playing together, not caring a damn for anything or anybody
as long as you're together—that's my idea of it.
If another girl happens to be the person, is it my
fault?"

"I suppose not. But it's—silly, Sally. You must
know that."

In her voice was a pity that struggled not to be contemptuous. "It's so queer of you. I can't make out
—nobody can—what's come over you!"

That pulled Sally back from the confessional.

"I may be queer, but I'm not quite mad yet. I won't
bite you."

Cecily had risen, and was powdering her nose at the
glass.

"I'm awfully sorry," she said vaguely. "But you
mustn't go on shutting yourself up like this. Come

to tea on Wednesday—I've got Jim's brother coming
down."

Passing the table, she glanced at the invitation card,
lying face upwards.

Barrington Hope—is that the man your friend's
marrying? I used to know a Major Barrington Hope,
in the war. Wonder if it's the same?"

Sally described him.

"Very twinkly eyes, and goes in for psycho-
analysis? That's the man. I met him once when I
was dining with Jim in town. He was in Jim's regi-
ment, at the time."

"Did Jim like him?" queried Sally, even voiced.

"He said he was a good sort. But a bit of a gay
dog, I believe. Jim told me he had rather a name
for looking on the wine when it was red, in those days.
Oh, but that was years ago, of course—I expect he's
quite different now," she added hurriedly, remembering that the gay dog in question was about to marry
Sally's best friend.

But Sally had already heard enough. When, left
alone, she sat down to answer Averil's invitation she
could not get the stupid words out of her head.
"Looking on the wine when it was red." Pen in
hand, she stared out at the laurel bushes by the gate,
shaking their gilded leaves under the evening sunlight.
A normal girl would have gone to the wedding—a little
sad, perhaps, at the end of one good time, but with
her eye already on the best man, and the chance of another good time. The normal girl would never dream
of spoiling her friend's happiness at the last moment,
by the repetition of idle gossip.

"But then she says I'm not normal," said Sally.
"And—is it idle gossip?"

# SURPLUS

She tried to put herself in Averil's place, to look at Barry through her eyes. Would she prefer not to be warned beforehand, if it were true? Desperately Sally tried to be unprejudiced against the man. It might not be true, or, on the other hand, he might have completely and permanently altered his way of life. And in any case, most people thought nothing at all of the very venial backsliding implied; merely, they thought it a sign of good fellowship.

But he was above all things astute. He could act the fatherly friend to the life, while all the time he was waiting for the right psychological moment to declare himself the lover. When Averil was once his, was it not at least possible that he would infect her with the idea that a carefully chosen dinner with liquid embellishments was worth a Kreisler recital, the scent of a rose, and a view of the Himalayan snows, all rolled into one?

"He'll drag her down, make her just a gay dog, like himself. He doesn't believe in souls—he'd rather pin his faith to a dinner at the Ritz. A bottle of the best in the hand is worth eternity in the bush, to him. I know it—I've got an instinct. Why shouldn't *I* act on my instincts, for a change?"

Action meant that she must warn Averil. It was not too late, even though the trousseau might be bought, and the church chosen. What did a trousseau matter, compared to being tied for life to that kind of man—she the artist, the fastidious!

"I know there may be no truth in it," she wrote quickly. "Or he may have told you himself already. But I'm not going to risk that. Don't be furious with me, don't think I'm trying to come between you for

209

my own selfish ends, this time! I'm putting myself
in your place. I should want to have a chance of
counting all the cost beforehand, and I should expect anyone who cared for me to give me that chance.
Whatever happens, I know you and I can't ever come
together again, so you must see I'm disinterested. I
just want you to have your eyes open, if you decide to
go on with it all the same."

She posted it quickly, before her mind should have
time to change. And then at once she began to wonder
whether Averil, the new Averil, would believe in her
good motives? Sally knew well enough what most
people would think of such an action. "Cat" would be
among the mildest of their epithets. Supposing
Averil were so like the others, now, that she would
think the same?

"It doesn't matter what she thinks of me, so long
as she's saved from making a mess of her life," said
Sally with her lips.

But her heart said:

"I'm not quite forgetting myself, even now. There
*is* just a chance she may come back to me, if she throws
him over—some day, a long way ahead."

If only, for once, that accusing undertone could
have been silent! But Sally had none of the strong,
silent heroine stuff in her, and though she heard it,
she ignored it. She told herself that if there was
any such thing in the world as a love that lasts, then
Averil would have to forgive her interference, to come
back to her, in the end. If Barry were out of the
way—

For the idealist who is also a coward will fight to
the death rather than surrender her belief in the particular person or thing which she has once taken to be

SURPLUS

the manifestation of her ideal. To find the perfect
friend in Averil—to lose faith in her, and keep one's
faith in friendship—Sally was not strong enough for
that.

# CHAPTER XVIII

IT is a hard thing to be afraid of sleep, because of the dreams it brings. Always the same dream, constantly repeated, from which one wakes shivering and sweating, arms stretched towards a dream figure with averted face.

Averil had been married nearly a month, and Sally was recovering from influenza, as the doctor called it. The attack had started with the receipt of Averil's reply, saying that she already knew all she wanted to of Barry's past—"thanks all the same, if you mean it as a friend."

It had culminated on the night when Sally wired:

"Ill, must see you at once."

And the even more formally worded answer had come from Dr. Hope, to the effect that he did not think it wise for Averil, who was already tired with shopping, to leave London three days before the wedding.

So, for once, Sally achieved completeness. The failure of her perfect friendship was undiluted by any element of nobility, romance, or hope. It was a more commonplace failure than any her worst forebodings had pictured, and more cruel. To end this friendship —this—as all women's friendships are supposed to end, as so many of them did end! Because of a man. Why, didn't everybody laugh and shrug their shoulders whenever a woman's partnership was suggested? "Yes, that'll be very nice—until a man turns up!"

# SURPLUS

The suggestion being always that the girls will immediately forget their work and become bitter rivals, clawing each other for possession of the prize.

Though, in this case, things had not been quite like that, the commonplaceness remained the same, and the cruelty. Averil had changed towards her, because of a man. Averil no longer cared how much she hurt another girl—because of a man. At his bidding, she had cheerfully turned her back for ever on the friend who threatened her married peace. To her, the tale of their life together was already as a scroll that is rolled up, stored in a musty corner of her mind. Occasionally, she might take it down and glance half scornfully, half pitifully, at its faded writing. But never once would she regret—because of a man. (And because, incidentally, she never regretted anything.)

When Sally realised, with regret but without surprise, that her influenza was not going to prove fatal, she made up her mind, at last, that she must get away to some place where no one would know what had happened to her. For the tragedy that other people laugh at is intolerably hard to bear.

There was Mrs. Mayhew down the road, for instance, who had lost her son in the war, and whom everyone excused when she took to drugs in consequence. Yet she had a devoted husband left, whereas Sally had—no one. There was Sheila Drake, whose *fiancé* had jilted her on the eve of their wedding. Everybody took it as perfectly natural that she should be broken-hearted, everybody rallied round her and did their best to cheer her up, even when her heart had been mended by another young man.

But Sally was expected to go on behaving just as

usual, though the only creature in the world she truly loved had left her to a future just as empty as Sheila Drake's had been. The general opinion being that her future was *not* empty, considering she still had a home and family—uncongenial perhaps, but still a family—while many girls had none. And if she felt it was empty, then the fault was hers. As if one said to a cripple:

"You may have lost your legs, but you have a pair of perfectly good and expensive wooden ones. Why worry?"

The decision to leave Leamingham, to which she forced her mind as one forces a jibbing horse at a leap, was accelerated by a visit from Barbara Rickaby, Mrs. Rickaby's youngest daughter. Bar was really exactly the kind of daughter one would have expected, under the circumstances. She was the assertive ego, freeing itself with violence from the bath of treacle in which it finds itself immersed. Her hatred of sentiment was positively vicious, surpassing the natural distaste for emotionalism that belonged to Averil. At twenty-three, she was a promising student at the London Hospital for Women, and had already decided to specialise in surgery, that branch of the profession being the least sentimental she could find.

She was so seldom home that Sally did not even know her by sight. Her face was small and piquant, her shining red hair was brushed back into a tight knot, long hair being her one concession to her mother's importunities. When she came into the room, she brought with her a wind that was certainly bracing, if somewhat bleak.

"Mother's sent you this book," she said, handing over a slim volume with an old flagged garden, complete with grey lady watering mauve flowers, on the cover. Something in Sally's expression must have caused her to add:

"D'you really like reading that sort of thing?" Sally explained that she was bored enough to read anything, "Even this—er, this sort of thing," she added, with a ghost of a smile.

And Bar Rickaby decided that the invalid was not such a fool as she had been led to expect. She remembered that this "poor neurotic girl"—how mother always exaggerated!—was also by way of being a motor expert, and she seized the opportunity to make enquiries as to the best motor cycle to purchase for her own use.

When Sally had advised her, she was curious enough to add a question as to why the motor cycle taxi had been given up. Informed of the fact that there was no capital to buy another, she said:

"Oh. Bad luck."

Her interest in somebody else's affair was already exhausted. But the very ease with which she dismissed the subject made Sally querulously determined to pursue it. Bar evidently had a contempt for the girl who stayed at home and lived on her father, an idle parasite. At the moment, Sally would have liked nothing better than to tear down that burnished hair and rub it full of furze prickles—anything, to make it look less capable, less splendidly ordained.

"Do you know of a post going anywhere?" she asked.

Well, Bar had heard of two girls who were making a great success of a motor garage, but they employed only men. Also a girl she knew had secured a jolly post as under-secretary to an M.P.—but, of course,

now she came to think of it, the said M.P.'s wife and
the girl's aunt had been old friends.

"Supposing I did find something, do you know any
girl who would share rooms with me?"

"Why, don't you like living alone? How funny!
Why not try a girls' club, then?"

Sally thought that over. She had once been inside
such a club, and had been shown the spotless little bed-
rooms, all the same cell shape with the same pale
green walls. She had lunched at a separate table,
too—among a crowd of silent girls, each with a paper
propped in front of her, too busy bolting her food to
talk. She had seen the drawing room in the evening,
with a few of the girls—those who had no appointment
with a boy—gossiping together in corners over their
camisoles and jumpers. ("He didn't look too pleased
when I asked him, but he didn't dare say no." "That
Miss Wilson in the outer office wears real silk all the
way up. How she can afford it, unless—well, that's
what *I* said——" "Charley not coming to-night?
All right, s'long as he's not out with another crowd!")

Was not that alternative even worse than living
alone?

But Bar, and the others like her, had no fear of
loneliness. Sally could see her, cool and collected,
making herself at home with a book on anatomy, on
her quiet evenings. No visions of an empty future
would come to trouble her serenity. She had her
career, she had friends—"ordinary" ones—whom she
could see when she was in the mood for sociability.
Bar lived her own life, and wanted nobody to help
her live it. She was independent in spirit, not in
name only. Desiring marriage no more than Sally
desired it, she asked nothing of the world except suc-

cess. She was reasonable enough not to ask for love and a home, as well.

Sally thought of these things, and a burning determination seized her to be like Bar, since she could not be like Cecily Torrow. Cold blooded people ought to be capable of acquiring unbreakable hearts to match —if they were not, it was a piece of abominable injustice.

"I *will* be one thing or the other!" cried Sally, in effect, and the only way to harden herself was to leave the sheltering backwater of her father's house, and strike out for the open.

It proved extraordinary, the number of superlatively wonderful positions that were held by the friends of one's friends. Mrs. Rickaby had a niece who had gone off, only last week, as companion to an artist— a lady artist—in Algeria, and had nothing to do but pose—in costume—for her two or three hours a day. And Cecily Torrow knew of various girls who were earning fabulous sums a year. All most interesting— but it advanced Sally no further in her own quest. If one could only meet these fortunate individuals, learn from their own lips how they did it!

Then one day she saw in the paper a request for a lady typist, with perfect French, to help in a tea shop run by "Belgian ladies" in New Oxford Street. And when Madame Lamie had agreed to take her on a fortnight's trial, there was no longer any reason, any excuse for holding back.

So Sally left Leamingham as suddenly as Averil had once left Salter's Ridge. She knew that if she did not do it at once, the impulse to do it at all would desert her. She waited until it was settled before writing to tell Miss Landison, who was the only person who had appeared to understand some small measure of the disaster, and had not looked on it as a farce. And then, when the day of her departure was fixed, she did not write after all. She was not going to tell Miss Landison that she had given in to fate at last, that she was about to do what she had said she never would do—try to stand alone. Miss Landison would only smile, and perhaps write back a letter full of nice phrases about the joy that comes from doing the right thing, and the beauties there are in life for those who live alone and look for them.

Sally no longer trusted her judgment of Miss Landison, or of anyone else. She was prepared for that Sybil-eyed woman to burst forth with just those tactless, smug remarks that one would not have expected of her.

Everyone else seemed to greet the news with approval. Her father said it sounded a rather unsuitable position for his daughter, but that if it was respectable—she must satisfy herself on that point—one could not afford to be too particular, nowadays. At least it would be something for her to do, and though her pay would not suffice to keep her entirely (Oh, yes, it will," said Sally grimly), it would be a help, a great help.

Bar Rickaby said it would provide a stepping-off place from which she could hunt round for a better job. And Cecily declared that a tea room was a place where Cupid lurked in every corner. With this thought in her eyes, she gave Sally instructions for knitting a particularly lacy silk jumper. When Sally informed her that her work would be in the office, alone with Madame, she said:

"Oh well—you never know."

# SURPLUS

"You never know"—the slogan of youth undying, meaning that always round the next corner there may be something wonderful, which will make the journey worth while. But for Sally it had lost all meaning. She went up to London expecting nothing, hoping nothing, not even for a glimpse of Averil, who would probably still be on her honeymoon. Nobody saw her off at the station, because Cecily's husband particularly wanted her that morning, and Colonel Wraith had a match on.

As she sat squashed in the corner of a smoker, going off to be a typist in a third rate tea shop—and lucky enough to get the chance—a picture of Averil's honeymoon came to her. Averil on the terrace of Monte Carlo, with the vivil colours that she loved all around her. Averil laughing under a lace edged sunshade, with the other promenaders staring after her tilted, eager head—or sipping an absinthe, with Barry at her side.

"I'm glad one of the partners is happy, anyhow—now it's done. I'm glad—I *am* glad!" she told herself fiercely.

She was aware that that was not the way it should have been said. She ought to be able to rejoice so much in Averil's happiness that she could forget her own unhappiness. As it was, she could say from her heart: "I want Averil to be happy,"—as long as the wish was a generalisation. But she did not want to hear any details of that happiness. Nor to be told that Averil preferred her town flat to Moss Cottage, that she had enjoyed a motor trip with Barry as much as the expeditions in "Georgina's" sidecar.

And Averil's babies, if they came—those least of all could she have borne to see, she thought. They would

219

be Averil's and Barry's, shutting the rest of the world
into outsiders. Not half a loaf, even, but a few
crumbs, would have been left then for the perfect
friend.

. . . . . . . .

The work at Madame Lamie's consisted mostly of
correspondence relating to the sale of "Belgian
brioches," for which delicacies Madame had a growing
private custom in the suburbs. Her own English
being extremely faulty, the idea had occurred to her
thrifty soul of getting a typist to take the whole business of their dispatch off her hands. So Sally also
had to pack and address them, ready for the carrier's
van. And in the afternoons, when business in the
shop was slack and Madame was "resting," she had
to help Julie and Amelie, the waitresses, about the
temporarily deserted tables, cleaning and rearranging
them. And anybody who wasn't a "lady" and didn't
know French could have done that.

It was deadly dull, but it needed no self confidence,
no daring. Sally, her wiry limbs gone slack already
from the stuffy, sedentary life, sat huddled in her
chair, doing just what she was told and no more.

"I'm fated to be a clerk-of-all-work, so it's just as
well I've given up trying to be anything else," she
thought, remembering her time with Sampson's.

But there was an enormous difference. That had
been on the way to a big position. And at least it
had been within the sound and smell of engines, the
clamour of steel on steel, the thrill and tremor of
power imprisoned. Even the letters she typed, then,
had been all concerned with things that were destined
to go out into the open air and get a move on.
Whereas now, she had to write of cakes and rolls, sur-

rounded by the soft chatter of feminine tongues and the odour of frying.

When a slack moment came Sally read the picture-papers, and let the jumbled impressions they conveyed flow over her mind in a sticky mess, obscuring thought. Occasionally Julie or Amelie brought her a cake with a shy smile, and lingered to chatter about their young men. But she never really listened.

Meanwhile, the evenings after six were terribly solitary, in the small bed-sitting room on the un-fashionable side of Westminster Bridge. But Boniface Road was in sight of the river, and it was as far from Farthing Lane, and reminders of the old days, as she could get.

Bar had given her a vague invitation to look her up some time, but she was out on the first occasion, and Sally did not repeat the experiment. Now she had made the plunge and set up on her own, she was afraid of sinking back into her old state of dependence on somebody else. Loneliness made you lose control of yourself so easily! She foresaw that loneliness might drive her to the vain humiliation of beseeching Bar, for whom she really felt more fear than affection, to give up her own rooms and come to Boniface Road. So the less she saw of Bar the better.

To start out on the whole wonderful home making business again with a strange girl, instead of Averil, was a mockery against which no good resolutions would be proof. Besides, living with any woman must always be a strictly temporary affair—Sally would never forget that again. And, however temporary the arrangement was, it meant getting used to her, beginning to cling to her in some degree.

Never again would come the dream of perfect

SURPLUS

friendship, the pain of its dissolution. But to expose oneself once more to the danger of expecting permanent companionship from another woman—could there be a worse folly?

## CHAPTER XIX

GRADUALLY Sally felt herself slipping back into the bad habits of which Averil had temporarily cured her. And she did not care. She grumbled now, when she felt like it, at the things that did not please her about the room. Why suffer discontent in silence, when there was no understanding smile to commend her forbearance? And why not talk to oneself, when there was no gently teasing protest to stop one? Why bother to eat, instead of reading, at meals?

Besides joining a lending library, she took in a daily paper, the one that provided the most reading material (quality immaterial) for the lowest price.

The divorce cases of the moment were, of course, too prominently displayed to escape anyone's notice, and after a time Sally found herself studying them instead of passing them over quickly in search of more promising material. Though she would not admit it to herself, she was really trying to find in them a justification of her attitude in regard to Averil's marriage. These were the sordid records of the things which befall those who, too late, find out that instinct is not an infallible guide to happiness—that even motherhood, that "greatest glory of womanhood," does not always suffice.

But then she noticed that humanity continued, undeterred, to take the risk. On other pages of the paper were always accounts of couples who had met each other for the first time at the altar, and were apparently consumed with pride at the fact. Or of blissful *fiancées,* overwhelmed with congratulations, sailing across the world to marry men they had not seen for five, ten years perhaps—long enough for mentality and disposition to have changed completely, in both cases. Also of Czecho-Slovaks or Roumanians, or even of Irishmen, who had advertised their desire for an English wife, and had so many eager applicants for the post that they were obliged to call in the services of the Chief of Police to help them decide.

It was obvious that the general public—"Paterfamilias" and the rest—felt admiration rather than contempt for these individuals. They had no censure, though much false sentiment, for the conditions that created the woman of the streets. They had only fellow feeling—a smile and a dig in the ribs—for the man with many mistresses. As long as people acted according to nature, how could "Paterfamilias" blame them? Of course not—they were all right.

The library novels did nothing to weaken this impression. That winter a particular cult, which might have been called the cult of Pure Nature, was at its zenith. Some of the younger novelists—and a handful of older ones, to whom net sales were still a consideration—had conceived the idea of turning the emotional unrest, that had been brought to a head by the turmoils of peace following the nervous strain of war, into a direction that should lead to their own profit. The public wanted to "let itself go," but it was restrained, being British, by an inconvenient suspicion that it would be ashamed of itself next day. Therefore it should be told—it would like to be told—that letting itself go was a perfectly right and natural process.

So it came about that several of the books Sally picked out at random from the "A class" shelves contained a culmination episode, wherein the heroine suddenly realised her obligations as a "mate" to her man—or to somebody else's man, as the case might be. In this great moment, she realised how pale a pretence had been the "palship" that was her idea of love—until the light dawned. She saw, with a clarity that varied according to the author's reputation for calling a spade a spade, that friendship was only a small and unnecessary adjunct of love. (And while the process of realisation went on, the author had a splendid opportunity for a scene that would not have disgraced a French farce.)

Only, of course, the whole thing was so "virile," so "clean minded," so "pulsing with the Life Force," that no reader could find anything but food for the highest aspirations in it. The said reader was just to be swept irresistibly back to the great Heart of Nature—always in capitals—after the artificialities and subterfuges of modern civilisation.

And the plan worked, and the books sold in their thousands, the public being ready as ever to be swept in a congenial direction by an old force under a new and higher sounding name.

But Sally noticed chiefly that friendship was counted a thing of naught. Whenever a female professed unadulterated friendship for a male character, and there were no signs in the first chapter of the subsequent light-dawning, it was safe to bet that she would turn out to be the villainess. Either she was lying, or else she was a sexless, race suicidal creature, who

SURPLUS

was trying to lure the male from his ancestral search
for a mate, for her own cold-blooded and abominable
purposes—such as possessing herself of his ten thousand pounds per annum.

And if by chance some careless writer produced a
hero who could spend twenty-four hours in company
with a pretty woman without wanting her as a mate,
the critics were down on that hero with all the contemptuous abuse to which they could lay their pens,
and wilted the book out of circulation. Upon which
the author, if he were wise in his generation, proceeded to explain that the said hero was only suffering
from suppressed impulses, or inhibitions, or complexes,
or whatever psychological jargon of the moment happened to occur to him, and altered the last chapter to
show how a famous psychologist lifted the curse and
restored him to normal virility again. And left him
in the arms of the lady, or upon her breast, or clasping
her ankles—anywhere, so it was sufficiently obvious
that love, real Larve, had come at last. After which
the book went merrily into twenty editions straight
away.

"Fear not them that kill the body, and after that
have no more that they can do," said a wise Teacher.

Shall we not rather fear them that prate of life,
even from generation to generation, for the body—
and mention the soul as an afterthought, if at all?

Sally began to think about the love of a woman for a
man as compared with friendship. Unbelievable as
those writers and their readers would have termed it,
she had really not thought much about it before in
her life, except in a vague, impersonal kind of way.
In her early society days, for instance, she had taken
it as perfectly natural that she should enjoy the thrill

226

of a kiss, now and again between dances, without experiencing the faintest desire to marry the kisser. Certainly, she had felt surprise at many of the unions entered into so light-heartedly by the girls she saw around her, but this she had accounted for by ascribing an extra fastidiousness in such matters to herself. Some people can eat anything, others have to choose their menus carefully, if they are to avoid indigestion. The fault—and the loss—was the men's, that she had loved none of them. Or so she had considered, up till now.

And then had come Averil—and she had taken her friendship for Averil as the greatest and finest love that could possibly happen to anyone, man or woman.

Now, for the first time, she saw that friendship as others must have seen it—as a no-account thing, as rather an obstacle than otherwise to the finding of real love. Why, even the best known authors, whose fame was so great that they could afford (so Sally imagined) to paint life as it really was, never dreamt of depicting a woman whose case at all resembled her own. Except as an Awful Warning.

Climbing up the steep stairs when her day's work was over, knowing there would be no one waiting for her at the top—no deep sea eyes to glow with welcome—she had to read something till far into the night, to sleep. Consequently, she went straight to her book, and imbibed a harrowing description of an "unmated" woman, who thought she was perfectly happy with a girl friend, but later found out what she had missed and, in despair, ended her career in an asylum.

"Is that how I shall end?" thought Sally.

It was the inevitable effect of cumulative suggestion

on a mind already deprived of its critical faculty by a long period of worry and loneliness. She did not stop to consider that the novelist in question evidently classed his awful warning along with vegetarians, and collectors of art pottery, and other would-be spiritual, highbrow folk who are generally considered quite mentally sound, in spite of their idiosyncrasies.

She began to think of herself as a pitiable freak, on a level with the poor dwarfs selling squeaky toys down Ludgate Hill. All the spectres that Averil had kept at bay came out and jibbered at her—"You're a failure, you're wasting your life!" they cried, louder than ever.

And now a new voice cried from the printed page— "You'll always be alone, quite alone."

She remembered the curiosity in Mrs. Rickaby's eyes, the pity in Cecily Torrow's, the contempt in young Bar's, and magnified them tenfold, as is the way in solitary musings. Remembered, too, the pronouncement of Barry Hope, on the evening of the hypnotising.

"Repressed instinct. . . . It means you're bound to have an uncomfortable time in life." And "Friendship? That's quite a different thing."

Because she had tried to find happiness with another girl, she had outraged the law. She had chosen friendship in the place of love—the love of Nature and the novelists—and the penalty must be lifelong.

She was a pariah, belonging to no type, and nobody wanted her. Girls who lived as Bar did, alone and glorying in their aloneness, did not want her because she could never be like them, however hard she tried. Because, in spite of all her efforts, she was soft at

228

the core, sentimental perhaps, needing love to carry her through life. And the others, the women who were married or wanted to be—who were novel heroines with the glass off—had also no part with her, because they wanted a "mate," and she wanted merely a friend.

They might be sorry for her, but only in the way one is sorry for a lunatic. They might try not to flaunt their possession of the greatest thing in life before her starved and hungry eyes. (Another writer invariably uses this phrase to describe the eyes of the surplus females in his books.) But that was all they could do for her.

She began to study the couples in restaurants or tea-rooms, watching them and their covetous or serenely contented expressions. When, occasionally, she visited the cinema, she always seemed to find herself sitting behind a couple holding hands. And when the lights went up, she would wonder how that anæmic, giggling girl could possibly want the pimply, sticky-handed boy, or he want her—she supposed she ought to envy them. But she knew it was only the dream friend she wanted in the empty seat beside her, so they could laugh at the funny bits together.

It was all very well to agree with oneself to forget Averil, but how was it possible? She was there, in every familiar tune the cinema orchestra played, that they had heard together. When Julie Lamie called Amélie "little one" in her broken English, there was Averil calling to "Tins" the arrogant, with his waving tail and beautiful leopard coat. When, coming home along the Charing Cross Road, there was a new poster on the hoardings, it was for Averil's name she looked instinctively—that tidy, thick black slant of letters across the gaudy background. But she never did see the distinctive signature. Evidently Averil was finding her new career of marriage too engrossing to admit of a rival, as yet. Or else she had decided that poster painting was not, and never would be, her *métier,* so that it was not worth while going on with it.

Once, delving at the bottom of her trunk, Sally came upon the smudged design of "The Armour of the Modern Woman." She had forgotten it was there, but now she took it out and propped it up on the table. Staring at it, she saw how the crude colours had faded, so that the rough pencil outlines showed through in places. The modern woman, with her spear and breastplate, but minus a face. Now it would always be unfinished, incomplete, that design.

Was not the incompleteness of that symbolical figure like the model who had sat for it? Like Sally herself, who was neither one thing nor the other—neither completely finished as to the hardening process, equipped and eager for the battle all alone, nor an old fashioned woman, ready to sit at home and take what fortune sent her in the shape of a husband. Modern enough to be "cold blooded," indifferent to the sex claim *per se,* keen on a career—but old fashioned enough to go to pieces without love.

That poster was beautiful no longer. She was not going to look at it any more—but there was a characteristic bit of Averil's drawing in the feet.

She was putting it away again, when she felt something cold and hard in the trunk. A tarnished silver frame—and inside it was the newspaper cutting with the picture of the cattle breeder, "Mr. Glen Carnier, part owner of an East African farm——"

# SURPLUS

"He was keen on you, Sally," Averil had said once, in joke.

Well, he was the right kind of lover for her—a blurred picture, a thing of paper, instead of flesh and blood. A lover who would keep her company in effigy, would at least stick to her always, thinking it no sacrifice, demanding nothing in return.

Sally put him in the middle of the mantelpiece. She did not trouble to polish up his frame.

But when a dream waked her, as it often did, she would stare up at the place where the ceiling was and listen to her heart's beating. The photograph was no kind of company, then. There was nothing there, behind the dark, no miracle waiting to spring out on her. No presence to say to her, as was said to Job:

"You have suffered enough now, for your teaching. Now you shall have it all back, all the happiness I did not mean to take utterly from you."

Averil was gone for good. If Sally were ill, she would not know, or, knowing, would not care any more than she would for a stranger. If Sally died, she would not lose an hour of her sleep. She would not even wonder if they would meet in the next life, because by this time she would agree with her husband that there wasn't one.

"It's unfair!" she cried. "I love a woman with all the strength of my heart, and I'm sneered at, laughed at, condemned to solitude as if I'd committed a crime."

But anger could not alter the facts. Right or wrong, she was alone, she must go through life without the companionship of one creature who would live or die for her, for whom she could do the same. She must be always faced with the stern decree that for a woman, marriage is the only—though not infallible—safe-guard against loneliness.

"I'm so terrified of loneliness! But I must suffer it all my days, because men and women must go each to each other and the Devil take the hindmost—which is me."

The Essential Essence, the illimitable Life Force, was not like a petty, personal God. It would not swerve a hairsbreadth from its course to spare one girl. It hated a freak, as it abhorred a vacuum, and its law was that the freak must cease to be one, or perish. Was that law to be altered, because one human atom had not gone the way appointed?

"If there's no more individual life for us, then I've lost my one chance of happiness. But if there is, and we do go on after all, then it'll be worse. I shall still care for Averil, and she won't want me. If only I knew for certain that this is the end!"

As passionately as Sally had once defended her belief in immortality, she now wished to disbelieve. But doubt would not become negative certainty, at her wish.

That is the trouble with death, the charlatan. He will hold out to us, inexorably, the cup of Lethe—when we cower away from it. But when we cry out to him for that same cup and no other, he smiles—and offers a ticket marked "Eternity lottery" instead.

# CHAPTER XX

ONE morning towards the middle of March, Sally arrived a little late at Madame Lamie's. She had walked, for the sake of the exercise, and she had stopped on the corner of the Strand to buy a bunch of early violets from a street seller. There was no real reason why she should choose that particular morning for an extravagance she had never committed before, and the violets would certainly be faded by the end of the day. Nevertheless, she tucked them into her belt with decision. It was almost as if she were celebrating some achievement.

Perhaps the achievement was that she had got used to an existence wherein nothing ever happened, and nothing ever would happen. It seemed that she was to go on till further notice, typing letters in the morning, doing odd jobs in the afternoon, and walking on the Embankment on fine evenings, with an occasional Saturday at the Zoo, or Sunday at a Queen's Hall concert.

It was a wonderfully safe kind of life. Nobody sneered at her for her softness, or blamed her for her selfishness. She did not have to struggle to keep a happiness she knew would elude her at the end, to claim sacrifice, in claiming faithfulness, from the one she loved—and to know that she claimed in vain. There was no longer a dream beckoning out of the mist.

Instead, there was a certainty of little pleasures,

SURPLUS

such as a box of new laid eggs from Leamingham
(Colonel Wraith had taken to fowls), the acquiring of
a cheap hat in the sales, or, more rarely, a theatre with
Bar and her friends.   When the latter was in prospect,
it was always a revue that Sally chose, nowadays.
Serious plays invariably held a character, an incident,
a speech even, that recalled what one wanted to forget.   Change the scene ever so little, and almost any
stage sorrow might be one's own.   Then one came
home and cried half the night, and what was the use
of that?   It was nearly six months, now, since Sally
had felt like crying.

There was, too, the relief of knowing that the worst
had happened.   Only physical troubles could touch
her now—a lingering illness, or the loss of sight or
hearing.   And that, she felt, would not happen, because it would be adding the spectacular high lights
to a dull, rather obscure little play, turning it into
something more resembling a popular melodrama.   So
she could cross the streets, now, with an unconcern
that was no longer recklessness.   People whose presence in the world was of no use to anyone were of all
others the most unlikely to meet a violent end.

She had found out a method of getting used even
to being alone.   By reading a great deal, and otherwise resolutely reducing the amount of time during
which thought was possible, a lasting state of coma
of the brain could be induced.   She felt, and con-
gratulated herself on the fact, that she was no longer
a rebel.   It was easier than she would ever have
imagined, to acquiesce in things as they were, to give up
wanting impossible things, so that she could have torn
the stars out of the sky to get them.   Instead of a twisting knife under the breast, to have a ball of cotton-

wool, seeming to absorb pain, to smother it at birth.

She had lately dared to test her forgetfulness, as a skater circles closer and closer round a patch of thin ice. She had been to the Academy as soon as it opened and studied the cases of miniatures, comparing their numbers with the catalogue, where once they had dreamed of seeing the senior partner's name. Once, too, she walked down Farthing Lane, past the spot where she had said good-bye to Averil for the last time. The window of the first floor room was shut now, but the ghost of Dina's hateful laughter seemed to float down from it. And Sally walked on at an even pace. It no longer mocked her, because it was so far away, because it had belonged to another life.

Surely that freedom from emotion must mean that she had left off caring for Averil? Sally did not examine herself closely on the question—she had almost given up the old habit there, too—but she had come gradually to see that it must be so. She could pass whole days and nights and weeks now, without thinking of Averil at all. That love of hers had been an excrescence with no real roots. The perfect friendship had been, indeed, a dream friendship, existing only in her own imagination, which had seized on poor Averil and put a false halo round her.

While she was not actually thinking of Averil, she could see how impossible it had all been, that idea of friendship love. Well, the great thing now was to steer clear of love of any sort, which was not only possible, but easy.

There had been changes at the tea shop, too. A new waitress—a Swiss baggage, who wore shorter skirts, and a bigger bow in her hair than any stage imitation. (But somehow Sally liked seeing her about the place, and often watched her.  She had dark, attractively bobbed hair, that curled inwards.)

And, three days ago, Madame had launched forth into an orchestra.  It consisted of a piano and a violin, and it performed from one o'clock till two; Sally had not yet heard it, as its performances coincided with her luncheon hour.  But she knew that Madame was on tenterhooks lest the venture should prove an expensive failure, and that suspense had not improved her usually placid temper.

That morning, she expressed herself with some freedom on the subject of unpunctuality in employees.

"Ten minutes yesterday, 'arf hour to-day—to-morrow you come not at all, hein?  In my country——"

Sally smiled wearily.  Madame was always talking of the wonders of her country, of its hard working men, of its housewives who rose at dawn and went to bed at midnight.  The old Sally would have retorted "Why didn't you stay there, then?"  This one merely said:

"Sorry, Madame."

Staying on late that day to finish the letters, she was made aware that the door at the end of the little passage between her office and the restaurant had been left half open.  There was a tune that wandered through it, a complaining undertone to the dulled clatter of tongues and china.  With part of her mind Sally heard it, while with the rest she typed addresses.

But the music pursued her, would not let go till she recognised the tune.  It was Massenet's "Élégie"—surely an unusual choice for a third rate tea room violinist?  She wondered why it should bring with it an indefinable fear, as of a footstep in the dark to a child lying awake. Then she knew why. The last time she had heard that tune as a violin solo it had been played by Mavis Barron, and Averil had been at the piano. It had been one of Averil's favourites.

Idly curious, Sally got up and walked down the passage. Softly, though no one would have noticed in any case, she opened the door a little wider, and looked across the room with its clutter of tables and the smoke brooding above them. Suzette, the new waitress, was leaning over one of the corner tables, laughing at something a young man was saying to her, so that the great green bow bobbed up and down in her hair. Against the further wall, almost opposite Sally, stood the piano, in all its glory on a small raised platform.

The violinist was not looking at the music, and her head was bent over the instrument. Silver pale hair she had, coiled in a loose coronal that could belong to no one else but Mavis Barron.

Sally stood just inside the doorway till the piece was finished. The restaurant was blotted out, and in its place was the damp patched ceiling of Moss Cottage, and the open window, with fir stems swaying close outside. Instead of an air heavy with rancid fat, there was the scent of ripe pine needles under the sun—and the old feeling that the tender, wailing tune had gathered up, made perfect, all the joy and pain of a dream come true, that yet might not be immortal.

Mavis played it her own way, leaving the tinkly piano to follow her in protesting jerks. Never once did she raise her eyes. It was as if she too were immersed in a dream that the violin was translating to her.

# SURPLUS

When the last high, soft note had died, there was a perfunctory clap or two.

"Let's hope she gives us something cheerful, after that," said a woman next to Sally's ear.

And then, with a click, the shutter of memory closed, and she was back in the present. She remembered that Mavis had profaned the laws of hospitality, and used Moss Cottage as a trysting place for an intrigue with her employer's husband. For that reason, if for no other, the obvious course to pursue was to give her a wide berth.

Yet when two o'clock struck, Sally went back into the restuarant, just to find out when Madame was going to sign the letters. She did not mean to speak to Mavis, only to have another glimpse of her. But at once she saw that Mavis and Madame were together, standing in an angle of the screen that guarded the "service door," invisible to the majority of the lunchers. Madame sat with her chest thrust forward, emphasising her words with angry gestures of her fat pink hands, while Mavis stood before her saying nothing, holding her violin case in front of her.

It would have been easy to go back to the office, leaving things to take their course. Instead, Sally found herself standing close behind Madame, who was reaching her peroration.

"After to-day, you play only what Miss Rosens tell you, or you go, and I find another girl who play so much better. You see?"

Miss Rosens was the pianist, a lean Jewess with an unerring scent for the latest syncopations in revue hits. So Mavis was to take orders from her? Sally stepped in front of the pair.

"What's the trouble, Madame? I know this lady."

238

# SURPLUS

(She had been going to say "Miss Barron"—but was that the name, now?)

Mavis withdrew her gaze from the distance, at the words. Her hair was as bright as ever, but her cheeks had lost their delicate flush, and the lines of her mouth were harder. She looked like a doll that had suddenly become a grown-up woman, and is dazed with the change. And she wore a wedding ring.

"Sally Wraith!" she said quickly, and made a movement to step forward. Then she stood still again, while Madame looked from one to the other, her sharp eyes missing nothing.

"If this Mrs. Gathorne is a friend, you tell her I engage her to play for my customers, not for her own self. They 'ate the sad tunes. She ought to know that."

"The 'Élégie' is by a French composer," said Mavis. "I thought it would be suitable."

"And tell her also she must dress smarter. She should dress like Miss Rosens, not that dark costume she have on now. In the smart restaurants, always the orchestre wear pretty colours."

Sally pictured Mavis in the magenta silk affected by Miss Rosens, with its tiny sleeves and the row of crystal buttons down the front.

"I expect Mrs. Gathorne would rather wear a plain uniform," she said. "Why not a green linen dress the same colour as Suzette's bow? But if she'd rather wear her own dresses, I shouldn't bother her about it, Madame. She was one of Seroni's best pupils, you know. You'll never get another like her."

She spoke so earnestly that Madame wavered.

"Tea room music must be different," she said, but in a sweeter tone.

239

# SURPLUS

"Very well, Miss Rosens shall pick the programme in future," said Mavis.

Sally walked with her to the street door, although Mavis had not asked her to, and she did not really want to.

"Thanks awfully, you were a brick," said the silver girl, in a voice devoid of expression. She was already over the threshold. In another moment the maelstrom of the street would swallow her, and there would be no need to meet her again. Sally always used the back entrance, when she went out to lunch.

"You're living in London, then?"

Mavis nodded.

"And you're not a star—yet?"

"No. I'm not a star. I never shall be," said Mavis, smiling faintly.

Suddenly Sally decided to test herself once more. If she could pass this test, then she would know at once for all that the sore place in her mind was anæsthetised, that the ball of cotton wool had done its work. Mavis was a living part of the past. Could she be dissociated from it, judged on her own merits, as one would judge a stranger?

"Look here, we must have a talk. Can I meet you anywhere—this evening, say?"

Mavis studied her in silence for a moment.

"I play at a cinema till seven to-night. It's down Wandsworth way. And I have to get home early."

"Wandsworth? I live on that side of the river. Come to a scratch supper?" And then, seeing that the other was about to refuse, "Do come!" she added.

Mavis was still looking straight at her, unsmiling now.

# SURPLUS

"I suppose you know I'm living with St. John Gathorne, and his wife hasn't divorced him?"

But Sally made a gesture that swept aside the information.

"That doesn't matter. You'll come?"

It ended in her coming to the room in Boniface Road, with its window that looked out on to the row opposite, and down an alley that cut the row in half, showing a narrow strip of the river at the end. And at first it was very difficult to find anything to talk about, till Mavis said that she had expected to find Averil, and asked after her.

'She's married Dr. Hope," said Sally calmly. "Didn't you know?"

"I haven't heard any Salter's Ridge news since I left. So she's married him, has she? Of course anyone could see he was keen on her, but I didn't think she was on him."

"Nor did I." (How easy to dismiss that topic!) "But I say, what are you doing playing at Lamie's? And at a Wandsworth cinema?"

"They do some quite decent things at the cinema," said Mavis, "only one has to change in the middle of a piece so often. Going straight from Chopin's Funeral March to a foxtrot—you've no idea how funny it is!"

She smiled, and Sally smiled back. But she thought:

"Here we two sit grinning at each other, talking about nothing in particular. Yet the things that have happened to us both since we last met——"

It was a strange sensation, in those days, to feel curiosity about another's life, and it was not strong enough to override barriers. If Mavis did not wish to talk, it was not worth trying to make her. So they ate their supper almost in silence, sitting on the

241

SURPLUS

window ledge, and when they had finished Sally pushed
the little table to one side.

"We needn't bother to wash up, Mrs. Jones does it
in the morning."

At that, Mavis laughed for the first time.

"You haven't changed so much after all, Sally.
You always shirked the washing up," she said.

"Changed—have I changed?" asked Sally.

She was really proud that the change should show
so clearly. But Mavis's answer disconcerted her
oddly.

"You've got fatter. Yes, there's a fat, sleepy look
about you. I don't believe you ever take any exercise."

"Not much," admitted Sally.

She would have explained that the change went
deeper than the surface, if the absurdity of the situation had not struck her. She had wanted—she knew
now that she had wanted—to hold out a helping hand
from her lonely security to Mavis in the depths. It
had been so delightful at lunch time to play, for once,
the rôle of champion of the distressed. But apparently
the position was now reversed, and it was Mavis who
was taking an interest in her.

"Don't let's talk about me," she finished slowly.
"I want to know why you—what's happened to your
career?"

"I've changed it," said Mavis, "that's all. What
about yours?"

"You saw mine this morning—or, no, you didn't
come into the office, did you? I'm through the little
door on the left. 'Yours of the umpteenth inst.
to hand'—that's me."

They looked at each other across the rickety table,
those two who had been going to climb so high. And

242

suddenly the wall of reticence that surrounded Mavis seemed thinner. Bit by bit she began to tear it down, sitting with her chin in her clasped hands, telling little things in half sentences, leaving Sally to piece the story together. How Gay and she had found out they cared for each other. How she had tried to keep away from him, but the opportunities for meeting had been too many.

"That cottage of yours, in the woods," she said, "we had so much time to talk, when he was seeing me home, and it was Mrs. Gathorne who insisted on his doing it, at first. I supposed you hated me for it, when you found out?"

"We were accused of having helped you to run away with him," said Sally, and at the sudden distress in the other's face, wished she had put it less bluntly.

"I never thought of that—but I might have. It's the kind of thing people would say! I did think of telling you all about it, too, on that last day I came. I would have told you, Sally, if you'd been alone."

"You mean you didn't want to tell Averil?" said Sally, amazed.

"She wouldn't have understood about loving—like that. You would."

The enormity of it kept Sally speechless. Averil, who had thrown aside so easily her own career, her partner, to go with a man—and she, Sally, who was cold-blooded—

"You'd have understood that I had to do it," Mavis went on, "because he needed me so awfully much. I was the only person who could give him any hope, any faith in himself. He'd never had a chance to be himself, because of Edith's contempt. He knew she only

243

wanted him as the father of her children—well, I think
nobody could have helped knowing it."

"How did she take it?" asked Sally. She remembered her own description of Mrs. Gathorne—"a cow
as to the eyes, but a devil about the chin."

"I think—it sounds a beastly thing to say—but I do
think she rather enjoyed being an injured martyr, with
every scrap of right on her side. So much so that she
keeps it up. She says it's against her principles, divorce. Of course she's got plenty of money of her
own, and Gay settled all the capital he had—it wasn't
much—on the children. I saw to that."

It was quietly said, but Sally noticed how the muscles of her mouth quivered.

"It was awful, taking him away from the children,"
she burst out suddenly. "I didn't mean to. I'd said
good-bye to him, when I left Salter's Ridge. And
then all the winter he kept trying to see me in town.
And he told me nobody wanted him at home, and I'
knew it was true. Even the children don't want him
—they all take after their mother, and it's her they
care for. So I had to choose—oh, Sally, be glad you've
never had to make a choice like that!'

Then she said she must hurry off because Gay would
be all alone, and he was in a bad mood. And when
she had gone, Sally realised that she did not yet know
why Mavis was playing ragtime, under the direction of
Miss Rosens, at Madame Lamie's, instead of giving
her own recitals in Queen's Hall. But there would be
other chances of hearing that. The extraordinary
thing was that she had been told "You would have
understood loving like that."

But Sally did not lie awake half the night wondering why Mavis had said it. Her mind, kept lying

fallow for such a long time, refused to grapple with the problem. Instead, she turned over and went to sleep.

In the summer that followed, she saw a fair amount of Mavis. They both, for differing reasons, stood "outside," and it seemed inevitable that they should draw as near together as their respective zones of isolation permitted. With Mavis, Sally could feel herself an equal, as she never could with Bar Rickaby and her associates. Bar had so many other interests. Each time you met her there was a vagueness in her eye, a visible effort to remember who you were, so that you felt impelled to repeat hurriedly your name and address, adding, "You asked me to tea in this restaurant on this date, therefore it's up to you to settle the bill."

But Mavis had no ties save the one. Her people, Sally learned, had washed their hands of her, and her friends had none of them been informed of her address. She never spoke of them, or, indeed, of anything that concerned her life before the great plunge had been taken. And Sally found that the sight of Mavis did not bring back, after that first time, the vision of Moss Cottage. Mavis was no longer the soaring genius intent on her music as Sally had been on her perfect friendship. She now directed all her efforts towards another goal, and in so doing she had become a stranger, cut off from the past.

What that goal was, Sally found out when she met St. John Gathorne. For a long time, Mavis would not take her home with her in the evenings, would not even disclose their address, except that it was "cheap and nasty." And then one night she capitulated, at a thought that came to her as she looked at Sally in the street—Sally in an old cotton dress, with rather

245

shapeless black hat, and the corners of her mouth drawn down, even when she smiled.

"All right, come along," said Mavis. "But don't blame me if he bites you. He's not—not ill, of course, but not very well, these days."

Certainly, St. John looked anything but well. His face was more parchment-like than ever, he stooped more, and he had a terrible cough. In the grip of a paroxysm he shook so that Sally thought his chair would give way. But when it was over he picked up the thread of his discourse exactly where he had dropped it, and Mavis, though she watched him all the time, said nothing about it. Evidently that cough was taboo as a subject between them.

There seemed no change in him, in other ways. When once he had realised that Sally came as a friend, he seemed rather pleased than otherwise to have a fresh listener, other than Mavis, to whom he could pour forth his disgust at the state of the world. And the burden of his raging, though the very opposite of what it had been in the Salter's Ridge days, was still directed against his own constraining circumstances. Mavis, he said, had made a parasite of him—insisted on doing it—when all he asked was to be allowed to go on giving the public what it wanted, and keeping them both on the proceeds. He supposed Sally knew what an exceptional chance Mavis was throwing away—the chance of becoming a woman Kreisler, after another two years' training?

Sally admitted that she knew.

"But why?" she said. "That's what I still don't understand."

"She hasn't told you? Well, Miss Wraith, she's got it into her head that she wants to be the bread-

winner of this partnership. It's an idea some of you
women have gone crazy on, since the war. And her
excuse is that she wants me to paint a real picture!
As I keep telling her, it's pure madness. I lost all
ambition in that direction years ago, and now I've
forgotten how to paint seriously at all. I simply sit
here wasting my time, while she pays the bills."

"Gay! Don't listen to him," implored Mavis.

But he went on, in his sharp, irritable voice:

"I'd got to enjoy doing my pot boilers, too. And
they've paid better lately. If Mavis had the sense to
go on with her career and leave me to go on with mine
in my own way, we should be knocking up quite a decent income between us. As it is, we're damned poor,
and likely to go on being. I loathe roughing it like
this"—his scornful gesture repudiated the room, which
had struck Sally as a miracle of cosiness, after her
own—"But when a woman wants a thing, and keeps
on fussing till she gets it, what's one to do, for peace
sake?"

Sally could not trust herself to give a civil answer,
so she turned her back on him.

"You'll spoil your style, with the awful stuff you're
playing now," she told Mavis. "You'll never get it
back again."

Whereat Mavis frowned at her, shielding her face
from him.

"You don't think much of my style," she laughed.
"If you think it can't stand a year or two's rest. Be-
sides, I'm learning all sorts of things at Lamie's, things
I couldn't have learnt in any other way."

And that, thought Sally, was probably the case. But
were they things that would help her to become a great
violinist?

247

# SURPLUS

Afterwards, when they were alone, Mavis explained that St. John must not be taken seriously.

"He simply hated my giving up the training, for my own sake, only he saw he was making me too unhappy by refusing to let me, so at last he gave in. And now he tries to make you think he minds because of the money, just out of devilment. He's like that."

"But was it absolutely necessary for you to give it up? Couldn't you have carried on somehow——"

"How could we?" demanded Mavis. "It takes time to paint a portrait when you're right out of practice, and more time before commissions come in—and meanwhile you've got to live. Gay's only known as a commercial artist, now, and that won't help him at all. He's got to start all over again from the beginning, before he married. But he'll come to the front soon enough, once he gets a start."

Because Sally was silent, she felt it necessary to say more.

"Isn't it his turn to have a chance of doing the kind of work he really loves, the kind he was born to do? All his life up till now—all his married life, and he married young—he's had to paint girls' heads for magazine covers, and Cupid smoking somebody's cigarettes for the advertisements, and things like that. Because they were the only sort that would sell quickly enough to please his wife. And during that time, I never played a thing that wasn't my idea of good stuff. I was being encouraged to do my best all the time, and he had to try and do his worst. Oh, I know people say that a good advertisement is worth more than a bad portrait—and perhaps it is, if you can put a bit of your heart into the advertisement. But St. John couldn't. He hated it because he knew all the time he

248

ought to have been painting great portraits. He hated
it so much that it was killing him. That's why he's
not so fit as he ought to be, now."

"And you?" said Sally. "Oughtn't you to be doing
your best, too?"

"We've only changed over for the time being, that's
all. When he starts selling his portraits, I shall go
back and finish my training."

"How many has he painted, so far?" queried Sally.

"He's busy getting together sketches for a portrait
of me," Mavis answered stiffly.

So Mavis had given up the certainty of becoming a
star, in order that this selfish worm Gathorne should
have his problematical chance—and he had not even
finished one portrait yet, after all these months! Sally
felt the more furious about it because Mavis herself
had uttered not one word of self pity. Mavis seemed
to think it perfectly right that her career should be
sacrificed for her man's, and that doctrine of feminine
abnegation was one that Sally had always held in
detestation. Why *should* the world be deprived of
Mavis's music, so that St. John might have time to
dabble about with his paints and accomplish nothing?

For she did not believe he meant to accomplish anything. He had just accepted her sacrifice as a right—
the immemorial male right—and now felt himself at
liberty to grumble at her in front of a third person.
It was certainly difficult to put much faith in St.
John's good intentions, on the face of it.

Sally would have distrusted all this interest of hers
in Mavis's affairs, if it had shown signs of leading on
towards affection. But admiration was all she felt
for the silver girl at that time, and there was nothing
close or clinging about that sentiment. It was impos-

# SURPLUS

sible to forget—at least, Sally took care that it should
be impossible—that Mavis was very much in love with
a man.  Therefore between Mavis and herself there
was a great gulf fixed.

# CHAPTER XXI

MAVIS had begun to ask awkward questions. Wasn't it rather a pity that Sally should sit day after day in Madame's office, doing odd jobs that any board school girl of twelve could accomplish equally well, when there was nothing to prevent her from going back to the motor trade? Informed that women were not wanted in that trade, she said:

"But there are some in it already."

To the fact that Sally had no capital, she opposed that most girls hadn't—nor had they all a friend in the trade. And Sally, driven into a corner, declared at last that she was sick of fighting against odds.

"This job gives me a certain living, of sorts. What's the use of giving it up, and getting nothing, most likely? If you'll actually find me a better one that I can step into——"

At that point, it was Mavis's turn to have no answer.

Then one Saturday afternoon they went for a walk on Hampstead Heath, and Sally went to sleep on a bench in the evening sunlight, to be roused by Mavis's hands on her shoulders.

"You're in terrible condition, Sally. Fancy getting tired like this, after the gentle stroll we've done! You need more fresh air and exercise, that's what it is."

"If you'll kindly tell me how I'm going to get it?" said Sally sleepily.

"Join a tennis club—or run up and down the Embankment, anything. You're just letting yourself go to pieces, as it is. Look at that old dress of yours—why don't you make yourself a new one?"

"What's that got to do with it——" began Sally.

"A lot. Nobody could be much of a success in a dress like that. D'you know, when I first knew you in Salter's Ridge, you were the very last girl I should have said would be content with the job you've got now?"

But even the reference to Salter's Ridge did not rouse Sally. She had given up sticking up for herself, since she had given up being angry with Averil. She felt no inward necessity to answer Mavis back, as she looked at her on the other end of the hard green bench.

"I may be a failure," she said slowly. "I don't say I'm not——"

She went on looking at Mavis, admiring the sun in her pale mass of hair. Possibly Mavis misinterpreted the look, for she said:

"I expect you're thinking I've got no right to speak like this. But at least I'm doing one thing no one else could do—and I'm not failing in that."

And Sally thought she meant that she was giving St. John his chance as an artist, only. Which was all that Mavis, being a simple soul, did mean.

Though that conversation had no immediate effects, it would not quite go out of Sally's mind. She begun to see that it might be one thing to acquiesce in one's own failure, and another to have that failure recognised as such by Mavis. Certainly, there was no one who cared whether she lived and died a tea-room clerk or not, except her father—and he would be satisfied if

252

she went on making just enough to keep herself. He had written her to that effect only recently, saying he was glad she was now really settled and happy. Her brother, he told her, had had to give up his appointment with Messrs. Tomlinson, because the prospects had proved not good enough, but there was every indication that a better post would soon materialise.

No, nobody cared, but one person knew, apparently —knew how much she had meant to do, knew the extent of her failure, and despised her for it. And contempt was what she had left Leamingham to escape!

Mavis had taken to suggesting 'bus rides with walks at the end of them and other strenuous amusements, for the evenings. But Sally reminded her that St. John hated walking with women—they always wanted to stop somewhere, it was like taking out a dog that wasn't trained to heel, he said—and that she ought not to leave him alone.

Then, one particularly hot day, she insisted they should be extravagant and go on the river. There was reason for a celebration of some sort, since Gay had really started on the great portrait.

St. John did the poling, with frequent pauses for coughing, and many unnecessary collisions. And Sally, who could have done it a great deal better herself, lay and watched him with a lazy joy in her heart that she could see what a fool he was making of himself, and had not Mavis's blinded eyes.

It was a great advantage, to have a free, open mind, able to assess things and people at their just value, without getting frightened or angry when they did not come up to some impossible standard of your own. "The red mist of illusion"—who was it wrote of the virtue there was in release from it?

# SURPLUS

St. John was in an almost genial mood, that day. He apologised twice for splashing them, and told Mavis to use his coat as an extra cushion. He threw back sentences to them, detached but less bomb-like than usual, describing an art show he had attended that morning. One or two of the exhibits had been really quite good. Talleyn had a portrait of a girl —his latest, probably—that had distinct depth of colour, though the hands were out of drawing. (And last time Sally had heard him mention Talleyn, back in Moss Cottage, the adjectives he had applied to that eminent artist had been nothing short of legally libellous.)

And then, when the punt and its occupants had stretched themselves under a tree, Mavis somehow dropped a teaspoon overboard, and insisted they should soak themselves to the shoulder in an effort to retrieve it.

"That's a woman all over," said St. John, when at last the effort was abandoned. "All this fuss over a spoon that cost sixpence halfpenny, and yet she's lying on my new coat and creasing it all up, without turning a hair. Paid for it herself—of course, she has to buy my clothes—so I suppose she doesn't mind throwing the money away."

Mavis only laughed, but Sally said:

"Why is it like a woman, particularly?"

"Don't ask me. It's the nature of the beast to be like that, I suppose."

"I can't imagine why everyone thinks it necessary to generalise about women in the way they do," said Sally. It was the sort of thing she would have said with a snarl in the days when the red mist of illusion was on her, but now she said it with a smile. "How

254

can you tell what all women will do, just by what one of them does? It's as if we were all specimens under a glass case—'This breed grows white feathers in winter.' "

The subject had dropped, like the spoon, to the bottom of silence, when Mavis fished it up again.

"Gay thinks a lot of women, really. He thinks it's jolly plucky of us to go out and work as we're all doing."

"As long as you stick to your own jobs," agreed St. John.

"There you go again," laughed Sally. " 'Our own jobs'—that means our jobs are bound to be different from yours, and they're not, except when it's a case of physical strength. It means our brains—all of them—are fundamentally different to all of yours, and they're not—only you like to think they are, so some of us pretend. Why can't women occasionally be judged as human beings, instead of women? There are too many of those silly tags—'Her logic was very good, for a woman'—'She ties a knot quite tight, for a woman.' Which side started the 'sex war,' and who does all the talking about it now, eh? You'll never hear a girl who's got a good job mentioning it. Who wants to keep the sexes as far apart as possible, and make life as difficult as it can be made, even now, for the woman who wants to do anything interesting besides being a woman? It wasn't a working girl who invented the surplus women scare," pronounced Sally. "It was a married man, and his wife told him he was being clever."

"We don't mind what kind of work you do," said St. John. "I don't, anyway. If you can do it as well as the men, but you can't."

# SURPLUS

"Mavis——" began Sally.

"Oh, Mavis! She does everybody's job."

He was looking at her as he spoke, and Sally saw the transfiguration of his habitual saturnine expression into an eager boy's. And saw that to Mavis it was worth while to put up with the loss of her career and her friends, with an old-fashioned conscience that could never be properly broken in, with St. John himself, his moods and his hopeless incapacities—just to be the cause of that sudden, momentary change.

When Sally got home that night, she wondered whether she had assumed too easily that it was necessary to fail in both directions, love and work? Because she could never have the kind of love she understood she had crushed the craving for it, so that only the tip of its adder tail still writhed occasionally in the dust, and had trained herself to want nothing. She had argued, truly enough, that all her ambition had been for two, and that success in her career was not only impossible, but utterly worthless, alone. Now she wondered whether there was enough virtue in success for its own sake to warrant a genuine effort?

"Shall I put success—money making, Rolls Royce owning, Paquin-gowned success—in the niche from which the false idol of friendship has been cast out?"

Thus Sally, who had at least the normal instinct for high flown phrases, would have worded the matter.

Pacing up and down the narrow room, she caught the solemn glance of the solitary picture on the mantelpiece. That man—any man, for that matter—would agree that, of course, success was the next best thing to love. (Many of them even put it first.) That bull breeder would despise nothing more than a hu-

256

man being who sat down and let herself go to pieces, because she had missed love.

Sally started work by polishing up the frame.

A few days later, it occurred to her that it would be good to show Averil that her defection had not meant ruin, after all. If she could only make a name for herself, somehow, so that Averil would come to hear of it! It was pretty certain that Averil, on the day she read of Sally's accession to partnership in a famous firm, would merely smile and say, "I'm so glad, but I'm not surprised. I always knew it wasn't true, when she said she couldn't get on without me."

But still, she might be a little sorry—

And then Sally realised to what a pitch Mavis's urgings, and an afternoon spent with a pair of lovers in a punt, had brought her. Here was the old knife beginning to twist again in the closed wound. She was beginning to think of Averil again, of what Averil would do and say, and of the fact that she would not be there to hear her say it. Of Averil regretting, wanting to come back to the firm—

It was the foredoomed result, Sally saw, of letting Mavis into the ring fence, of ceasing to stand completely alone. Mavis had told her to "go on trying." But why should one go on trying? It was like telling a swimmer, who has at last resigned herself to the waves, to struggle up to the surface again for one more gasping breath, with the certain knowledge that she must sink in the end. It was the cruel kindness of the doctor who gives a stimulating drug to the sufferer from an incurable disease.

Besides, success is hard of access, if one goes after it merely as a cheap form of revenge. To shout, "Garn!" and put five fingers to one's nose—it is the primitive avengement of an insult, but it does not carry one very far, without a steadier underlying purpose.

So this second flowering of ambition had no roots. For the Sally who had got used to catching 'buses, and wearing cheap ready-made clothes, and eating roast mutton every Sunday in her room, had no desire for anything that was not safe and cotton woolly. She wanted chiefly to make the Sundays come as close together as possible, and the weeks slide into months before she noticed the change. She was determined not to begin wanting anything else again.

Sally saw less of Mavis, after that. And Mavis was so busy sitting for St. John in the hours when she was not working, that she did not notice Sally waited to be asked, now, before coming round.

Then, on an evening when summer had decided to give place to autumn, but was in the mood to make her departure as unpleasant as possible for the conqueror, Sally strolled out across the bridge and down the Victoria Embankment, following the gleam of water as a pointer follows her nose, but without conscious volition. The day had been heavy and airless, neither hot nor cold. One wished it had been one or the other, so that there might have been something definite to complain of.

London lay still in the gathering shadows, like an animal that has been hunted the long day through, and sinks exhausted into cover. A few couples sauntered up and down, brushing Sally as they passed, too lazy to give her road, too indifferent to hold hands. The trams, the rush hour over, ground at long intervals over the shrieking metals, sullen and remorseless as cars of Juggernaut. Even the river seemed tired, as she crawled at low water between the mud flats. On the opposite bank, the warehouses seemed to be leaning up against each other, a mass of contorted outlines, grey and monstrous.

Sally leant over an embrasure, and the rough stone parapet was damp to her bare elbows. She stood so still that a sparrow hopped on to her shoulder, found it was not good to eat, and hopped off again. It was not a good day for exercise. She wondered if she had been foolish to postpone her fortnight's holiday, when she might have gone to Eastbourne with her father. Listening to his golf all day, and a concert in the evenings—yet the air might have braced her up for the coming winter.

But why, after all, want to be braced up? As long as you could go on getting through the day's work, sleepiness was a comfortable feeling. Her thoughts went back to the morning, when Suzette had left hurriedly, with a box on the ears as a parting gift from the proprietress. As she was ramming her absurd tulle hat over her flaming face, she had shouted so that the customers must have heard.

"Bien, je m'en vais. This life, it kill me. Moi, je dois vivre—I must be alive!"

Suzette was very young. She did not know, yet, how life got hold of you—letting you run free for a little space, like a cat with a mouse, then gripping you again in its claws.

"I'm all right as I am," said Sally to herself. "I've got enough to eat. I nearly always sleep at nights, and my work's not too hard. And I know I mightn't like a better job, even if I got it. Only fools go hunting for trouble. Mavis—Mavis is a fool. She'll be sorry, when he dies of that cough, and leaves her all

SURPLUS

alone, without a career, with nothing. She'll see then
that my way's best."

A solitary gull was picking its way across the mud
at her feet, and Sally watched it, thinking how dirty
it looked, how far removed from the white winged
tribe that flash in the sunlight. Behind her, footsteps
whispered, going their own ways, not interfering with
hers.

"This is the only happiness that lasts—this not
caring. If I'd only known that all along! But better
late than never. I'm happy now, anyway."

"You don't look it," said a voice at her side, and
she realised that she must have been thinking aloud,
as usual.

Casting a sideways glance at the owner of the impertinent voice, as she drew away, she saw a man,
rather tall, with no hat on, and hair turning grey at
the temples. He had clear blue eyes, and his tie had
been carelessly tied. It was not till she got to the
last detail that Sally recognised him. His face had
grown so much thinner.

"You don't look pleased to see me, either," added
Glen Carnier.

"I'm surprised," she answered.

But she was not really surprised. Since Mavis had
come back from that other life, why should not this
man also? And Averil had never known him, so it
should not have hurt at all. She smiled at him, then.

"I knew we should meet again all right," he said.
"I knew you hadn't just dropped into space, though
it looked like it, when you didn't answer my letter."

"Your letter? Did you write, then."

"Of course. When I got back from Scotland, I
went straight to Sampson's garage. You remember

260

SURPLUS

you never gave me your home address? And that
fellow Sampson told me you'd gone. He said he
made it a rule never to give away his employees' addresses without their permission, but he promised to
forward a letter. So I wrote and told you I found
I had to go back to East Africa sooner than I'd expected, and I asked if I might call, wherever you were.
And when you didn't answer, I concluded you had no
use for me, without the commissions for your friend.
You rather—" he seemed to wonder how she would
take the end of the sentence—"you rather gave me
the impression you wouldn't have, you know. But I
wrote again, from the boat, to apologise."

"I never got those letters," said Sally.

She could see Sampson throwing them both into
the waste paper basket, delighted at the chance of doing her a bad turn that could never be proved against
him. He had thought, of course, that there was
"something up" between his lady demonstrator and
her only male client, and had determined that no nice
little romance should come of the business, so far as
he was concerned. It must have happened very soon
after her dismissal, when she had told him what she
thought of him as an employer.

"I'll go round to-morrow and wring that Sampson's
little neck, if he's still alive."

Carnier spoke with such earnestness in his quiet,
hesitating voice, that Sally stared at him. She liked
the heavy lines of his shoulders, and the way he
stood still before her, without the nervous flick of fingers, the shifting of weight from one foot to the other,
that marked the men one saw at a place like Lamie's.
He looked securely rooted, somehow.

A mist rose up from the river and the mud flats

261

now, so that one could not see any water line. The lights from Charing Cross Bridge struck through it, pale pyramids with blurred edges. Then all the clocks in London began to strike the hour, one after another, one against another, Big Ben's hollow dirge chiming in. It was the loneliest sound in the world, and Sally shivered as she listened.

Then she saw that the man beside her had changed his position. His figure, now, came between her and the river. His eyes were darker than she had remembered. They were not unlike another blue pair—eyes you had seen at once would never flinch, never betray you.

## CHAPTER XXII

THE stock farm had done well in the last three years, and Carnier was now in a position to buy out his partner and run the show alone. He had come "home" in July to fix up the business arrangements, and for a six months' holiday, which was the last he expected to have for many a long day. The overseer he had left in charge was a good man, but not the sort to take big risks in the owner's absence. And such risks had to be taken almost daily, if any undertaking out there was to succeed.

All this he told Sally within a week of their meeting, and the information was volunteered, because she did not ask him a single question. She accepted without question, also, the fact that he often waited for her outside Lamie's at six o'clock. He seemed to have very few acquaintances in London, beyond his solicitors, and some of the constantly changing succession of overseas club members. Sally put that fact in the forefront as a good reason for letting him eat supper with her occasionally, instead of condemning him to a lonely meal in the club. So at her choice they patronised all manner of alien restaurants in Soho and Seven Dials, each paying their own bills with great solemnity. Until one day he said he wanted a change and took her to Simpson's, where she let him pay for them both because, after a really square meal, she was too overcome with astonishment at the extent of her own appetite to think out, at the moment, any convincing reason why he should not.

# SURPLUS

Carnier had a way of not seeming surprised at anything, and it wàs very restful. When, in response to his enquiries, she told him she had given up the motor business because her friend had left her to get married, he merely said he was sorry. He did not want to know what her friend's marriage had to do with it, nor did he exclaim at the unsatisfactory nature of her present employment. He did not, even by implication, advise her to get out of her groove and start struggling again.

Instead, he talked of his own work, of the droughts that burnt up every blade of green for a hundred square miles, of desperate rides across the river bed to get the cattle safe on high ground before a sudden flood came down. In his slightly drawling voice, with the frequent little pause between sentences, he made her see the wide grass lands and the wide, burning skies, flecked with hovering vultures, and feel the wind that blew on the uplands, coming from far away, no smoke tainting its virgin freshness. And Sally listened as a child to a fairy story, enchanted as much by the sound of the words, as by any meaning in the tale itself.

When she introduced him to "Mrs. Gathorne," it was with the intention that he should ask her to join them on these excursions. She knew that St. John would not come, and she was sure it would do Mavis good to get away from him occasionally. He was working hard on the portrait, now, and his state of mind was vicious in the extreme. For nothing and nobody had he a good word, and in his fits of blasting depression he was continually telling her "to go away and leave him." But Mavis was not to be beguiled, when Carnier duly invited her. She said she had so

264

little time at home that she could not afford to lose any
of it.

"Home," thought Sally. "Two furnished rooms—
what a home!"

But Mavis smiled on the two, and hoped they would
have a good time.

"I'm glad you're taking Sally about a bit," she said
to him. "It'll do her good."

Sally had the feeling that she was being handed
over to another keeper—she, who had with such difficulty attained a state of wanting nobody to take care
of her. The impression was heightened when Mavis
said to her, one day coming out of Lamie's:

"You can tell him about—us—if you like. He's
the sort it wouldn't make any difference to."

"But why should I tell him?" asked Sally. "What's
it got to do with him?"

"Nothing—if you don't want him to know," said
Mavis enigmatically.

Soon after that, Sally got away early one evening,
because he was meeting her up west, and they were
going to a supper dance at the Savoy, though she had
pleaded for the Palais de Danse. But he had insisted
that he needed to get as far as possible from the back-
woods, for a change, and as it was his treat she was
obliged to concede the point.

She had no dresses now that were not in the fashion
of the year before last, so she bought one ready-made
on her way back from work. Black had seemed the
easiest choice—and then she had seen a sale remnant,
a little leaf-green diaphanous thing, square-cut at the
neck, with a sprinkling of tiny crystal beads on the
girdle.

"Green is Moddam's colour," had said the show

girl, and Sally had positively blushed to hear she still had a colour.

Yes, it suited her, though her shoulders were too thin for those narrow shoulder straps. It gave her a look of lightness, like an elf who had just flown in on the way from his woody home, all dusted with dewdrops, and couldn't stop. She even tried a few steps, swaying slowly, hands behind her head. It was such a long time since she had danced, and she knew none of the new ones. Then she remembered that he would not know them, either, and that anyway there probably wouldn't be any really new ones—there never were, really.

When she got out of the front door, she found he had a taxi waiting for her.

"How can you—the expense——" she began, but he only laughed at her.

"Never mind the expense. I've only got a holiday once—we're only young once. Come on and dance!"

"I'm not what you call young, whatever you may be," Sally told him. But she protested no more about the taxi.

"I'm forty-five," he told her, "but I feel about thirty to-night. That's the best age. You know what you want, and the best way to get it, if it's a thing that can be got at all. You don't waste time trying experiments."

And the realisation that, on her approaching birthday, she herself would say good-bye to the twenties, came to Sally with none of the shock that realisation usually entails. For she had not kept her last birthday at all, because it was bound up with so many memories, that day—and anyhow, who wants to keep a birthday all alone? She had just thought of herself as growing steadily older, and wished, sometimes, that she could hasten the process. Now she felt that he was right, and that thirty was not such a great age, even for a woman, nowadays.

In the cloakroom, she was ashamed of her plain, dark coat, with its sensible collar. She did not like to think of Carnier waiting, more than ever like a steady rock among the swirl of couples passing and repassing in the lounge, for *that* to come out to him after the dance was over, when the other women's partners could claim the wearers of the wonderful wraps she saw glistening from their pegs. She decided they would leave early, before anybody else.

But they stayed till the band left. He danced with the surprising ease and grace so often shown by apparently clumsy men, and it did not seem to matter what steps they were doing, so long as they kept moving. The music was a muddle of syncopations, all with that effect of heart-rending misery—as of a cow mourning her calf—produced by a leader with a saxaphone. But that did not matter, either, and it was all to the good that intervals were practically non-existent. She found herself changing her step exactly when he changed his, knowing which way he was going to turn just one fraction of a second before he did it. She had not forgotten how, and that was the only thing that mattered.

On the way home, she did most of the talking. It was extraordinary that she felt hardly tired at all, considering her lack of practice. She told him so, and asked him to feel how limp her biceps were.

"No muscle at all," he agreed, gripping her arm hard, then dropping it quickly, "why, three years ago

you looked as brown and fit as anything. What have
you been doing to yourself?"

"London doesn't suit me," she said.

Then, because his tone had been genuinely interested,
and because they were walking down a quiet street
that seemed to stretch away into infinity—because she
was tired, suddenly, of not telling anybody—she told
him of Averil's marriage, and how the breaking of
that partnership had broken her, and how she had
wanted to die, but had been afraid of not doing it
thoroughly enough. She used the past tense through-
out, and she did not speak belligerently, but calmly,
as a person still under the influence of an anæs-
thetic will repeat the most idiotic dream to the
surgeon.

Only two things she did not mention. One was
the word "love." And the other was the fact that
his photograph, cut from a newspaper, stood on her
mantelpiece. It was too much to expect, that he would
be modest enough to believe the peculiar reasons why
she had placed it there. And as it happened, it *had*
been in some sort a link between them—Carnier, the
stranger who had remembered her all this time but
whom she had forgotten, had kept a watch on her by
proxy, till he should meet her again in person.

"I was a fool," was what she did say.

And Carnier did not contradict her. Only, after
a little silence, he remarked:

"As far as I'm concerned, it's lucky for me you
two parted company. You wouldn't have had a word
to say to me, otherwise. You only bought my old
machine because you wanted me to get commissions
for her."

"And you never did," said Sally, laughing. It was

the first time anything about the transaction had struck her as even remotely funny.

"And I never did," he repeated. "Do you remember telling me that nothing for nothing was the only motto, in business? I'm still in your debt."

"Oh, no, not now. Look at the suppers you've given me!"

"All right," he said, "if that's the way you're going to take it out, then there's plenty to make up. Say I'd got her half a dozen commissions at five pounds each—it'll have to be the Carlton to-morrow."

Again Sally laughed. The night air seemed to have gone to her head, unlike champagne, which merely made her sleepy. It was a subtle elixir brewed of moonshine in Thames water.

"As if I meant that——"

But next morning she remembered what she had told him, and saw that it was far too much. It made him an accessory after the fact; it let him, definitely, into the ring fence. He knew more about her, now, than Mavis did—Mavis, who had been part of the life at Moss Cottage.

"I shall get so that he means something to me, so that I miss him when he goes away," said Sally to herself, in terror.

So she refused to meet him that night, or the night after. But on the third night, when he waited for her outside Lamie's, the disappointment on his face was too much for her resolve.

"Why don't you come and play with me?" it said. "There are so many delightful things we might be doing—why waste time like this?"

Besides, she found that she had not missed him at all, not more than Bar Rickaby would miss any one of her numerous acquaintances. There was nothing you could teach Sally about missing people, and she knew there had been no pang in not finding his tall figure waiting for her.

She had told him things she had told to no one else, but that was simply because the telling had been so impersonal. He had been—not a father confessor, that was too superior—but someone who had just listened kindly, drawing no conclusions of his own as to her past conduct, giving no unasked advice as to the future. Just a safety valve, perhaps. And, having once told him, she would not need to repeat the experiment, but could face his departure with indifference. So the ring fence was not necessary, as far as he was concerned.

He told her he had bought a couple of horses to take back with him, saddle horses, that ought to be exercised. Would she ride with him on Sundays?

"How do you know I can?" she asked.

"I didn't know," he answered, "but now I've found out, you can't get out of it."

"I've no habit," she objected then.

But she wore a rain coat. And the horse was a four year old, and a bit of a puller. There was a snap in the air, and he tossed his chestnut head and shied at an inoffensive old lady who was leaning over the railings. He was faster than Carnier's mount— well, no, perhaps there wasn't much in it, when they were both extended. It was hard work, pulling him up, and Sally's hands tingled, her shoulders ached deliciously, as the horses stood side by side, their breaths mingling in little gusts on the still air. Good for the muscles, that.

By the end of October, her face was brown again,

instead of a pasty yellow, and her eyes were bright. Madame Lamie noticed the difference. She also noticed that her "secretary" was increasingly inclined to find fault with little things she had hitherto ignored —with the eternal smell of fried fat (Why couldn't the kitchen door be kept shut?), and the way the marble topped tables always looked dirty, however much you cleaned them.

She was beginning to be sorry that there was nothing more interesting to tell Carnier about her own work. The tea room seemed so sordid after the restaurants they patronised together, the customers so dowdy, Suzette's successor so tawdry in her imitation Spanish comb and the green glass brooch that just clashed with her dress. All the staff, from Madame downwards, had no faintest interest in their work as such, apart from the amount they could make out of it. They all, and herself with them, seemed to be going round and round through the daily routine like trippers on the galloping horses, only that, unlike the trippers, they pretended they were getting somewhere. Was it buying safety at too dear a price, to remain enrolled among such company?

Carnier did not say so, but she gathered he thought she was not really suited to any career, and that the fact ought not to worry her. He could not see the hopeless problem of it, and thereby he gave the first indication, to Sally, of a disinclination to see an insoluble problem in anything. Like Averil, he judged that all the difficulties of this life could be solved if one kept right on with living—as the seasons follow each other, no matter what storms may temporarily arrest their sequence. And with the next life he had, till the moment might come for entering it, no concern.

# SURPLUS

And Sally, though she regretted his attitude to her job, found that it made no difference to her liking to be with him. After all, one could not have everything. She no longer expected to find any human being who could sympathise with every side of her, her love of sport, her too extravagant ambitions, her vague and her sharply defined fears. That perfect understanding belonged to the perfect friendship, which no longer existed even in her dreams, which never could exist.

Mavis, to whom she repeated the conversation, showed even less surprise than she had felt herself.

"Of course he's not keen on your getting another job," she said. "Can't you see what he wants?"

Sally saw, immediately, though she tried not to.

She had long ago forgotten that a man had ever wanted her, in that way. She knew that she was not the marrying sort, and it seemed to her that every man she met must know it, too. Her sexlessness, she thought, stuck out of her like the prickles on a porcupine. Glen Carnier had liked going about with her because they were both lonely, and both keen on sport and dancing. Wasn't that reason enough?

She considered him with new eyes next time they met. And she noticed how quickly he swung towards the sound of her footsteps, how the serious brown face changed as if a mask had been lifted from it, setting free the laugh in his eyes. All the time she was speaking to him he watched her. When she changed her mind, for no reason at all, and said she would rather not do a theatre that night, he gave way at once, without a question, though she knew he had been looking forward to the show.

And it was the same on other nights in other little

ways. He gave way not because he thought her choice of an entertainment was the right one, but because he wanted to give way. Glen thought of her as so much a woman that he considered it her prerogative to change her mind as often as she liked, about little things. He listened to her opinions with deference, and if he felt obliged to disagree with them did so almost with apology. He noticed when her shoelace came undone, and insisted on going down on his knees to tie it for her—metaphorically speaking. Like many Colonials who, from inclination or from pressure of isolating circumstances, have mixed with post-war women very little, his views about them were the views of ten years ago. He was still inclined to put them on a pedestal apart, as creatures of a finer clay, to be guarded lest they break—not, when they changed their minds unreasonably often, to be cursed for it.

One evening he brought her a present, a pair of dainty silver spurs, engraved with her initials. And she said, with the feeling that it was being forced out of her, that he waited for it:

"They're lovely—but I shan't want them any more after you're gone. You shouldn't have done it."

"After you're gone." It was out, and it sounded worse, even to her, than she had dreamt it would. It made her realise how quickly she had got used to having someone to talk to in the evenings again, to not being alone. The ball of cotton-wool had worn thin so pitifully quickly after all! It was a wisp now, and beneath it was the ache. "Why should I be alone always? It's not fair."

"And I thought about you all the time out there," he was saying. "When I was riding in at night—

273

the bungalow's on top of a little hill, you know—I used to make believe I could see you, leaning over the verandah railings."

"That was pretty silly," Sally caught at a straw. "I should have been in the kitchen cursing because the pastry wouldn't set—no, I shouldn't have got as far as that even, I can't cook at all. You'd just have come in and said, 'Sardines for supper again!' "

But he didn't laugh.

"Can't you come, Sally? It's a dull kind of life to offer you, I know, and I suppose I'm a selfish brute to ask you. But if you knew how much I wanted you!"

Even at that moment Sally could not help thinking, "That was what I said to Averil—that she must stay with me because I wanted her so much. Was it a good reason after all, then?"

"You wouldn't have to cook," he was explaining. "I'd get you a native girl. And it's not too fearfully lonely—well, not compared with other districts. There's another farm five miles away and we'd have the little car——"

"That's enough—I don't want a complete catalogue! And I should have to have some kind of work to do, if it was only cooking."

She had spoken sharply, but he came a step nearer, put out a tentative hand. They were on the doorstep of her lodgings, and Sally had her back against the door.

"Does that mean you will—that you'll think it over, anyhow?"

"If you really knew me——" she began. Then, "All right, I don't mind thinking it over. But that's all I can promise—understand?"

She did not wait for his answer, but ran inside and shut the door on him.

That night she started thinking it over, putting one argument against another, her brain ice cold, though her face and body burned beneath the bedclothes.

It came to this, that she dreaded going on as she was—as nothing, accomplishing nothing. The cherished happiness of indifference was gone now, and she had begun to be afraid of the future again.

"If marriage is the only way to escape being alone then it's now or never for me. I don't appeal to men, as a rule. Why should I? They don't to me, except as pals, perhaps."

If she married Glen she would have a home of her own, not somebody else's. A place where she belonged—a house she could experiment with, making it come alive, room by room, corner by corner. She would have simple, obvious, necessary things to do, and not much time to think about them. Keeping the house clean, planning improvements, entertaining Glen's friends occasionally, helping with the cattle too, perhaps. No problems, no wondering whether she ought not to be doing something else, no one to tell her she was wasting her opportunities.

"But you don't really care for this man—as much as you did for another woman."

"What's that to do with it? I've found out now that friendship isn't meant to take the place of love. Besides, Averil liked the look of his picture. He's her sort—like her in many ways. I shall get to care ever so much more for him than I thought I did for her."

"You can't be sure," persisted the inner voice.

# SURPLUS

"But one's never sure of anything! He's the nicest man I ever met, anyhow. And he wants me (ah!) he wants me to make a success of his life, to keep him from being lonely. If I do that, I'll have made a success of my own—like Mavis. It'll be one kind of success instead of another, that's all. And I should never do anything worth doing in the motor business now, it's too late. I'm too much of a coward—I should soon give up the struggle again."

And the voice said smugly, tritely:

"That may be true. But there's more in marriage than companionship. Have you thought over the other part?"

At which Sally lost her temper with it.

"If I did it—but I'm not going to, so don't worry —but if I did, I should be a proper wife to him, of course. I'm not the kind of woman who takes all she can get out of marriage, and then expects to pick and choose what she'll give in return. I should be a skunk if I tried to do that!"

"Especially considering you don't really——" began the voice. But Sally turned over and shut the ears of her mind.

Next day was St. John Gathorne's "Private Exhibition." The full-length portrait of Mavis was finished at last, and it hung at the end of the little room, with half a dozen small sketches, mostly with her as model, at each side—as it might have been a sacred ikon, surrounded by votive offerings.

The guests were few, but important. They consisted of more or less well-known critics, the editor of one of the papers St. John had formerly worked for, an agent famed for his power of spotting real talent among unknowns, and a couple of journalists who appeared as profoundly bored with the whole proceedings as small boys at a mothers' meeting. They had all accepted the invitation promptly, and it was sufficiently obvious that eagerness to see the mysterious model with whom St. John Gathorne had set up house accounted for the promptness. Rumours had spread about that she was something quite out of the common, with red bobbed hair that curled like a nigger's, and a hooked nose, and a German accent.

Finding only Mavis, with her white complexion and smooth, pale coil of hair, they were as obviously disappointed.

"Can't imagine what he sees in her," Sally heard one of them murmuring. He had a round face and little twinkling eyes, and he reminded her of someone, she could not quite remember who. "There aren't many attractive models about these days, I know, but still——"

He launched into a low-voiced description of a certain nymph at a studio dance he had attended the other day.

Sally was the only woman present, besides Mavis, and she had been allowed as a great favour to bring Glen Carnier. And he was the most anxious of them all to see the picture.

St. John had painted Mavis as he saw her, as the Madonna woman, achieving all her triumph vicariously, through her man—suffering with and for him, yet rejoicing in the torture. In her eyes was a little smile that said:

"It's all right, I'm here to take care of you. I'll make a path to Heaven for you over my body, and you needn't mind how heavily you tread, because I shall be perfectly happy as long as you get there."

# SURPLUS

It was undoubtedly a great picture. The critics talked about the unusual qualities in the lighting, and the journalists, not to be outdone, admired the values in the lines of one of the wrists and in the draping of the plain dark gown. The agent promised to bring a new American customer of his to see it, a canned-fruit king, who wanted a portrait of his latest wife.

"She's got him in leading strings, and he told me her orders were it must be something out of the way. This ought to do the trick. She'll be tickled to death if you make a saint of her."

And Glen Carnier stood in front of it, towering over them all, and said:

"It's pretty good."

Which St. John did not recognise as the biggest compliment he had ever had or ever would have.

So the party was a success, and after the others had gone Sally hugged Mavis in the middle of the room, for the first time since they had met.

"He'll be famous in no time," she cried. "He'll get heaps of commissions now. You'll be able to——"

But Mavis was looking over her shoulder at St. John, who was doubled up in a fit of coughing.

"It's been too much for him," she whispered. And aloud, "Have you taken your medicine to-day? I thought not! I'm just going upstairs and I'll bring it down."

"For God's sake don't," snapped St. John.

But she turned to him from the door and their eyes met.

"I'd better come up, too," he said, and there was no snap left in his voice.

They stayed away a long time and it grew darker

in the room. The coals fell in and died down to a red glow, making even the scuttle look beautiful and mysterious. Sally sat on one side of it, in the only armchair, and studied Glen's profile, which was all she could see of him. She thought, with a curious little catch of the breath, how sad the shadows beneath his cheekbone made him look. There was a good deal of grey in his hair, too—but his eyes, she remembered, were young. Perhaps that was because he had lived so long among open spaces, where the only problems were the big natural ones, like droughts and floods and famines, and the other outdoor catastrophes. She could not remember the exact shade of blue— then they were looking at her, and she saw that in the half light they were almost black.

"Sally," he said quietly; and again, "Sally!"

She had not seen him move, but he was bending over her, sitting on the arm of her chair. She felt his hands on her shoulders, gripping hard. They were like fate, saying, "You don't know what you want, but I do. I've made up your mind for you!"

They were drawing her back against him, and she had to set her teeth in the effort not to let her head fall where it would be comfortable, at rest.

"I can't, Glen. I'm not the marrying sort. I'm— I'm just the opposite of tnat picture!"

She pointed desperately to the face of the Madonna woman where it gleamed out of the blackness—the woman who was content to do her man's job by being the influence behind him. But he still looked at her.

"I don't want a picture, I want you, you queer little devil. Ah, you like me to call you that? I thought you would! Just because you're nothing of the sort."

His hand was under her chin now, and the muscles

279

of his fingers were steel against her throat.  Perhaps
it was because of that she had to whisper.

"I can't.  No, listen, there are things—I'm
afraid——"

"Afraid of me, are you?  All right, I'll let you
go.  There!"

Suddenly his arms fell away from her, and the
sensation of flying on and on through the bright air,
away from everything that had ever harmed or trou-
bled her, was removed.  She felt as though a para-
chute had dropped with her from a great height, and
deposited her, cold and a little sick and trembling all
over, on the ground.

Involuntarily she turned, to see how far away he
had gone—and at once he was close to her again.

"It's loneliness you're frightened of, Sally, not me.
Are you afraid now—now?"

# CHAPTER XXIII

SALLY never knew quite what it was that made her write and tell Miss Landison, first of all, that she had promised to marry Glen Carnier. Perhaps it may have been some idea of burning her boats, of cutting off escape. Perhaps, again, it was that Miss Landison had said, "I learnt to stand alone." Well, Sally would show Miss Landison that there was another solution to her own difficulty. Standing alone was all very well, but if one could not bear it, one could not, and there was an end of it.

And Miss Landison answered, "If you've found the right man, you'll be happier than if you'd not had all that unhappiness before."

Sally sat a long time with that letter in her hand, telling herself it was a very nice one. Of course, Glen was the right man. He loved her a great deal more than anyone else had ever loved her, and that alone was proof enough.

Often, now, he told her about things that had happened in his boyhood. Of his life in a north country parish (his father had been a sweated parson), and of the struggle he had had to keep out of the Church himself, because he had always wanted to be a farmer. And of the struggle in East Africa, where he had made his way, without capital, from farm hand, *via* plate-layer, miner, God knows what, to the owner of a prosperous estate. And at the end he would say:

"It was a bit of a hard time, but it doesn't seem to matter at all, now I've got you."

She made up to him for everything he had ever suffered, for kicks and curses, for days under the grilling sun and nights out in the poisonous jungle mists. He had tried to fall in love, after the manner of lonely men. Even last leave, in the months before he had met Sally, he had come over with the express intention of finding a girl to go back with him.

"But then I saw you, in your prim overall, looking like a caged beast that was hoping someone would happen along and let it out." ("Thanks!" from Sally.) "And I knew it was no good trying to find anyone else. Knew it was you I'd been waiting for."

And Sally wondered whether he noticed the silence that followed. She could not say the same to him, though she knew he was expecting it. "All my life I waited for you to come"—one could not say that twice. Sally at least could not.

She had promised Madame Lamie to stay at her post till after the Christmas rush, so that left her only a fortnight at home in Leamingham, before they were due to sail. Colonel Wraith, informed of this plan, answered much as Sally had expected. To wit, that his prospective son-in-law appeared to be desirable in every way from her account, and she had now reached a time of life when she could be trusted not to rush into such a step without due consideration. So he saw no reason to withhold his consent, and would look forward to making the young man's acquaintance after Christmas.

"That's the kind of father for mine!" Glen rejoiced.

But Sally thought that if a daughter of hers had been going to journey so far with a stranger, she would if necessary have chartered an aëroplane so

SURPLUS

as to find out, before the matter went further, whether in her opinion he was the right man.

Father had not even seen Glen's photograph. Sally had a proper one now, a large one, just as artistic and expensive as Averil's collection had been. She liked to feel that her paper lover was now a real one, like them. It was taken full face, and gave a good idea of his expression when he looked straight at you.

And Colonel Wraith called him merely "the young man," using the generic term for suitors of all ages.

Mavis, on the other hand, was almost too personal in her enthusiasm.

"I knew it would happen," she cried. "I knew you'd meet someone, and that it would be a big thing, when it came—that's why I didn't want you to let go."

And in a half whisper she added:

"I envy you. You'll be able to have kiddies. It'll be safe—for you."

It was the first time anything in the nature of a complaint had come from Mavis. So this was the pain Mavis hid behind her laughter, this was the price she had to pay for what she had done? Sally seemed to see further into other people's hearts, at that time, than ever before. And she saw that the bitterest sting, for Mavis, must lie in the fact that St. John could not share this greatest pain with her. He had never wanted children, and even now he did not really want them. Sally had no reason for being sure of that, but in her new omniscience she was sure.

Then her thoughts drifted from their case to her own again. "You'll be able to have kiddies," Mavis had said. Yes—only the trouble was that, like St. John, she had never wanted them up till now.

283

# SURPLUS

To sink one's own individuality in a child's—to go home early in the evenings, however interesting the company, because of seeing the child in bed, tucking it up, listening to its breathing. To spend one's days planning out its little clothes, to boast to every chance acquaintance that it had been put on four-hourly feeds, or weighed a pound more than the baby book said it should. To sit at home (the nest provided for them by that strong man, father) in an atmosphere of talcum powder, soap and flannel, crooning to baby about the wonderful things father was doing out in the great world—all these things her spirit had rebelled against. Something inside her had said:

"I want to fulfil myself—my spirit, not my body. It's my very own self, and you won't cheat me into believing I can hand it on to a baby. I can't—and if I could, I don't want to!"

Now, taking herself in hand, she found she could believe that it would be an ideal existence. One could leave off theorising, regretting, leave off trying to find one's own happiness in ensuring that of a child. It would be an occupation, too, during the long hours when Glen was busy on the farm. Even if one didn't love it so frightfully much as a tiny baby—but people said you did, whatever it looked like—it would grow up. It would be four and five, and then one would love it. And later still it would be a prop for one's old age. And Glen, of course, would expect it, and it was his due.

"The greatest thing in the world." Sally thought, exulting, that if she could have a fine, healthy baby she would have done what most people considered the highest duty of a woman. At long last, everyone would admit that she was not a useless creature, a

284

failure. She concentrated on the picture of a sturdy
toddler with his father's eyes, and her own brown hair,
and a mouth that should turn resolutely up.

It was so much easier than she had thought, being
like the majority, and she went about intoxicated with
the sensation. She made Glen take her with him to
choose the ring, a regulation half hoop of diamonds,
set in platinum. She held his arm when they crossed
the streets, and enjoyed—actually enjoyed—the
strange feeling that she was one of a million other
women who were never quite satisfied, quite at their
ease, unless their man was near to take care of them.
She bought a fat cookery book. She even asked
his advice about the trousseau, and discarded one
quite charming hat because he preferred her in another.

Once, greatly to her surprise, Glen rebelled.

"I never see you alone, these days," he said.
"We're always rushing about to shops and restaurants,
or else we're with the Gathornes. Am I never to have
you all to myself?"

"You'll have too much of me soon," smiled Sally.
"All me and nothing but me. Can't you wait another
month?"

But it ended in her going with him down to Ches-
ham, and spending the whole of a surprisingly mild
November Sunday afternoon wandering through leaf-
less, deserted woods. Some of the trees were larches,
standing out from the ruck like young princesses
among a crowd of dairy maids. They ate their tea
on a little hill, sheltered behind a clump of them, looking down on to a narrow, winding path caked with
dead twigs and needles.

It was very like the path through the forest, behind

# SURPLUS

Moss Cottage. So like that Sally remarked, apropos of nothing:

"You remember when I told you about the—the girl I was living with, and how I did all I could to stop her getting married? What did you really think of that—of me?"

Glen, standing there cleaning his pipe, looked down at her in astonishment, for it was not like Sally to stammer when she asked a question.

"I thought—I thought how lonely you must have been," he said with a smile. "Poor Sara!"

So he too could not believe that a sane woman—a woman, for instance, whom one wanted to marry—could possibly cling to another girl for any other reason than that the mate had not yet materialised. His smile, like Barry Hope's, said, "You hadn't met the right man yet—you hadn't met me."

But Sally could not leave it at that, though every nerve in her cried "stay."

"I suppose you think she was quite right to leave me as she did?"

"I think, from what you told me, she did it in a cruel way," he said judicially. "But she had to do it somehow, if she wanted to get married. You must have seen that yourself by this time, my child! Supposing a girl—oh, any girl, the best friend you had—came along and asked you to live with her now, eh?"

Sally was silent, considering the point he had raised. What would happen if—

But he took her silence as an acknowledgment of defeat in the argument. Quite often she would let him have the last word—that blundering, kindly word —because it was fun to see his naïvely pleased expression at the thought he had convinced her. Besides,

286

SURPLUS

her brain was not yet supple enough to enjoy pro-
longed discussions, however friendly, after such a
long period of lying fallow. And he had not known
the old Sally well enough to be surprised.
"Don't let's worry any more about what you did
and she did, and which of you was right. All that's
done with, it's a back number. The only thing that
matters now is that you and I won't ever be lonely
again."
And Sally, acquiescing, thought, "If *he* thinks that's
the only thing that matters, then it is."
And then, the day after he had received his first
portrait commission from the canned-fruit king, St.
John Gathorne went down with acute pneumonia.
The doctor said he would need careful nursing.
"There's no constitution—nothing to fight with but
spirit. Plenty of that, though. If we pull Mr. Gathorne through, it'll be because he refuses to die."
Truly, Sally thought it was the last moment of his
career that St. John would have chosen for such a
proceeding. She spent the next five nights on a sofa
downstairs, doing what she could to help. And whenever Mavis left the sickroom for a few seconds, the
invalid's fretful murmur would send her flying back.
"Mavis, where've you gone again? This damned
bandage has slipped. You should have told that fool
of a doctor it was too tight."
Or *"Can't* you come in or out and shut the door?
The draught's cutting me in half!"
Then, as the fever mounted, his murmur changed to
a harsh shout.
"Dickson says it's no good—he wants pigwash, he's
paid to want pigwash."
And "You never did, Edith—not in the beginning,
287

even. If you'd cared—I didn't do it just to spite you. It's no good cursing me. You never cared, I tell you!"

And the little smile still shone in Mavis's eyes, set in their dark hollows.

But on the fifth day he lay in a heavy stupor, and she beckoned Sally inside.

"He's asleep," she breathed. "Don't you think he's looking better, Sally? Just a bit more natural colour? The doctor's coming back at ten o'clock, he says the crisis will be to-night."

Looking down at St. John on his pillows, Sally could find nothing cheerful to say. To her, he looked so frail that a draught would blow him away, and his "natural colour" might have been put on with a brush, in two hard spots over his cheek bones. His fingers, clutching the counterpane, were so thin that one felt they must be sharp to the touch, like knife blades.

Mavis had leant close to listen to his breathing, when he opened his eyes.

"Mavis," he said, in his ordinary drawl.

He did not seem to see Sally, and she drew back to the doorway, asking whether she could fetch anything. But Mavis had crouched down beside the bed, and did not answer.

"Has it been worth it—to you, too?" he said.

"Worth it? Oh Gay, you know! But shut up— you're not to talk nonsense. You're to go to sleep at once."

"I'm going—to sleep."

Indeed, his voice sounded sleepy. But it seemed there was something else he had to say first, some argument between them he had to finish.

"It's one of the things I've never believed in. But I'm not so sure—now. If you're right—if we do get another chance——"

He mislaid the thread of consciousness, and Mavis kept her hands still over his, so as not to wake him. Sally was stealing from the room, when suddenly he raised himself on the pillows.

"Don't forget—the fiddle!" he cried, in a strange, hard voice.

Then, as if the effort of remembering it, at last, had been too much for him, he sighed and lay down to sleep.

.      .      .      .      .      .      .      .

It was entirely Sally's doing that Mavis came to Boniface Road to live, as soon as the funeral was over.

Left to herself, she would have stayed where she was. She seemed to think that where one lived was a matter of no account, and showed so few signs of breaking down that Sally watched her anxiously, fearing the collapse would be all the worse when it did come.

But Mavis was too busy to waste time that way. She had to make arrangements for taking up her training again. She had saved just enough to make this possible, if she lived on practically nothing, and got through it with the least possible delay. So she practised all day long, and in the evenings she talked music. No one would have guessed that she had just been left more utterly alone than Sally herself had ever been, in a world that looks askance at a new made widow who shamelessly discards her wedding ring and calls herself "Miss Barron."

Yet that was what Mavis did.

"I'm going to tell the truth, now, anyway," she informed a protesting Sally. "He always hated all that hole-and-corner business, but he saw it was necessary, so he pretended he enjoyed it. He called it 'laughing up our sleeves at Mrs. Grundy.' But I know he was longing all the time to laugh in her face—so I'm doing it for him, now."

It was for his sake, too, that she was going to be a star after all.

"It always worried him, my giving up my training. You remember what he said the very last thing? Well, I'm not going to let it worry him any more."

Sally was abashed before her calm, her certainty. Somehow it seemed to bring back in vivid relief her own grief crazed behaviour after the loss of Averil. But Mavis had the certainty that her love had been returned—that if they two went on at all, they would go on together. That must make all the difference.

"Supposing you weren't sure St. John had cared? How would you bear it, now?" Sally ventured once.

And Mavis answered, her eyes on her portrait, that was never to be sold:

"It would be pretty hard. And yet—if you'd really cared yourself—there would be that to remember."

Glen Carnier agreed at once to Sally's suggestion that they should postpone their departure till the next boat, so that Mavis might be safely settled in her work before they left. He kept out of the way entirely for the first few days, but after that he began to call round for Sally, and carried her off as often as he could. He said they had surely discussed Mavis and her affairs enough for the present, with so many arrangements of their own to make, and so little time left in which to make them. And Sally smiled at his tone, knowing all their arrangements—which were very simple, after all—had been made long ago.

It was better for her, Glen persisted, not to spend all her time in an atmosphere of gloom, seeing that she was quite pessimistic enough already. When Sally assured him that Mavis was perfectly cheerful, he asked whether she couldn't stand *his* company, for a change, and told her he had taken seats for a show entitled "Howls of Mirth," at the Hippodrome. She loved him for making her sit through it.

But once or twice she caught herself staring at him, when he was intent on the stage. Was this distinguished looking stranger—she felt sure "distinguished" was the right word—with his hair that was thinning at the temples, and his mahogany wrinkles, the man she would be living with, all alone, in less than a month's time? She tried to picture him pulling on his boots in the early morning, before she was out of bed—tieing his tie, slowly and clumsily, before her mirror—removing a two days' growth of stubble from his chin.

And when he was ill—everyone is ill sometimes—she would camp by his bed, as Mavis had done by St. John's, and do everything for him. But supposing he were irritable, and cursed her for trying to help him, would she still like doing those things, still think him the nicest man she had ever met, and the straightest, the strongest?

"I should hope I'd have a certain amount of decency," she told herself fiercely. "If one's feelings were to change because a man was ill, or cross, or a cripple, even——"

They walked home by the Embankment, as usual, past the spot where they had come back into each other's lives, and down on the other side of the river towards Lambeth Bridge. To-night a gusty wind was getting up, and the smell of coming snow was in the air. The water was so black that one could not see it beneath one's nose, except beneath the lamp arcs. Out in midstream a belated tug was taking advantage of the tide, towing a couple of barges. Sally could hear the determined "chunk, chunk" of her engines, as she cut into the wind. The last barge had a single, smoky yellow light burning in its deck house, as swiftly it flew by towards the sea, past the dark factories on the opposite bank, past the "Hovis" tower, with its dazzling challenge.

At the turn homewards, Sally paused to watch it.

"Glen," she said suddenly. "You're taking a big risk. Supposing you get tired of me?"

"Mighty big risk!" he scoffed.

"But I'm awfully hard to live with, other people have found that."

"That's only because they didn't love you enough—as I do."

He turned, and it seemed to her that he was fighting his way across leagues of space, though he could have touched her without moving.

"I believe you're still afraid—these last days, I've thought so. You're afraid you don't care enough yourself, not that I don't. There isn't—somebody else? Not now, I mean? Of course," he added hurriedly, "there have been other men. I'm not fool enough to insist on being the first, as long as the others were only to mark time with. As long as I'm the last—the last, and the best——"

"You're the first man who's counted," she told him gently.

"Then what's the trouble? There is something.

If only," he said passionately, "If only I could get behind your eyes and think with your mind, just for
once! You're *not* to have a trouble you won't let me
share. It's selfish of you, it's absurd———"

Then it occurred to him that this was only one of
her moods, the moods you had to discount in dealing
with the essential Sally. He remembered the girl who
had helped him to buy the ring, and when he put it on
as soon as they were alone, had kissed the back of his
wrist before he could stop her.

"It's only that you've got so used to expecting the
worst that you can't expect anything else. You're not
expecting to be happy, but you will be. You've told
me there's never been another man who counted—well,
that's of course, seeing you belong to me and always
have done. D'you think I'd let you marry me, if I
wasn't sure of that? If I had you in my arms this
minute, would you dare say it wasn't true?"

And Sally knew that she would not.

Then it was Christmas Eve and Sally had persuaded
Mavis to come out to dinner with them.

"If you won't, we shall all three sit here and mope,"
she had threatened.

So they went to a quiet place in Jermyn Street,
where the service was faultless, and the tables far
enough apart to allow of private conversation. Theirs
was in a secluded alcove, near the door.

Mavis was wonderful, that night. She talked, and
laughed, and drank their healths—she even drank her
own. Only towards the end of the meal her gaiety began to flag. The occupants of the other tables were
so merry—the family party with the grown-up son and
the flapper daughter, adoring the dissipation, the solid
city man, entertaining somebody's cousin in shell pink

and gold, the exquisitely coiffured lady with the white velvet complexion, escorted by the chubby faced undergraduate trying to look a man of the world.

And Sally, noticing Mavis's thin pretence of a smile, thought that perhaps they ought not to have brought her, after all. She had better be got out of it at once, anyway.

As she stood up, Sally looked towards the end of the long room, which had been hidden from her by the alcove. At the first table she noticed three people were sitting—two men and a girl. The girl wore black, and as she lay back in her chair while the men chatted, Sally could see the curve of her cheek, and the feathery dark hair curving away from it. Then she turned her head, and Sally caught the aftermath of the smile in her eyes—like a light coming up from the bottom of a cloudy sea.

Why had she not known that they were bound to meet again, sooner or later? The dark girl's expression was certainly a little like Glen's, but full of a warmth, an eagerness his did not possess.

She was Averil, unlike everybody else because more wonderful. She sat there, fearless and sure of herself, taking every experience life offered her and extracting from it something mysterious, unique—but never telling how she did it. The perfect friend to the little man opposite her, as she had been to Sally. Loving him by now, probably, as she had never loved Sally— with the real love, the only kind worth having. Ah, but it wasn't the only kind worth having!

Sally had a panic fear that she would shout those words aloud. But her lips were saying:

"Come on, Mavis, let's go home, I'm tired. Oh, bother my bag, I'm always leaving things behind!"

# SURPLUS

Quickly she shepherded her little party towards the door. Then she said she had left her handkerchief behind, after all, and sent the other two on ahead, to get a taxi. Which gave her a minute—only one minute—to stand in the doorway and look back at Averil's table.

The girl in black had a whiter neck and arms than the sun-tanned Averil of Moss Cottage—she carried herself more gracefully, and her gown had obviously been made for her. The hand that lay on the arm of her chair was a consciously beautiful hand, though its strong, square-tipped fingers were unchanged. If she were to turn just then, would she see only the selfish girl who had tried to block the road to her happiness—or would she, too, look back and remember?

And at last, as if drawn by an invisible magnet, Averil did look towards the door. But the glance was a casual one, immediately withdrawn. Her thoughts were busy with something else—a very important thing—a dream of her own, that she had only just learnt was to come true.

## CHAPTER XXIV

SALLY had gone straight upstairs to bed, not staying behind, as usual, to say good-night to Glen. She had told him she was tired—wasn't that good enough?

But she could hear his voice and Mavis's below her, long after she had reached her room. She could not bear that—he must go right out of the house, before she could think. She opened her door to call to him, and at once it was evident, from the clear sound of the voices, that he was halfway down the stairs already.

"The sooner I get her away, the better, then," he was saying. "She mustn't meet that girl again. Of course she'll soon forget, out there. But I wish——"

Sally shut her door again, softly. She had forgotten how closely Glen was concerned with her new discovery—of course, one could not think of love, now, without thinking of him.

She pulled a chair up to the window and opened it as wide as it would go. Christmas Day already, and the promise of snow turned to rain. "God so loved the world"—even if one no longer believed it, it was a beautiful idea. And the number of kinds of human love there were—noble and ignoble, little and big. Or did their greatness depend not so much on the kind of love as on the extent to which it filled one's heart?

"If I can't see it clearly to-night, I never shall. If I can stop being vague and sentimental——"

# SURPLUS

She knew, now, that her love for Averil had not died—was as strong as it had ever been in the days of their partnership. And a love that could last like that, outliving Averil's contempt and her own disbelief and neglect, a love that never had been or could be returned, could not be of no value. She had known, as she looked at Averil, that at a word, a gesture, she would have followed her to the other end of the world, or to a boarding house in Bloomsbury. Was that a love to be ignored, crushed under?

"This sex instinct—all the books I've read, and the people I've met who have worshipped it, sneered at me because I had so little of it, till they made me hate the very word, made me at last believe that the biggest love couldn't exist without it. And they made as big a mistake as I did in being afraid. It's necessary to the business of keeping the world supplied with population, and there's nothing ugly about it, nothing to be afraid of, or to hide in dark corners. But—it's not necessary to love."

It came upon Sally with the force of a new truth that love, and not the reproductive instinct, is the greatest force in the world—the only human attribute that is indestructible by time, that is certain to survive time, if humanity itself survives. And it had nothing whatever to do with the question of sex. The flower may spring up in a cornfield, or in a bare patch of earth—it is the same flower, as beautiful, as sweet scented. So love may exist alongside passion, or without it—it is the same power, greater than any instinct, greater than the atoms and rays and currents of which the scientists are busy building them a new conception of the universe, immeasurably greater than the brains of those same scientists. And to limit the full-

297

SURPLUS

est manifestation of that power to beings, between
whom the physical tie of matehood or parenthood ex-
sits, is like declaring that electricity can only be gener-
ated by one particular kind of dynamo.

Sally knew that she was an imperfect vehicle of the
power, because she could not find her own happiness
in knowing that the beloved had found it elsewhere,
with someone else. Not yet had that pinnacle of greatness in the scale of lovers been attained—and she
doubted whether it ever would be.

"But at least I've loved as unselfishly as I could,
and as deeply as I can. I've had the greatest thing
in the world, and nothing can take it away from me.
There are plenty of men and women—who've wanted
children, and had them, too—who still haven't got the
flower in their hearts. They may pity me, but they
would do better to be getting on with their job, and
keeping the race going. It's a good job, a splendid
job, but it isn't the only job, even for a woman. It
isn't mine."

Remembering Glen, she thought, "I wish it were—
but there's no use in being ashamed of myself because
it isn't. What I ought to be doing, and what I've
not done yet, is to find out what my job is."

All very fine and glowing on the crest of a great
moment—but at the tail end of the thought-packed,
rainy day that followed a sleepless night?

Sally had begun to be sorry she had given way, once
more, to her fatal habit of not letting well alone, by
the time it came to waiting for Glen alone in the sitting
room. Mavis—a tactfully commonplace, incurious
Mavis—had been safely disposed of at a concert, and
was now, too late, regretted.

Why not, after all, let things go on as they were?

298

# SURPLUS

There could be no good reason why she, Sally, should not take some love, as well as giving it. Glen already knew of Averil's existence. Even if she told him that she still loved Averil best, he would not mind. He would consider that a girl friend and a husband entered the lists for such a different prize that there could be no competition between them. Why not leave him in that belief, and leave him happy?

"I can go on giving him what I've given him up to now—a second best friendship, and all the passion I have to give to anyone. It's more than many people marry on, and it isn't as if I hadn't warned him. And I can't be alone again, I won't——"

Then Glen came into the room, solid and clumsy, smiling at her as if she belonged to him, now and for always, entirely. She had not remembered he was so lovable, that it would seem so impossible not to play the game by him.

"I heard you last night," she began quickly, before he could speak. "You said 'She'll soon forget, out there.' But I shan't—I shan't even try to, any more. Yes, it has to do with you. It means—oh, Glen, can't you see?—it means you met me too late. If I hadn't met Averil first, things might have been different, I don't know. But as it is—I'm a one-man dog, you see! I thought I had managed to forget her, and that the way I cared for you was good enough to get married on. But I find she still comes first—she's never been anything else—and I can't put you in her place."

"I don't want to be in her place. I want you to care for me as a woman cares for her man. You may fancy you don't, now, but you will later on. And if you don't—I'm willing to take the risk."

He was still smiling, holding his hands out to her.

"But I'm not willing," she cried desperately. "Do you think I could bear to live with you day after day, and know you were waiting, longing for me to change? I'm not the sort that cares more after marriage, just because of marriage. You know how in books the heroine says 'I'm yours, body and soul'? Well, I care first with my soul, and with my body a long way afterwards."

"You mean I put them the other way round?" His eyes were stern, now, as he stood over her.

"You're only pretending we don't understand each other better than that," he told her.

"But don't you see how much more possible our marriage would be if you *did* put it the other way round? If you didn't want the whole of me—if what I can give you was enough—but it isn't. You want the biggest love in my heart, and I can't give you that, because I've given it to Averil already. And that's why I can't marry you."

"Of course, you don't mean it," he said.

He had started to fill his pipe, but his hands shook, so that the tobacco fell on the carpet and lay between them, unnoticed, a little feathery pile.

"You've never been married, you're a child, you don't know what you're talking about. To say that this girl comes between us—you don't know what love is!"

"Don't I?" she said. "I think I know something about it. You've taught me, and Averil, and Mavis— It isn't thinking the one you love is splendid and wonderful when they're kissing you, or taking you out to dinner, or saying nice things about your eyes. It's feeling a thrill about them just the same when they've

300

got mumps, or when they're paddling on a cold day at the seaside, or when they've just missed a train, and are oozing with heat and fury. And I did feel like that about Averil—I do still—but I don't about you. I was sorry for you when you had a cold the other day, Glen, but I didn't want to be near you. It wasn't that I was afraid of catching the cold—I just didn't want to see you at all, because you weren't in your best form."

"Oh, didn't you? Well, you'll want to now——"

He had pulled her to her feet and held her at arm's length, exulting at her trembling. She knew that in another second she would be asking him to draw her close, so close that she could feel nothing, think of nothing but the beating of his heart.

"Let me go—don't touch me to-night. I'm awfully tired."

It was perhaps the only argument that could have made him obey.

"Poor Sally, you do look pretty used up. It's the worrying about Mavis," he said gently, as he released her.

And Sally thought over and over again, "I've got to make him see—I've *got* to make him see."

But it was so difficult to do! There was nothing in the room to give her inspiration. Only since Mavis's advent had this room been hers, yet already it had a more homely aspect than the one she had lived in for a year. A trio of etchings, purchased for the permanent home overseas, were temporarily adorning the walls, and a set of silken cushions—Mavis's home-made wedding gift—made the chairs luxurious. An unfinished piece of needlework of Sally's own made a splash of paleness on the table at Glen's back. There was a list of steamer sailings on the mantelpiece—no, the room was no help at all.

"You'd only be second best," she told him. "You'd only have half a loaf. Could you be satisfied with that, and give up expecting me to care for you one day as much as you want me to?"

"I think I've always known you didn't," he said slowly. "But——"

"But can you make up your mind to it that I never shall, and give up trying to make me? If you think you can, think again! I don't believe it's in your power to do that, any more than it's in mine. 'Love begets love'—it's true, up to a certain point, but everyone believes it goes the whole way. I never could believe Averil wouldn't come to think of me as I thought of her in time. D'you know," she said, "even last night I couldn't quite believe it? I felt that if only I knew the right argument to use, she'd leave her husband and come with me?"

"Well, then, if I did go on hoping—why should it matter? As long as I didn't worry you——"

"But I should know," she said. "We're not the sort who can bear being second best, either of us—we must be first or nowhere. Didn't you loathe the very idea that there might have been another man, before you, who counted with me? Weren't you jealous even of Mavis, because I was so taken up with her affairs?"

"Nonsense!" Then, like a guilty small boy, he qualified the denial. "We should have each other alone out there, and it would be different."

"It would be worse," said Sally. "A lop-sided love won't work to live with. I've tried it, and I know."

He had succeeded at last in making his pipe draw,

302

and leant back against the mantelpiece not looking at her.

"You mean you don't love me more than this girl loved you, then?"

"Averil did love me, in her way—only she didn't put me first. While I could make myself believe she did, or that she would one day, I was perfectly happy with her—but that wasn't often. She found the strain too much. Even if the man she married hadn't turned up she would have left me, I think, in the end. She couldn't go on living with anyone who wanted more than she had to give, and she couldn't keep up a pretence. I'm nothing like as strong-willed as she is; I couldn't pretend at all. I should know all the time that you wanted as much as you gave, and that I couldn't give it you. 'Nothing for nothing'—it's a good motto for marriage, too."

Her voice was so low that he had to bend close to catch it.

"That's all moonshine! This girl can't come back to you, anyway. Are you going to live alone, then, just because of her? When you're getting older——"

"Oh," she cried, "now you're talking like the books, and Mrs. Rickaby, and everybody else! 'Just you wait till you're forty,' they say, in a nasty, gloating voice."

Here was something to get angry about at last, and she seized on it.

"If I'm going to get cancer or go mad when I'm forty, because I haven't married and had a child, then you'd better start choosing the asylum, that's all. I'm not going to jump into the frying pan now so's to avoid the fire when I'm forty. One can't live life like that, all planned out beforehand. Do you want me to

sit down and calculate whether the chances of that
happening at forty outweigh the certainty that I don't
love you enough now, eh?"

She had wounded him at last and she saw it.

"You'd better go to bed and sleep it off," he said.

Then he looked down at her, huddled up in her
chair.

"Of course, I don't want you to 'calculate' anything.
But I think it won't be necessary, when we've said
good-night——"

His hand was on her arm—on her wrist, over the
leaping pulse.

"You're afraid of giving in!" he laughed at her.

"Please go, Glen," she said softly, not moving a
muscle. "You annoy me to-night. I simply don't
want you anywhere near me. Isn't that clear
enough?"

"Perfectly clear," he agreed. "Good-night," he
added, from the door.

She let the sound of his footsteps die away till there
was no more chance of calling him back. Then she
put her forehead down on to her wrist, where his hand
had touched it. Not to have let him kiss her once
even. But if she had, he would have remembered that
always, and gone on hoping always that the whole of
her heart would one day follow the kiss. Human
nature was like that—would always rather cling to
a false hope than accept the hopeless truth. But
truth *was* kinder in the long run. One could get used
to truth, make some kind of a working arrangement
with it, so that one could go on living with it.

Glen might always care most for her, but he was a
normal, human man. He would find some other girl
to live with him, keep his house for him, bear him chil-

dren.  He would be able to do that and keep his memory of her.   Whereas if he married her he would grow to hate her with the searing, unwilling hatred of love unreturned, even while still loving her—to curse her in his heart, as she had cursed Averil.

Later Sally told herself that surely, after all, one more kiss wouldn't have hurt?   A kiss, that is supposed to mean so much more to the woman than it means to the man.

"He's coming back to-morrow," she whispered. "He's not gone for good."

# CHAPTER XXV

MISS LANDISON lay on her couch in the broad window as if she had not moved since the morning Sally had said good-bye to her. Her face might be a little thinner now, but with the light coming from behind her, it was impossible to see. Only the climbing roses had grown unchecked above the sill, and their briars tapped against the panes, while at the bottom of the garden the larches soughed above a littered lawn, still agitated by the night's violence.

Sally had obeyed a sudden impulse and come down to Salter's Ridge, leaving a note behind for Mavis, containing the bare information that she would be back in the evening. For Glen she had left no message —it wasn't necessary, she would see him again so soon.

She had reached a point where she could no longer go forwards or backwards on her own initiative. It was as if she stood on a narrow plank above a ravine, frozen there, midway, by giddiness—she wanted to be pulled one way or the other, in whichever direction was the safest. And in this case there was no doubt as to which way that was. She wanted to be told by a calm, unprejudiced third person that she was a little fool, and that it was madness to refuse whatever happiness, however imperfect, she could get out of life. To be told that, at her age, she could not afford to be so particular—that she was only giving way to nerves, and that a little sea air would soon make her see things in their right perspective again.

Sally did not look at her audience while she told the story, because it was easier to keep one's voice impersonal while keeping one's eyes on the floor. And Miss Landison only interrupted once, quite at the beginning, when she was describing the terrible time that had immediately followed the dissolution of her partnership with Averil.

"I might have warned you it was bound to happen, but it wouldn't have made things any easier for you. From the first, I was sorry I had ever brought you two together. But I couldn't have known you would care for her so much, and once you had met her, it was too late. I could only sit back and let things take their course. Even if you'd asked my advice——"

"I nearly did, once or twice."

"You'd never have taken it!"

And Sally knew she would not, if it had involved leaving Averil. So she went on with the story.

"And I told him I couldn't marry him—that was last night." She finished, and waited for the deluge.

But Miss Landison had got her part all wrong.

"And what are you going to tell him to-night? You'll have to make up your mind," was all she said.

What was the use of asking for advice—with the full intention of taking it, this time—if you were simply told to make up your own mind?

"I *had* decided," she said slowly. "But——"

She glanced up then, and noticed that the decision was being left so entirely in her hands that she was not even being watched. The invalid's eyes were fixed on the book she had been reading, that now lay face downwards on her lap. Sally could see the title.

# SURPLUS

It was the very sea book she herself had read aloud to Averil, while they crouched, out of the draught, before the log fire at Moss Cottage. It was the call to adventure—adventure she had meant to share with Averil, just they two together in the ship's prow, questing over a heaving, night bound, sea.

If she married Glen, she would voyage with him, on a well found liner—would pass the little coast lights twinkling through the dark, and watch the traffic of strange harbours, and smell strange, warm, scented airs, with him at her side. And while his arm was round her, she would forget the thrill of new places, new chances, would forget, even, that he was not the foreordained partner of adventure.

But what of the longer voyage, the marriage voyage? It would not all be swift, effortless gliding, with nothing to do but watch the gleaming wake over the stern. There would be interludes of sickness, and storms, littering the beautiful white decks with wreckage, and days of scorching calm, with a fatally damaged engine and no port in sight. And then, when she was all alone with one companion, and he was not the right one—

"I'm not going back to London," she said suddenly.

It was as if, in that book with the faded covers, lay a power that overcame her vacillating will, her failing courage. The power of a dream that was dreamt for two.

"If I see him again, I shan't be able to leave him. But I must—I was right last night, when I told him so."

"You're sure?" said Miss Landison gently. "You've thought what it means, giving him up?"

And Sally hid her face, but she whispered:

# SURPLUS

"I'm sure—and I know what it means."

"And you feel, at the bottom of your heart, that you're doing something noble—eh, Sally?"

Miss Landison had not moved, but her voice had grown closer, more intimate, at last the voice of an equal, not an oracle.

"That's how I felt at first, when I did what you are doing, many years ago."

"You? But——"

"I was as big a coward as you are. I also was afraid of second best. You didn't know—no, I don't think anyone knows in Salter's Ridge—that I was just going to be married, when my horse threw me, out hunting? But I was, to the only man in the world. Afterwards, when the doctors said I should never be well again, Dick found out he didn't care enough——"

"The brute—oh, the brute!" muttered Sally.

"Not at all. He only did what you and I did—looked after his own happiness. And soon afterwards I was offered a love that was the real thing, by a man who had wanted me all along, who didn't care whether I was whole or in pieces, because I meant the whole of life to him. But—I wouldn't take it, though I cared for him more than anyone, except Dick."

"You thought it wasn't fair to him?"

"That's what everybody imagined I thought. All my friends and relations went about saying how marvellously unselfish I was, giving up my only chance of happiness to save him from being tied to an invalid for life. And at first I agreed with them, on the whole. Then he also had a hunting accident—a fatal one—through putting his horse at what he must have known was an impossible fence. And then I began to see that I didn't deserve all that pity and admiration.

And it made me so ashamed that when my people died I came away here, where nobody knew anything about me. I saw that I'd done it for my own sake—because I wanted to keep all my thoughts free for still remembering Dick, not to have to try and forget him. But a truly unselfish woman would have kept that first great love unlessened in her heart, and yet have had enough to give to another man who needed it."

She paused, and Sally wondered why it had never occurred to her that Miss Landison had a story of this kind behind her self-sufficient isolation. But nothing about the woman had suggested the folly of having allowed herself to remain faithful to the wrong man.

"Love isn't a small thing, like hate, that can be given to one object only at its deepest. It's got no limits, it's a widow's cruse. But it's easier to believe that it's exhaustible, and let one love have its way with you, never minding how much other people suffer."

"Is it?" whispered Sally. "I wonder—I thought it was how you were made, that some people couldn't love more than once. The selfish people, perhaps, like me. I couldn't ever be satisfied with second best, and unless I was, how could I make the man happy? Besides, it isn't *right* to be satisfied with it, once you've known the best. It isn't—surely it isn't!"

But Sally had come to the final unbridgable gulf, across which each human looks at every other, and can come no nearer. Miss Landison would not see that point of view.

"It's never anything to be proud of, to be selfish," she said. "But we're doing what we can, under the circumstances. We're learning to stand alone, as women in our position must, when they won't take

310

second best. I started years ago, and you're starting now."

" 'Our position,' " repeated Sally. "But you aren't like me. You loved a man as other women do."

"I preferred the memory of a man who didn't love me to the arms of one who did," corrected the invalid. "Judged by the standards of the majority, I stand alone. Most people prefer second best to nothing."

"It's not the same," persisted Sally. "I put a woman first. Other women have done what you did, but no other woman has done that."

"How we all cling to our own particular cross, and the brand of fate on our brow that is different to anyone else's, and deeper, and harder to bear!" smiled Miss Landison. "Don't flatter yourself, my dear, that you have the monopoly even there. And if you have—why, everybody else has one just as peculiar. There isn't such a thing as a completely ordinary person—how can there be? 'Human nature is always the same at bottom,' that's the biggest untruth that ever was uttered, and I've had plenty of time to think it over. Human nature is the only thing that always varies. They say"—she pointed to the book-lined shelves—"that civilisation has only put a superficial veneer on humanity, not changed it. But isn't it humanity that invented civilisation?"

Sally did not know, nor care. What sort of letter was she to write to Glen, and how best could she prevent him following her? And supposing that in spite of all he found her, what would happen then?

"I have an idea there may be other women—and men too, perhaps—who have done what you did, and who also feel they're bound to suffer alone."

But Sally had had enough of vague speculations.

"That's all very well," she cried, "but it doesn't help me to live. I daren't go back to Madame Lamie's while Glen's still in England, because he'd find me, and I daren't risk meeting him again. I shall have to go off, as you did, to a place where nobody knows me —but *I* shall have to work. It'll end in my being a fourth typist again, and staying one, I suppose."

She shivered at the prospect.

"But you've decided to go through with even that?"

"I hate it even more than I did before," Sally told her. "But that won't stop my going through with it. As you say, there's nothing else to do."

Miss Landison's eyes searched her face. Then she said:

"We're companions in crime, Sally. I can't leave you my little income, because that ceases at my death, but this house is mine to leave, and the proceeds of selling it go to you. You won't have long to wait now."

But Sally caught the invalid's hands in hers.

"You're not so much worse—surely you're not!"

"You're sorry?" smiled the woman on the couch. "I believe you are. Child, don't you see now why I wouldn't ask you to stay here with me before, when Averil first left you? I knew you would have stayed if I had; but it would have meant your hating to let me go when the time came, and it had to come so soon. We should have been like fellow castaways on a desert island, we couldn't have helped depending on each other. And then, when I left you, you would have been lonelier than ever. For the same reason," she added, "I won't leave you this house to *live* in. You'd grow into the hermit's life, and be unable to tear yourself away from it. Because this way of standing alone has been forced on me—I couldn't go out into the world and work—it doesn't follow that it's the right one for you."

Sally wished, not for the first time, that any way were forced on her. Even physical infirmity would be tolerable if it brought with it the one clear call to lie back and bear it—that, and nothing else. If it relieved one of the ceaseless obligation to go on struggling after the unattainable. A cripple need not reproach herself with being a total failure if she had done the one thing—borne her sufferings bravely.

"I did what I could for other people here on the spot," Miss Landison was saying. "I formed a taste for good books in a certain number of shop girls and gardeners' boys, and that was something. I keep in touch with them even now, and they come to see me whenever they can, and bring their children. But you—if you stayed on in this house alone—I believe you'd just sit down and bury yourself and wait for the end. Isn't that near the truth? And you're too young to do that—it wouldn't be playing the game."

It sounded so drearily familiar that Sally drew back, chilled. She foresaw that she was going to be advised to choose that well trodden path for the unmated, social service. To become a district visitor, a welfare worker in the slums, an organiser of children's outings and babies' crèches—for all of which occupations she had unstinted admiration, but about as much inclination and aptitude as the pirate chief has for assuming the cassock. If Miss Landison was going to make this a condition of her legacy, then she, Sally intended to refuse it.

"I don't like 'other people,'" she said. "Only persons, and one or two at that. And I don't see any reason at all why I should go out of my way to help the others. They haven't helped me—they've left me to sink or swim on my own. Except you and Mavis Barron. I'd do anything to help either of you, but as to 'other people'——"

"I'll tell you a secret," said Miss Landison. "It wasn't for love of the other people themselves, at first, that I tried to help them. It was a kind of private debit and credit account with myself that I couldn't escape. You may find it the same, or you may not—but I think you will. It's the only way you can justify yourself to yourself, in refusing to make any compromise with life, and thereby bringing misery to someone else, who has deserved nothing but good from you. Have you thought at all of your man's feelings, when he finds you really mean it, and are never coming back to him? You've taken a great love from him, and in return you're giving him nothing but trouble. Well, then, each time you do something for a stranger, you'll feel you are wiping off part of your debt to him. I can't explain it, but it is so."

"But how——" began Sally at once.

"You can buy a share in a motor firm, to start with. Now, at once, with a lump sum advanced under my will."

"Motor firm"—it was as unexpected an answer as Miss Landison could have chosen, at the moment. It let loose a whole crowd of old thoughts that had lain forgotten under new ones, old ambitions—little, perhaps, but better than nothing—that might still be brought to life again, and this time kept alive.

"They'll have a rather different welcome for the woman who comes to see them with her pocket filled," she thought.

"She must choose the right firm, though, and that would take time. Meanwhile, she could go to one of the big Coventry firms and get a first hand working knowledge of the business."

So there was the plan, outlined already, that would have to be carried through immediately,\before there was time to flinch from the difficulties in the way. A plan with no warm enthusiasms and eager hopes fluttering about it, but a steady object to pin one's thoughts to in the years ahead.

And here was the woman who was making it all possible, lying still and listening with a smile in her dark eyes. She would be left behind, with nothing but her thoughts—with the knowledge that, in helping one more of the "others," she had cancelled a little more of her debt, earned what Sally still called the right to keep the flower of love unchallenged in her heart.

Suddenly Sally rebelled against the air of inaccessibility that still clung to her. Why did not Miss Landison hold out her arms, instead of her money, why should not they two stay together, make common cause, as long as they could, even if it were for a little time only?

"We've only just begun to know each other," she said. "I can't take your money, and go straight off and leave you——"

But Miss Landison cut her short.

"I'll try and stay here long enough for you to report progress," she said, "but you must be quick!" You understand just how much I want you to do something worth while with that money? If you didn't, I'd leave it to somebody else. It's got to get you a footing, and once you get it, and can look round you,

315

don't for my sake miss any chance of helping somebody else. You've got to be another link in my chain.
Is that a bargain, my dear?"

Put like that, it was an unavoidable point of honour.
But Sally's nod of agreement carried with it none of
the heroic glow she would have welcomed. She had a
suspicion that at the bottom of any scheme of hers
to help others would lie, still, the desire to be of more
importance herself. To prove that she was just as
necessary to them, vital to their happiness, worth just
as much in the scheme of things as any wife and
mother.

And another impulse, too, perhaps—when she had
said to herself, "I don't know what my job is, but I'm
going to find out," she had meant a bigger job than
becoming a partner in a motor firm, surely? Something for other people—she saw, now, that she had
meant that. She too wanted to be unselfish, though
not for Miss Landison's reasons. Since she would
not give children to the race, could not, like the Madonna woman, find her fulfilment in being the influence
behind a man—since she was freed from the ordinary
ties and duties of love, she must pay her footing otherwise among the company of lovers. Love and service
went together inseparably. Because the object of her
love wanted no moon dropped into her lap to play
with, no smallest sacrifice or gift except the negative
one of allowing herself to be forgotten, she must find
another outlet for the urge.

But it would be hard. She was the scapegoat, cast
out from the herd, the one whom it is expedient should
suffer for the good of the multitude. They had no
use for her, except in so far as she would conform to
their standards. If she would give herself up to work

# SURPLUS

among the sick and poor, well and good—a very proper course to adopt, they would consider it, and one that showed there was, after all, some use to be found for such as her. But failing this, they also wanted only one service of her, and that a negative one—to accomplish her days in self supporting, decent obscurity, with the least possible amount of inconvenience to anybody else.

Unless, after all, Miss Landison were right, and there were others like her scattered over the world?

"I wonder," thought Sally, "if my job is to teach some other unmated woman that she hasn't missed the greatest thing in the world, if she's had a great friendship?"

## CHAPTER XXVI

SALLY went walking in the dusk at that day's end, choosing the high road, past the lane that led down to Moss Cottage.

The mountain mist lay so thick on the trees that they dripped with it, in a monotonous cadence, all along the forest fringe. The road surface was hard and shiny wet, and the echoes of her footfalls, mingling with the sighing and rustling of damp branches, were as the sound of an army following; halting, stumbling, but always close behind.

She knew that she would never again feel quite the same crushing loneliness. There went with her all those others who have been turned back from the golden gates of paradise on earth, because their passports are made out in a strange, unknown language. The inventor who has brought forth a brain child that the world calls a monstrosity, whose desk is littered with plans for an aëroplane that could never even rise a foot from the earth, yet who prefers those plans to any human infant. The patriot, who captures with his own hands a citadel his leaders have no use for, defying friend and foe alike from its walls. The explorer, who scorns ease, beauty, life itself, in the futile effort to scale a peak that is unclimbable, whereon success would be rewarded by nothing better than a few stones and a cloud—while at his feet roll vast plains, equally unexplored and equally exciting, and teeming with game into the bargain. All the dreamers who prize their dream above reality, and follow their flickering

SURPLUS

will-o'-the-wisp away from the broad, steady arc light of reason. And the rebels who would rather go on kicking against the pricks to the bitter end, than settle down to the yoke, humbly aware that it might have been heavier. All these—though most of them would have denied it—went the same way as the girl who refused to marry because her deepest love had been given to another girl. But they were ghosts; and she was old fashioned enough to need a warm human hand to hold, and the sound of a human voice saying, "We two, whatever comes, belong together!"

So, after all, it was down an empty road that Sally Wraith went forward into the mist.

(1)

THE END

**Sex Variant Women in Literature** by Jeannette Howard Foster.
Literary history. 448 pp. ISBN 0-930044-65-7          $8.95

**A Hot-Eyed Moderate** by Jane Rule. Essays. 252 pp.
ISBN 0-930044-57-6          $7.95
ISBN 0-930044-59-2          $13.95

**Inland Passage and Other Stories** by Jane Rule. 288 pp.
ISBN 0-930044-56-8          $7.95
ISBN 0-930044-58-4          $13.95

**We Too Are Drifting** by Gale Wilhelm. A novel. 128 pp.
ISBN 0-930044-61-4          $6.95

**Amateur City** by Katherine V. Forrest. A mystery novel. 224 pp.
ISBN 0-930044-55-X          $7.95

**The Sophie Horowitz Story** by Sarah Schulman. A novel. 176 pp.
ISBN 0-930044-54-1          $7.95

**The Young in One Another's Arms** by Jane Rule. A novel.
224 pp. ISBN 0-930044-53-3          $7.95

**The Burnton Widows** by Vicki P. McConnell. A mystery novel.
272 pp. ISBN 0-930044-52-5          $7.95

**Old Dyke Tales** by Lee Lynch. Short stories. 224 pp.
ISBN 0-930044-51-7          $7.95

**Daughters of a Coral Dawn** by Katherine V. Forrest. Science
fiction. 240 pp. ISBN 0-930044-50-9          $7.95

**The Price of Salt** by Claire Morgan. A novel. 288 pp.
ISBN 0-930044-49-5          $7.95

**Against the Season** by Jane Rule. A novel. 224 pp.
ISBN 0-930044-48-7          $7.95

**Lovers in the Present Afternoon** by Kathleen Fleming. A novel.
288 pp. ISBN 0-930044-46-0          $8.50

**Toothpick House** by Lee Lynch. A novel. 264 pp.
ISBN 0-930044-45-2          $7.95

**Madame Aurora** by Sarah Aldridge. A novel. 256 pp.
ISBN 0-930044-44-4          $7.95

**Curious Wine** by Katherine V. Forrest. A novel. 176 pp.
ISBN 0-930044-43-6          $7.50

**Black Lesbian in White America** by Anita Cornwell. Short stories,
essays, autobiography. 144 pp. ISBN 0-930044-41-X          $7.50

**Contract with the World** by Jane Rule. A novel. 340 pp.
ISBN 0-930044-28-2                 $7.95

**Yantras of Womanlove** by Tee A. Corinne. Photographs.
64 pp. ISBN 0-930044-30-4           $6.95

**Mrs. Porter's Letter** by Vicki P. McConnell. A mystery novel.
224 pp. ISBN 0-930044-29-0        $6.95

**To the Cleveland Station** by Carol Anne Douglas. A novel.
192 pp. ISBN 0-930044-27-4        $6.95

**The Nesting Place** by Sarah Aldridge. A novel. 224 pp.
ISBN 0-930044-26-6           $6.95

**This Is Not for You** by Jane Rule. A novel. 284 pp.
ISBN 0-930044-25-8           $7.95

**Faultline** by Sheila Ortiz Taylor. A novel. 140 pp.
ISBN 0-930044-24-X           $6.95

**The Lesbian in Literature** by Barbara Grier. 3d ed. Foreword by
Maida Tilchen. A comprehensive bibliography. 240 pp.
ISBN 0-930044-23-1           $7.95

**Anna's Country** by Elizabeth Lang. A novel. 208 pp.
ISBN 0-930044-19-3           $6.95

**Prism** by Valerie Taylor. A novel. 158 pp.
ISBN 0-930044-18-5           $6.95

**Black Lesbians: An Annotated Bibliography** compiled by
J. R. Roberts. Foreword by Barbara Smith. 112 pp.
ISBN 0-930044-21-5           $5.95

**The Marquise and the Novice** by Victoria Ramstetter. A novel.
108 pp. ISBN 0-930044-16-9        $4.95

**Labiaflowers** by Tee A. Corinne. 40 pp.
ISBN 0-930044-20-7           $3.95

**Outlander** by Jane Rule. Short stories, essays. 207 pp.
ISBN 0-930044-17-7           $6.95

**Sapphistry: The Book of Lesbian Sexuality** by Pat Califia. 2nd
edition, revised. 195 pp. ISBN 0-930044-47-9        $7.95

**All True Lovers** by Sarah Aldridge. A novel. 292 pp.
ISBN 0-930044-10-X           $6.95

**A Woman Appeared to Me** by Renee Vivien. Translated by
  Jeannette H. Foster. A novel. xxxi, 65 pp.
  ISBN 0-930044-06-1                                                    $5.00

**Cytherea's Breath** by Sarah Aldridge. A novel. 240 pp.
  ISBN 0-930044-02-9                                                    $6.95

**Tottie** by Sarah Aldridge. A novel. 181 pp.
  ISBN 0-930044-01-0                                                    $6.95

**The Latecomer** by Sarah Aldridge. A novel. 107 pp.
  ISBN 0-930044-00-2                                                    $5.00

## VOLUTE BOOKS

| | | |
|---|---|---|
| **Journey to Fulfillment** | by Valerie Taylor | $3.95 |
| **A World without Men** | by Valerie Taylor | $3.95 |
| **Return to Lesbos** | by Valerie Taylor | $3.95 |
| **Odd Girl Out** | by Ann Bannon | $3.95 |
| **I Am a Woman** | by Ann Bannon | $3.95 |
| **Women in the Shadows** | by Ann Bannon | $3.95 |
| **Journey to a Woman** | by Ann Bannon | $3.95 |
| **Beebo Brinker** | by Ann Bannon | $3.95 |

These are just a few of the many Naiad Press titles. Please request a
complete catalog! We encourage and welcome direct mail orders from
individuals who have limited access to bookstores carrying our publica-
tions.